THE ADVENTURES OF PINOCCHIO

CARLO COLLODI (pseudonym of Carlo Lorenzini) was born in Florence in 1826. He was deeply committed to the political objectives of the Risorgimento: the self-government and unification of Italy, and sympathized with the democratizing reforms accompanying it. Professionally a civil servant, he devoted his most enthusiastic energies to his prolific writing as a freelance journalist and satirical critic of the social and political scene. Also the author of novels and plays, at almost 50 he was commissioned to translate Perrault's fairy tales into Italian. A further commission produced a modern version of a children's classic: *Giannettino* was an entertaining story which successfully disguised its didactic purpose; it was followed, until the end of Collodi's life, by a series of sequels. *The Adventures of Pinocchio* was originally serialized in a children's newspaper, with resounding success, and was published as a book in 1883. Collodi died in 1890.

ANN LAWSON LUCAS researches and writes on Italian—and comparative—literature for children and young people, especially the late nineteenth-century classics of Emilio Salgari (adventure novels) and Carlo Collodi (*Pinocchio*). Her monograph on Salgari (Olschki, 2000) and editions of three of his novels (Einaudi, 2001) were published in Italy. She has contributed as an Advisory Editor to OUP's forthcoming *Encyclopedia of Children's Literature*. She was Senior Lecturer in Italian at the University of Hull, and latterly Visiting Research Fellow in the Institute for Advanced Studies in the Humanities at the University of Edinburgh. From 1993 to 1997 she was a member of the Board of International Research Society for Children's Literature.

OXFORD WORLD'S CLASSICS

*For over 100 years Oxford World's Classics have brought
readers closer to the world's great literature. Now with over 700
titles—from the 4,000-year-old myths of Mesopotamia to the
twentieth century's greatest novels—the series makes available
lesser-known as well as celebrated writing.*

*The pocket-sized hardbacks of the early years contained
introductions by Virginia Woolf, T. S. Eliot, Graham Greene,
and other literary figures which enriched the experience of reading.
Today the series is recognized for its fine scholarship and
reliability in texts that span world literature, drama and poetry,
religion, philosophy and politics. Each edition includes perceptive
commentary and essential background information to meet the
changing needs of readers.*

OXFORD WORLD'S CLASSICS

CARLO COLLODI

The Adventures of
Pinocchio

Translated with an Introduction and Notes by
ANN LAWSON LUCAS

OXFORD
UNIVERSITY PRESS

OXFORD

UNIVERSITY PRESS

Great Clarendon Street, Oxford OX2 6DP

Oxford University Press is a department of the University of Oxford.
It furthers the University's objective of excellence in research, scholarship,
and education by publishing worldwide in

Oxford New York

Athens Auckland Bangkok Bogotá Buenos Aires Calcutta
Cape Town Chennai Dar es Salaam Delhi Florence Hong Kong Istanbul
Karachi Kuala Lumpur Madrid Melbourne Mexico City Mumbai
Nairobi Paris São Paulo Shanghai Singapore Taipei Tokyo Toronto Warsaw

with associated companies in Berlin Ibadan

Oxford is a registered trade mark of Oxford University Press
in the UK and in certain other countries

Published in the United States
by Oxford University Press Inc., New York

British Library Cataloguing in Publication Data

Data available

Library of Congress Cataloging in Publication Data

Collodi, Carlo, 1826–1890
[Adventure di Pinocchio. English]
The adventures of Pinocchio / Carlo Collodi; translated with an
introduction and notes by Ann Lawson Lucas.
(Oxford world's classics)
Includes bibliographical references.
I. Lucas, Ann Lawson. II. Title. III. Series.
PQ4712.L4A713 1996 853'.8—dc20 96–1472

ISBN 978–0–19–955398–3

13

Printed in Great Britain by
Clays Ltd, Elcograf S.p.A.

CONTENTS

ACKNOWLEDGEMENTS

I wish to express my warm appreciation of the help, encouragement, and pleasurable discussion provided at different times and in different ways by Peter Hainsworth, Judith Luna, and Fernando Tempesti.

INTRODUCTION

Pinocchio is world literature to the point where its Italian origins are probably largely unknown outside Italy. The statistics of its international success are extraordinary. *Pinocchio* is one of the most translated books in the world, maybe more even than the Bible.[1] The National Library in Florence has *Pinocchio* in Armenian, Irish Gaelic, Latin (*Pinocolus Latinus*), Dutch, Rheto-Romansch, and Slovene, not to mention Piedmontese dialect (*Pinòcchio an piemonteis*). In 1983 an international competition was launched in Italy for designs for 'Ex-Libris' labels to commemorate *Pinocchio*'s centenary.[2] Almost 300 entries were received from 18 countries, mainly in Europe and the USSR, plus one from Japan. The political map has changed dramatically since then, and it is noticeable how many designs from the Eastern bloc countries presented Pinocchio's misadventures in anguished images, interpreting him, it seems, as a symbol of freedom.

The story has been the subject of many, many re-tellings and abridgements, both in Italy and abroad, adorned with all manner of illustration from simple line drawings to lavish pop-up pictures. The Pinocchio industry goes well beyond the confines of publishing, and the famous—or notorious—Walt Disney film is the most obvious example; made over 50 years ago it toured Swedish cinemas in 1994 and is now promoted as a video in Britain. Other films include a Russian Marxist interpretation, an Italian realist, period drama, and three new versions are under

[1] In 1976 Pietro Citati asserted that more than 200 translations had been published throughout the world; Bibliographical Note, in Carlo Collodi, *Le avventure di Pinocchio* (Milano: BUR, 1976).

[2] *Ex-Libris dal mondo per Pinocchio*, Introduction by F. Tempesti, Fondazione Nazionale C. Collodi, Pescia (Firenze: Salimbeni, 1983).

consideration.[3] The puppet frequently treads the boards and in 1995 was packing the house in Johannesburg and London. Then there are cartoon-strips, toys, advertising exploitation, and every sort of bric-à-brac. The image and idea of Pinocchio have permeated international popular culture and become part of folklore.

The tale was a popular success immediately in the early 1880s. By 1983 there had been 135 distinct illustrated editions in Italy, more than one per year.[4] It was from 1922 that the Pinocchio industry became a phenomenon of mass production, unabated even in wartime. The production line included copious numbers of derivative publications by other authors. New adventures covered everything imaginable: Pinocchio the Explorer wearing a topee; on the Moon; his Betrothed (a reference to Manzoni's great novel of 1842); the Pirate/Railwayman/Cyclist/Policeman . . .; Pinocchio Robinson with fur cap on desert isle; even, in 1927–8, Pinocchio the Fascist. Then there are the 'Son of Lassie' titles: the adventures of brothers, friends, a sister, even indeed a son of Pinocchio. Moreover, the Italian *Books in Print* currently lists no fewer than 30 volumes of criticism and biography on *Pinocchio* and its author.

Italy takes children's literature seriously, and the nation recognizes the value of its greatest children's writer by according him a permanent memorial, theme park, and study centre in the form of the Fondazione Nazionale 'Carlo Collodi' in Tuscany, established in 1962 by decree of the President of the Republic of Italy. The Foundation has both a popularizing and a scholarly function, and the latter has played a significant part in the re-assessment in depth of Collodi's work. The recognition of the importance of *The Adventures of Pinocchio* as literature has developed enormously

[3] I. Mayes, 'Fame of the nose is growing', in *The Guardian* (London, 13 May 1995).

[4] R. Biaggioni, *Pinocchio: cent'anni d'avventure illustrate* (Firenze: Giunti Marzocco, 1984).

since its author's day, so that the story now has a dual role in terms of popular culture on the one hand and, on the other, as a literary classic.

Carlo Collodi: Politics and the growth of a writer

In the western world the second half of the nineteenth century produced a number of major classics of children's literature: in Italy *Le avventure di Pinocchio* (1883) is universally regarded as the masterpiece of the genre, while in Britain most people's choice might well be *Alice's Adventures in Wonderland* (1865). In some quite striking ways, these two stories and their authors have significant features in common. Both books were composed by confirmed bachelors, though the authors were surrounded at various times by children. Both men had been the eldest son in huge families; Carlo Lorenzini ('Carlo Collodi') was the first-born, in 1826, of ten children, only five of whom survived infancy, while Charles Lutwidge Dodgson ('Lewis Carroll'), born in 1832, was the third child in a family of eleven. In each case a parent died young. Other members of each family were to create exceptional lives: a maternal uncle of Carlo became a noted painter in Florence; Carlo's brother, Paolo, was to be director-general of the finest porcelain makers in Italy; one nephew of Charles would be his biographer, another became a professor of physiology at a London hospital. Both writers had been brought up in the country, where the magical life of nature captured their youthful imagination, and where the future story-teller took a leading role in devising the imaginative games played with either siblings or friends.

While Charles Dodgson was the son of a country parson, Carlo Lorenzini was the child of poor servants; his father was a cook in the service of a distinguished Florentine aristocratic family, the Ginori, and his mother a seamstress. She, however, had come from a background of rather more education, for her father was steward to another noble

Tuscan family, the Garzoni. Though he was born in Florence, Carlo spent many of his early years in his mother's country village, completing his elementary schooling there, and larking about adventurously with the country boys. Carlo showed intellectual promise and the Marchese Ginori made himself responsible for the boy's education, sending him to a Tuscan seminary, in Colle Val d'Elsa, for five years. Carlo, like Charles, had been destined for the Church, but having no vocation for the priesthood he proceeded no further. After two more years' schooling with priests in Florence he emerged at 18 with a good classical education. Like Dodgson, he was educationally privileged; like Dodgson, he worked in the secular world, in an intellectual profession, or rather two simultaneously, those of journalist and civil servant. At the age of 30 he first used the pseudonym which he later adopted for his *alter ego*, the writer for children; to 'Carlo' he added the name of his mother's village, Collodi, where the Garzoni had their estate. Usually explained as a tribute to his mother, it more probably expressed nostalgia for the carefree, country days of youth. So when Lorenzini published the volume of *Le avventure di Pinocchio* at the age of 57, he did so as Carlo Collodi.[5]

Lorenzini's life seems a bizarre, apparently incongruous one for the author of *Pinocchio*. Yet the more one knows it, the more *Pinocchio* is explained. When he left school, Carlo Lorenzini went to work at a noted Florence bookshop, the Libreria Piatti. The manager, Giuseppe Aiazzi, was a remarkable man, a historian and palaeographer who helped nurture Lorenzini's developing literary knowledge, not only in Italian and Greek, but also on French. His eventual expertise in French was to lead to several important

[5] The first known appearance of the pseudonym, a recent discovery, is as the contributor of an article published in the first issue of *La Lente*, January 1856.

scholarly and literary products later on; indeed it provided an essential stepping-stone towards the story of Pinocchio. Besides, the bookshop was a focus for Florentine intellectuals, journalists, and liberals and, both politically and intellectually, provided a crucial maturing ground for the young Carlo. It was a period of great political upheaval in what is now the state of Italy, but what was then a patchwork of miniature states of many kinds. This was the era of the Risorgimento movement, which sought to free the Italian regions which were under foreign rule and to unite the whole peninsula as one nation, a political condition not experienced since Ancient Roman times. Much of the north of Italy was ruled by Austria, and other smaller states came under Austrian influence, so that a prime necessity for the creation of Italy was the liberation of those areas. This meant war.[6]

At the Piatti bookshop, Lorenzini quickly absorbed and identified with the political aspirations of the patriots. He broadly sympathized with the ideas of Mazzini, the Risorgimento theorist, idealist, and insurrectionist whose aim was an egalitarian Republic of Italy. Perhaps more surprisingly, this part of Lorenzini's development was of importance in preparing the writer for children who was to emerge 20 years later. It is obvious that a child of poverty, whose chance for an interesting life, economic security, and a career in culture had been provided by an exceptional education, might recognize the need for others to be encouraged to learn. This, together with his spirit and humour, and his scepticism which queried the style of traditional education, nurtured the future writer of educational fiction. Because of his own patriotic and democratic inclinations, Lorenzini's educational objectives would be fused together

---

[6] H. Hearder, *Italy in the Age of the Risorgimento, 1790–1870* (London and New York: Longman, 1983).

with his aspirations for the new nation of Italy. But how could politics be relevant to *Pinocchio*, a children's entertainment, a fantasy? Like *Alice*, *Pinocchio* has hidden depths: it is, indeed, imbued with Lorenzini's most fundamental perceptions, not only of human nature, but of life in society; his sympathy for the poor, his criticism of social and political institutions, and his detestation of hierarchies are all here.

Lorenzini was not simply an ardent young patriot, then, but keenly aware of what was at stake socially in the long revolution of the Risorgimento. Although the new Italy would in fact be born a monarchy, many of those who argued and fought for it were inspired by the desire for a republic and the disappearance of the decadent, repressive old regimes, ranging from the Bourbon kingdom in Naples to the pro-Austrian puppet duchies in, and to the north of, Tuscany. Twice in a dozen years Lorenzini was to leave off his career to enlist as a volunteer in the Wars of Independence which preceded the unification of Italy. The first occasion was in 1848, the great year of revolutions in Europe, when Piedmont was at war with Austria, and when Lorenzini, aged 22, had been working for four years, during which time—in 1847—he had published his first articles in the *Rivista di Firenze* ('The Florence Review'). In April 1848, along with his brother Paolo and Signor Giulio Piatti of the bookshop, he joined the Second Tuscan battalion, Second Company, and left with the expeditionary force for Lombardy, the focus of revolt against Austrian occupation; there, on 29 May, he fought against the Austrian army in the unsuccessful battle of Montanara and Curtatone. In three vivid letters to Signor Aiazzi, he expressed youthful enthusiasm, of course, but what is more remarkable is the beginnings of the shrewd observation of human ineptitude which would characterize the mature writer. He was scathing about the activities of the regular army officers in command ('who possessed a 400 horse-power ignorance of

military matters').[7] The Tuscan volunteers were decimated,
but Lorenzini returned safely to Florence—still politically
impassioned, even if somewhat discouraged—and immediately embarked anew on his life in the literary world.

With his brother Paolo, and two friends, Lorenzini
promptly founded a politico-satirical daily newspaper, *Il
Lampione*; launched already on 13 July 1848, it may have
been partly the result of discussions while away campaign-
ing. Its existence was made possible by a recent (limited)
freedom of the press bill, extracted from the Grand Duke
of Tuscany by the leading liberals and democrats. It was
both a popular and a radical paper, aiming to combat bour-
geois conservatism, without supporting all of Mazzini's
ideology or goals. Its name meant 'lamp-post' and its purpose was 'to enlighten those faltering in the dark'.[8] Under
the editorship of Carlo Lorenzini it was to have much success for the next nine months. At the same time his second
career began on 2 August when, probably thanks to the
intervention of Aiazzi, who *inter alia* was the Tuscan Senate's archivist and librarian, he entered the service of the
Grand Duke as a civil servant to the Senate, a position
which was no doubt essential to him financially, but which
interested him little. During the life of *Il Lampione*, there
were both inspiriting and distressing changes in the politics
of the Tuscan capital: the formation of a democratic government, the flight in January 1849 of Grand Duke Leopold
II to the safety of the South and the Bourbon King Ferdi-
nand, his return and restoration in July 1849, supported
by the peasantry and the presence of Austrian troops in
Florence. It was this reversal in political fortunes which
caused the closure of *Il Lampione* on 11 April 1849. Not

---

[7] Letter to G. Aiazzi, preserved in the National Library, Florence, and
quoted in B. Traversetti, *Introduzione a Collodi* (Bari: Laterza, 1993), 17.
(*My translation.*)

[8] Quoted in G. Fanciulli, *Scrittori e libri per l'infanzia* (Torino: S.E.I.,
1960), 81. (*My translation.*)

only that, but Lorenzini's 'subversive' journalism cost him his administrative post, though this was restored on 1 June. Before long he was even promoted, undoubtedly again through the good offices of Aiazzi, to duties in the Senate archive.

The earlier relaxation in censorship had permitted the emergence of a myriad papers and periodicals in Florence. But the Restoration meant a new period of loss of freedom of expression. Nevertheless, for a decade, Lorenzini was to contribute quantities of journalism to a great variety of publications, but now mainly in the forms of social commentary and theatre, music, and literary criticism, rather than the more dangerous, though funny, political comment. What he wrote was mainly prose, but there was some bad verse as well; his work was often humorous, often in the form of dialogues and sketches, while his criticism concerned opera more than any other genre. Any journalism, however apparently innocuous, may have a political subtext and opera provided the ideal opportunity for double meanings. This was the glorious century of Italian opera, from Bellini, Donizetti, and Rossini (the composers best loved by Lorenzini) to the magisterial Verdi and finally Puccini. Opera was at once the most distinguished and the most popular of art forms in Italy at this time, and musical genius was frequently wedded to the subliminal expression of patriotism and nationalism.

In November 1853 a new theatrical journal was founded with Collodi as its editor. The *Scaramuccia* had been named after a comic operetta currently in vogue, though the name had a long history reaching back to the plays of Molière and the Commedia dell'Arte tradition. While provocative in style, Lorenzini's writing here developed a kind of cultural conservatism (which often rejected foreign influences— the other face of nationalism) that was to be a permanent trait in his critical persona. His association with the periodical nurtured a profound enthusiasm for all things theatrical. His knowledge of opera would later shape passages of *Pinocchio*, which, starting with the idea of the puppet himself, is saturated in the culture of the Commedia dell'Arte and of the theatre in general. Meantime Lorenzini began to write plays himself. The first was *Gli amici di casa* ('Family friends') in 1853, which he was banned from staging in public by the censors, but which was published, rewritten as a comedy, in 1856, and finally staged, after the Unification, in 1861.

One of Lorenzini's most striking characteristics in terms of his personality and his writing was wit. His humour could be facetious and adolescent, but at best produced resonant aphorisms on the *comédie humaine*. His most famous and most quoted pronouncement was uttered in the columns of the *Scaramuccia* in July 1854; it could be taken as a knowing piece of self-description, but was in fact levelled at contemporary novels in the fashionable, romantic *feuilleton* manner, against which he regularly inveighed. The article in question was entitled 'Fantasy' (and, after all, his own work was composed of a multifarious and kaleidoscopic manipulation of word and form): 'It is now our fate: no description is possible without probable digression'.[9]

His rebukes concerning *feuilleton* fiction found full expression in his own first novel, published in 1857, which took its title directly from the enemy camp of Eugène Sue, author of *Les Mystères de Paris* (1842–3); Sue was one of the most successful practitioners of the art of popular, sensational fiction-writing with a social conscience. Unlike the long line of 'mysteries' which explored the urban and the criminal, Lorenzini's *I misteri di Firenze* ('The mysteries of Florence') was a parody, poking fun at the genre, though it also embraced a form of realism, simple, unadorned, without illusion, anticipating the directness of *Pinocchio*.

[9] Quoted in Traversetti, *Introduzione a Collodi*, 32. (*My translation.*)

The story opens with a masked ball in a theatre, pointing forward to the theatrical elements, masks, and disguises which would later reappear as wholly integrated features of *Pinocchio*.

Lorenzini/Collodi had a complex character, perpetually suspended between irreverence and formality.[10] A close colleague of later years, Ferdinando Martini, wrote in his memoirs that Lorenzini, contrary to all appearances and all assumptions, was in truth a sad man, or, we might now say, a depressive. But he was 'a melancholic who made it his great entertainment to entertain others'.[11] Important features of his mature character were scepticism and even cynicism. His philosophy of life was summed up in one of his journalistic pieces thus:

Remember that poets rarely tell the truth, perhaps for the important reason that the truth is prose, and, often enough, bad prose.[12]

Even by his early thirties his military days were not yet over. Lorenzini's whole life was rooted in Florence, and yet in December 1858 he moved north to Milan to work for a publisher. Because he was addicted to—and unlucky at—cards, it has been suggested that he needed to escape gambling debts. At all events, his stay was short, for the Risorgimento movement was coming to its climax. On 10 April 1859 at Pinerolo, aged 32, eleven years after his first experience, he enlisted again as a volunteer, but this time in the regular army, and with the Light Cavalry of Novara he took part in the Second War of Independence. It had been one thing for young hotheads to join up and express their patriotic passions on the battlefield; it showed quite a

[10] Traversetti, *Introduzione a Collodi*, 64.

[11] F. Martini, quoted by P. Pancrazi, 'Vita del Collodi', in *Tutto Collodi per i piccoli e per i grandi* (Firenze: Le Monnier, 1948), xxiii. (*My translation.*)

[12] Quoted in Traversetti, *Introduzione a Collodi*, 69. (*My translation.*)

different determination and level of commitment in the mature, established writer and urban intellectual. Meanwhile, things were changing dramatically at home. On 27 April the Grand Ducal dynasty came to an end definitively when, after popular demonstrations, Leopold II fled again, never to return. (To Lorenzini this was a great triumph, symbolized by his giving a false birthdate—27 April—on his release from the army.) The beginnings of equality and democracy were seen in the establishment of a new Parliament by election and, after a plebiscite, Tuscany requested union with the kingdom of Piedmont-Sardinia.

After the Peace of Villafranca, Lorenzini returned to Florence in late August 1859 and plunged again into his career in journalism, contributing to scores of papers in the next twenty years, cured, it has been asserted, of his gambling habits. From February 1860 he was again given an official appointment; so it was that he joined the Commission for Theatre Censorship—a quaint case of the biter bit, or rather, the bitten biting. On 15 May he relaunched, after eleven years of enforced silence, *Il Lampione*. As if continuing a conversation, he opened his first editorial article, 'Let us again take up the thread which was broken off by the feeble, high-pitched voices of Reaction...'[13] In the same year he was commissioned by the new government to write a polemical pamphlet against a reactionary apologist for the *ancien régime* of the Grand Dukes.[14]

The year 1860 saw the culmination of the Risorgimento, with the near-complete unification of Italy. In that year Garibaldi, with his Thousand Redshirt volunteers, took Sicily and the southern mainland. The Piedmontese army invaded the Papal States which separated northern Italy from the south. Italy was now one, with the exception, for

[13] Quoted in Fanciulli, *Scrittori e libri per l'infanzia*, 82. (*My translation.*)

[14] C. Collodi, *Il signor Albèri ha ragione. Dialogo apologetico* ('Mr A. is right. A dialogue in vindication') (Firenze: Galileiana, 1860).

a few years to come, of Venice and Rome. Elections for the first Parliament of the new nation were held in January 1861, it met in February in Turin, and in March the Piedmontese king, Victor Emmanuel, was officially recognized as King of Italy.

Turin in the far north was remote from most of Italy, and in 1865 the political capital was moved to Florence, the cultural capital for many centuries. The Risorgimento period had been characterized by lengthy debates about the correct form of Italian to be used for cultural purposes, widely differing dialects being the natural, everyday languages throughout the diverse states. By the time of the Unification there was broad agreement amongst writers, greatly influenced by the example of the Milanese novelist Manzoni, that Florentine or Tuscan Italian was the finest literary vehicle. Now that Florence's pre-eminence was confirmed politically, various publications were produced to establish the language of culture. A Government Minister, Emilio Broglio, arranged for the production of a new and comprehensive dictionary of the Italian language according to Florentine usage, which would appear in four volumes between 1877 and 1897.[15] After a short visit to France in 1867, Lorenzini was invited in 1868 to take part in the compilation of the dictionary, a development in his work which was to bear fruit in the composition of *Pinocchio*, the work of a stylist who relishes all the potential of words. In particular, Lorenzini was asked to identify French neologisms in contemporary usage and propose good Tuscan alternatives. Florence's new political role was not to last long. Once Italy was fully unified, with the annexation first of the Veneto then of Rome, the capital was moved once again, to Rome itself.

Despite all his demonstrations of amused detachment,

---

[15] G. B. Giorgini and E. Broglio (eds.), *Il novo vocabolario della lingua italiana secondo l'uso di Firenze* (Firenze: 1877–97).

Lorenzini was not without a sense of cultural responsibility. Although keenly aware of his limited success as a dramatist, between the years 1853 and 1873 he wrote six plays in an attempt to improve the quality of the contemporary theatre. He expressed his continuing scepticism, even in the New Italy, concerning all things political, but at the same time his reliability and loyalty as a civil servant were rewarded by his promotion to First Secretary in the Prefecture of Florence. Shortly he was to turn his attention from the condemnation of small men to an approbation of little children, a wholly logical evolution, it might be argued.

It was two years later, in 1875, that his writing took a quite new turn, changing his life and ensuring his immortality. He was almost 50, and there were still six years to go before the creation of *Pinocchio*. Critics agree that there is a mystery surrounding the inception of the puppet story. But, in reality, the greatest mystery occurred in 1875 when the Florentine publishing house of the Brothers Felice and Alessandro Paggi approached Lorenzini to translate from the French some of the finest, pioneering fairy stories of the seventeenth and eighteenth centuries, nine by Charles Perrault (from the *Contes de ma mère l'Oye*), along with four by Madame d'Aulnoy and two by Madame Leprince de Beaumont. It is true that Lorenzini was a chameleon writer; variety and quicksilver mobility were the hallmarks of his writing life. And yet, why ask him to translate from French? Why ask him to tackle fairy tales? Why ask him, a novice in the medium, to write for children? Works of genius do sometimes stem from a publisher's inspiration. Lorenzini's highly acclaimed *I racconti delle fate* ('Fairy Tales')—the first whole volume to bear the name 'Carlo Collodi'—established a new, important partnership between himself and the Fratelli Paggi, and opened a new chapter in the history of children's literature.

Alongside the political revolution, substantial social changes had been taking place since the beginning of the century: the development of public education was one. Everywhere in Europe children's literature was becoming established as a new and separate genre. In Italy its evolution was intertwined with progress in political and educational thinking. A famous aphorism of the Risorgimento was D'Azeglio's remark at the time of the Unification that now Italy was made, what remained to be done was to make Italians. After Unification there was a cultural vacuum for the educated classes, whose energies and passions had been wholly focused for decades upon the political goal. Many saw the need for popular instruction on the subject of Italy itself and for 'unifying' reading matter. Under the Grand Dukes, the Paggi brothers' publishing house had espoused Mazzinian and republican attitudes. In the New Italy, their sense of responsibility towards the formation of the nation led them to embark upon a programme of educational books for the young.

The Paggi brothers now asked Collodi to devise a new and modern version of an old educational best-seller, Parravicini's *Giannetto*. This had been a typically improving and moralizing work for children, first published in 1837. In 1877 Collodi's *Giannettino* appeared and, while it was self-evidently an educational book, its style was vastly more natural and the instruction was presented within a fictional context intended also to entertain. The New Italy provided both a need and a market; people were responding to change, to modernity, and *Giannettino* was a great success. In 1878, Lorenzini was knighted as a 'Cavaliere della Corona d'Italia' (Knight of the Crown of Italy). There then followed a whole series of Collodi books for children, some specifically for use in schools, all instructive, all entertaining, though the balance between fun and information varied. After Giannettino had addressed geography and grammar, the children of Italy were acquainted with their nation through the three volumes of Giannettino's journey around Italy. These books were not only culturally unifying, but socially cohesive too. There was no talking down, and Giannettino is far from being the model boy of prim and proper 'Victorian' literature; on the contrary, he is ordinary, naughty, and scruffy.

Meantime Lorenzini, the writer for adults, was still in evidence, publishing collections of earlier journalism. An amusing and saddening meditation on life—his life and that of Florence—was brought out in 1881, with the title *Occhi e nasi* ('Eyes and noses'), by which he meant satirical portraits focusing on single features. Here, the irony that was to be such a brilliant characteristic of *Pinocchio* was deployed fully—and pungently. His 'Cheerful Stories' (*Storie allegre*), intended simply to amuse young children, were freer, more personal, than the *Giannettino* books, and added a new dimension to his work for children. In the same year (1881), having worked in public administration for 33 years, he requested early retirement and, at 54, left with a pension of 2,200 lire per annum. Of course his writing went on unabated.

Old acquaintance brought about the next development. A colleague in journalism, Ferdinando Martini, now an MP of the liberal Left, established and edited an ambitious literary periodical with some of the most distinguished of contemporary writers as contributors. Martini, with a commitment both to high culture and to the people, was a popularizer of high calibre. He decided to found another weekly, a top-quality children's newspaper to be published on Thursdays, the holiday from school. The end of the century saw great expansion in the field of journalism for the young, and this was to be one of several important children's newspapers to emerge. It was called simply *Il Giornale per i bambini* ('The paper for children') and was to have the finest children's writers figuring in its pages. The first issue was published on 7 July 1881; on page 5 appeared the first instalment of a serial story specially written for it by Carlo Collodi. It was *La storia di un burattino* ('The story of a puppet'), which featured on the front page in the next number and was printed irregularly in eight parts, with the last in the issue of 27 October. The story ended tragically—and provocatively—at Chapter XV with the puppet hanged on an oak-tree by thieving murderers.

The participation of Collodi in the new venture had been solicited well in advance, and after much pressing he had sent a wad of papers towards the end of 1880. Famously he had written in the accompanying note, 'I'm sending you this baby-talk; do what you like with it . . .'.[16] The story was an enormous success, but the young readers wanted more, especially as the hero had been left for dead. Eventually Collodi restarted it in February 1882.[17] Now it had changed its title to the definitive one, *Le avventure di Pinocchio* ('The adventures of Pinocchio'). Eleven more instalments appeared by June, and then there was another break, just as Pinocchio's happy ending seemed imminent. A further sequence of misadventures began in November until the final conclusion was eventually reached on 25 January 1883. The following month Paggi published the full story in book form, illustrated by the much-loved, somewhat scribbly, black-and-white line drawings of Enrico Mazzanti. It was the first of innumerable editions. By 1900 the eighteenth edition had been published and reprintings accounted for millions of copies. But Collodi did not live to see the full scope of *Pinocchio*'s success, especially its international renown.

From 1883 until 1886, he took over the editorship of the *Giornale per i bambini*, though more or less nominally. All the same, he supplied pieces for publication, notably

[16] Quoted by many sources, including Traversetti, *Introduzione a Collodi*, 104.

[17] In fact, Collodi contemplated lengthening the story from the start; his letter to the editor had continued, 'if you print it, pay me well to make me want to write a sequel'. Ibid. (*My translation.*)

another serial, about Pipì, the little pink monkey, who is warned 'Be careful! If you ape people so much, one day you'll become one yourself . . . and then! Well, then you'll be sorry, but it will be too late!' The flame of Collodi's ironical and satirical humour was still burning bright.

In 1886, his aged mother died. He himself now lived with his rich brother Paolo and Paolo's wife in a handsome apartment in central Florence. Between 1884 and 1890 three more of his educational books were published, the last being *La lanterna magica di Giannettino* ('Giannettino's magic lantern'). On 26 October 1890, a month before his 64th birthday, he suffered a heart attack as he went into the house, and died. At the time, he was, it seems, working on a sequel to *The Adventures of Pinocchio*.

Pinocchio

While thousands of children in different times and places have loved *Pinocchio* and *Alice*, some have not; Alice's adventures can seem frightening (or irritating) and Pinocchio's misadventures tiresome (or nightmarish). At the same time, only an adult can take pleasure in the satirical and parodic resonances of the books. Peter Hunt has said that there are children's books for children and children's books for adults, while Peter Hollindale asserts that a good book for children is a good book for anyone. On the inclusion of a passage of *Pinocchio* in his admired anthology of modern Italian literature, the distinguished scholar and critic Gianfranco Contini commented that the work is not 'children's literature' but simply 'literature'.[18] All the same, *Pinocchio* is honoured in Italy as the supreme example of Italian children's literature, and its author, Collodi, as an innovator and stylist of genius. Abroad, this reverence and its academic

[18] 'Questa è letteratura senza aggettivo, non letteratura per bambini . . .' (This is literature without an adjective, not children's literature), G. Contini, *La letteratura dell'Italia Unita, 1861–1968* (Firenze: Sansoni, 1968), 241. (*My translation.*)

ramifications often cause puzzlement, mainly for the wrong reasons. In Britain at least, we marginalize the serious study of literature for the young. The popular international image of *Pinocchio* is a commercial and inaccurate one, founded upon Walt Disney's wholesale distortion of the novel. Furthermore, Collodi's text is relatively rarely published in its entirety, compared to the innumerable abridgements, often booklets of single episodes in simply language for the very young. In examining the complete work, where, then, should one look to find evidence of its genius?

Part of the magic of *Pinocchio* undoubtedly lies in the depth and complexity lying beneath a seemingly simple and natural surface. *Pinocchio* amalgamates a number of apparently hostile opposites with apparently artless ease. To begin with, it is both traditional and innovative. The construction of the opening lines tells the reader this, while affectionately and conversationally engaging the attention of the child:

Once upon a time there was ...
   'A king!' my little readers will say straight away. No, children, you are mistaken. Once upon a time there was a piece of wood.

Collodi employs the traditional fairy-tale opening, but converts it to his own purposes, combining the pleasures of familiarity and surprise. If one is aware of his ideology and his satirical inclinations as a writer, then one can already see the beginnings of political satire and literary parody in this opening. Fairy tales generally tell of the exceptional. Here the children are recalled from the automatic hierarchical thinking inculcated by traditional stories and are invited to consider something very mundane, basic, everyday, something they have experienced—something real. It seems like just a little joke, and it does introduce the avuncular good humour of the book. Yet it has a much deeper, indeed fundamental, importance. The piece of wood will shortly change hands between two very poor old men, at the opposite pole, socially and economically, from kings. The reader is about to experience with them their cold, their hunger, their reality.

The folk tales and fairy tales of oral tradition always were methods of addressing real life, of course, but they were extended metaphors in which fantasy was dominant. Collodi maintains an extraordinary balance between fantasy, the unreal, the world of the imagination and, interwoven with it, the harsh truths of real life. It is clear all along that it is in real life that we belong, and eventually the hero's great ambition is to leave the fantasy world and belong fully to ordinary reality. He was not a piece of luxury wood, after all, but just firewood. *Pinocchio* is not a high-minded, moralizing tract, however; it is a fairy tale and fun, but not of a kind to promote unrealistic expectations.

Fairy tales were originally folk tales, narrated orally from time immemorial to all age-groups. With his opening lines, Collodi captured the tone of oral story-telling, but he had only recently played a different role in the continuum of the tradition. As the translator of Charles Perrault, Madame d'Aulnoy, and Madame Leprince de Beaumont, he had communicated the work of some of the finest and earliest of literary fairy-tale tellers, of the late seventeenth and early eighteenth centuries. Yet his was the age of the great collections of oral narratives. The Brothers Grimm published their volumes of folk tales between 1812 and 1822; in Italy the last quarter of the century was especially fruitful, with Comparetti publishing his Italian folk tales in 1875, and Imbriani his Florentine story-book in 1877, while Giuseppe Pitrè engaged in encyclopedic research in Sicily throughout the period (his Tuscan folk tales were to appear in 1886).

Some episodes of *Pinocchio* demonstrate a close affiliation to the fairy-tale tradition, whether popular or literary. One of Perrault's stories, *Le Petit Poucet* ('Hop o' my thumb'), has a little boy of spirit pitting his wits against an ogre. The ogre, who has a whole sheep roasting for supper, wants to eat the child and his siblings, and gets out his knife; the brothers go down on their knees and beg for mercy. In *Pinocchio*, the puppet-master, Swallowfire, is huge and terrifying, and his voice is described as like that of an ogre; he is roasting his supper of a whole ram but, having insufficient wood, he plans to put Pinocchio on the flames; taking pity on Pinocchio's old father, he decides on Harlequin instead, whereupon Pinocchio goes down on his knees and begs for mercy for his 'brother' Harlequin. In *Pinocchio* the Fairy's coach drawn by mice is reminiscent of the coach provided for Cinderella by her Fairy Godmother, and the poodle coachman in his Louis XIV livery is in keeping with this and other fairy tales. The Fairy's magic birds (the Hawk and the Woodpeckers), which do her bidding, also have traditional antecedents: pigeons, turtle-doves, and all the birds of the air come to aid the Grimms' Cinderella at her call.

The Fairy with Indigo Hair, who appears in turn as a 'Little Girl', as Pinocchio's 'sister', and finally as his 'mother', is the most overt link with fairy tales. Yet, in spite of a wealth of Fairy Godmothers, she comes as a surprise to latter-day readers: in many respects, she is so unfairylike, we think. To start with, it is a question of size. Her normal human scale does not match the modern stereotyped fairy. However, it was Shakespeare who gave diminutive fairies a literary existence in *A Midsummer Night's Dream*, and influenced the recurrent image of the fairy in modern writing. 'In contrast, the *fées* of the cult for fairy stories in France at the end of the 17th century were full-sized people with formidable characters,'[19] like the good Fairy Godmother of Perrault's Cinderella and the wicked

[19] H. Carpenter and M. Prichard, *The Oxford Companion to Children's Literature* (London and New York: Oxford University Press, 1984, 1995), 174.

fairy of his Sleeping Beauty. Naturally, it was Perrault's model that Collodi followed. In keeping with her size, the personality of Collodi's Fairy, in her sisterly and motherly guises, has nothing of the strange or the exotic that would link her to a Titania; she has notably human and humane qualities, warmth, kindness, pity, and responsibility among them.

She has only two characteristics which distinguish her from the normal and terrestrial. First, she has dark-blue or indigo hair, the unique feature which identifies her as supernatural (no wings, of course). A single defining or symbolic colour is a common device in traditional fairy tales, as in Little Red Riding Hood and the Bluebird, but can have the same 'unreal' connotation, as in Perrault's Bluebeard. The sophisticated (and Turkish) dark-blue of Collodi's 'turchino' was a colour which appealed to him, which had some symbolic value for him, perhaps denoting specialness, elegance, mystery. In his novel *I misteri di Firenze* ('The mysteries of Florence'), the first ephemeral sighting of a crucial character is at a masked ball, where this person is wearing a 'dominò di seta turchina' (a costume of indigo silk).[20] Secondly, Collodi's fairy can work magic, as when she summons the woodpeckers to reduce the size of Pinocchio's nose, or when, at the end, she transforms the puppet into a real boy, his hut into a pretty cottage, his frail, ailing 'father' into an active, hearty craftsman, and the contents of Pinocchio's pocket into 40 gold florins. These magical moments, however, are counterbalanced by her parental, persistent, gentle persuasion that Pinocchio must learn to be good and must be diligent at school.

The leitmotiv of metamorphosis runs all through *Pinocchio*, and the capacity for metamorphosis is dominant in the Fairy's magic. Without appropriate passage of time her own age changes, from little girl to concerned mother.

---

[20] C. Lorenzini, *I misteri di Firenze* (Firenze: Salani, 1988), 20.

Her essential nature is capable of change, too, as is her social status. At first she appears like a 'dead' doll; after being an industrious housewife, she is a grand lady wearing jewels in a box at the theatre; the last time Pinocchio sees her in the flesh, she has become a little she-goat with hair of an intense indigo colour.

The Fairy is not the only character to undergo dramatic metamorphoses. Pinocchio himself, instead of turning from puppet into real boy, first becomes, like his naughty friend Candle-Wick, a little donkey. So both Fairy and puppet are transmogrified from their quasi-human selves into animals, in keeping with another traditional, recurring motif. In old fairy tales, whether oral or literary, the animal and the fairy worlds are frequently intertwined. Shakespeare himself had associated the Fairy Queen with an ass, with similar punning and metaphorical intent to Collodi three centuries later. Indeed, the donkey is one of the most prevalent of animal characters throughout the folk-tale genre and specifically in fables. The reason lay in the familiarity of the donkey as beast of burden, so domesticated by people that the human–donkey relationship was a commonplace of life. Moreover the words for the ass had early taken on the popular metaphorical connotation of stupidity when applied to human beings. Collodi employed this tradition when he made metamorphosis into a donkey the just deserts of all the silly, lazy boys in *Pinocchio*.

Because of the intimacy between men and donkeys, and the manifold exploitation by the one of the other, the donkey is well placed to observe all human failings. As in Apuleius' satire *The Golden Ass* (also called *The Metamorphoses*), Collodi's donkeys bear witness to the stupidity and brutality of men. Collodi's Little Man who collects children to take them to the Land of Plenty and Pleasure is cold viciousness personified in his cruelty to the carriage donkeys, children once themselves. The idiotic Ringmaster puts on airs for the benefit of his audience, while making money out of the labour and humiliation of his performing animals, but heartlessly abandons the donkey, Pinocchio, to a harsh fate, once he no longer serves his purpose. The country bandsman is content to drown the donkey lingeringly, so as to have his skin for a drum. (In the Grimm Brothers' story 'The Musicians of Bremen', the tired old donkey escapes from his master to avoid being sold for his skin.) Finally, Donkey Candle-Wick dies of exhaustion in the service of a peasant farmer. In nineteenth-century Italy such condemnation of cruelty to animals was astonishing.

Collodi's device of the donkeys goes back to even earlier times than either the fairy tradition of *Peau d'Asne* or Apuleius (second century AD). The Fables of Aesop, who lived in the sixth century BC, are full of donkeys. There is the one which illustrates the stupidity of the suggestible old man and boy, who end by carrying the donkey to market, instead of riding it, causing mirth and pleasing no one (except the donkey). The ancient fables are moral tales in which animals often provide examples of virtue and vice; amongst the many typical participants are the fox, cat, dog, donkey, goat, owl, and grasshopper (or cricket). These all appear in *Pinocchio*. Collodi's animals are anthropomorphically characterized, with satiric intent, in just the same manner as those of Aesop's fables. His interest in the aristocratic French fairy tales of the reign of the Sun King may have extended to embrace La Fontaine's Aesopic fables in verse, where again cunning and stupid animals symbolized the greed and hypocrisy of human beings.

Collodi's Fox and Cat are superb examples in the Aesop–La Fontaine mould. The traditional fox often plays tricks on others, but is sometimes caught out himself. He invites the stork to dinner and puts down a flat dish of soup; the stork reciprocates with a tall jar of mincemeat. The fox is gluttonous but insincere; the grapes he cannot reach must be sour. He is a successful wheedler and con-man, persuading the crow that it is beautiful and must have a lovely voice, so she 'sings' and drops her lump of cheese. Collodi's Fox and Cat are also insinuating and plausible tricksters, callously seeking their own gain at the expense of others, whose trusting *naïveté* they exploit without scruple. They too receive their come-uppance, for *Pinocchio* likewise is a fable or moral tale, though the didacticism is disguised. (Long before, Collodi had used the same metaphorical notions: the final chapter of *The Mysteries of Florence* is entitled 'The foxes in conclave'.) Even one of Collodi's most distinctive creations in *Pinocchio* may have Greek ancestry. The voice of Aesop's grasshopper irritates the owl, which eats it and sleeps in peace. The admonitions of the Talking Cricket irritate Pinocchio, who kills it and does as he pleases.

A characteristic of the fairy tale is the presence and, importantly, the interaction of both humans and magical creatures, including witches and wizards, giants, ogres, dragons, and monsters. Alternatively, the (so-called) fairy story may be populated by a combination of humans and animals (Goldilocks and the Three Bears, Little Red Riding Hood). *Pinocchio* has all these types of participant: Swallow-fire is a kind of ogre; the Serpent on the road is a kind of dragon; the Green Fisherman is a kind of monster; the Little Man is a kind of wizard or goblin—or the Devil. There is only one (multiform) fairy, and there are only a few human characters (usually realistically drawn), but there is a veritable menagerie of animals, common and rare, European and exotic, which have several functions, especially human caricature. This was one of Collodi's (double) innovations as a writer for children. We now take animals in children's books for granted, but it was an idea that was only just taking root in the second half of the nineteenth century; previously it was for adults that animals had been given sophisticated roles in social satire. Two pioneering stories in the 1870s, both by women, one in Italy and one in Britain, had established the possibility of writing about animal protagonists: one was Ida Baccini's *Le memorie di un pulcino* ('The memoirs of a chick', 1875) and the other was Anna Sewell's *Black Beauty* (1877). Both these stories used animals naturalistically, not symbolically. A precedent closer in kind to Collodi was Lewis Carroll's creation, in *Alice's Adventures in Wonderland*, of animals that talk and behave like human beings. Like the animals in *Pinocchio*, Carroll's are connected with the fable tradition and are there to illustrate human foibles. His White Rabbit and Mad March Hare are kith and kin to Aesop's Hare in the race with the Tortoise. Carroll has a sleepy Dormouse where Collodi would have a lazy Marmot. Both were initiating new procedures and new languages in the children's literatures of their respective countries; both were doing it by modernizing aspects of an ancient art.

Collodi was innovative, too, in his choice of protagonist, for the puppet represents yet another dimension in his complex system of characters: unlike the animals, Pinocchio is an inanimate object, who magically springs to life. (He is not, however, a toy, which would rank him lower than children; he is a 3-foot, 'working' puppet associated with the world of entertainment, and Geppetto/Joe had intended to make a living out of him.[21]) In both *Alice* books, Carroll had used a similar conceit, albeit alongside a human heroine: in the world beyond the Looking-Glass the chess pieces are alive, while in Wonderland the pack of cards is animated, with dramatic results, the Courtroom scene being quite as fearsome and life-threatening as the episode backstage at the puppet theatre.

The figure of the puppet, Pinocchio, with his unique personality, capacity for comedy, and narrative function, was without precedent. Pygmalion's statue was given life in the

---

[21] Pinocchio is included as a toy in L. R. Kuznets, *When Toys Come Alive* (New Haven and London: Yale University Press, 1994). He is frequently perceived in that way overseas, influenced by Disney, by book illustrators, and by Easy Reader versions.

story recounted in Ovid's *Metamorphoses*. Latterly, life-sized automata had occasionally taken leading roles in narratives for adults: Mary Wollstonecraft Shelley had created Frankenstein in 1818, while in 1816, the German author of several fairy stories, E. T. A. Hoffmann, had written *Der Sandman* ('The Sandman'), inventing the mechanical woman later converted into *Coppélia*, in the ballet by Delibes. But these are not true analogies: they have to do with man's desire to play God and create both life and perfection; the modern ones are sinister stories, bound to end in disaster. Pinocchio does not have to be coaxed into life; he already possesses life before he is out of the wood, and he causes tribulation accidentally while, of his own accord, longing to be an ordinary boy. He is an astonishingly bold (and cheerful) character, affectionate and never vengeful or antagonistic to humans, never inert or passive, never ruled by or dependent on human beings. Collodi's puppet did not derive from other narratives but, as in the case of Madame Eugénie Foà's *L'Histoire d'un polichinelle* ('The story of a Punchinello puppet'), his place of birth was the theatre, that archetypal arena for the co-mingling of reality and artifice.

For nearly thirty years Collodi had been passionately interested in the theatre and in cultural manifestations connected with it. He was knowledgeable about the Commedia dell'Arte, the Italian theatre of stock characters, stock situations, improvisation, masks, wit, and slapstick comedy, the theatre, that is, of Harlequin and Columbine, Pulcinella, Brighella, Pantalone, and, indeed, Scaramuccia. For centuries there had been marionette versions of Commedia dell'Arte performances, as well as live ones. The significance of the mask and the stock character permeated popular culture at all levels of society, as in the masked balls in Florence and the costumes worn for Carnival in Venice (a city prominent in the history of comedy in Italy). In the Commedia dell'Arte there ran not just a comic but a satirical vein of comment on social mores. Typical situations derived from social conflict and the moral victories over adversity of humble characters. The Venetian playwright Goldoni developed the idea of the hero-servant who was livelier, funnier, more active, more attractive, more appealing, and above all cleverer than his master, the aristocrat. The concept spread to the French theatre and to opera, most remarkably in Mozart's treatment in *The Marriage of Figaro* (1786), its text being by his Venetian librettist, Lorenzo da Ponte. (Here women, as well as servants, are altogether better than the 'noble' male.) The political implications for democracy and equality in the real world are plain to see. *Pinocchio* was another part of that evolution, a prose narrative which used some of the characters and conventions of the old comedy (a theatre of the people, incidentally), and which depicted the honest poor jovially, while mercilessly exposing the failings of the privileged classes.

Obvious borrowings from the theatre in *Pinocchio* include the puppet himself (and Mazzanti, the first illustrator, gave him the typical frill at the neck and waisted tunic of Commedia dell'Arte costumes); then there is the puppet theatre with Harlequin and other familiar characters, the use by the Fox and Cat of disguises masking their faces, the puppet shows in the Land of Toys, and the circus sequence embellished with the paraphernalia of the theatre and the music-hall manner of the Ringmaster. Less obviously, the very form of *Pinocchio* is theatrical, demonstrated in the episodic construction of the novel in strictly separated scenes, and in the use of much vivacious dialogue, which often has the flavour of quick-fire stage repartee, matching the style of the quick-witted improvisation of the Commedia dell'Arte:

'Good morning, Master Anthony,' said Old Joe. 'What are you doing there on the floor?'

'I'm teaching the ants their numbers.'

'Much good may it do you.'
'What brought you here, my friend?'
'My legs....'[22]

The 'Much good may it do you' is redolent of the Commedia dell'Arte style, and it is reminiscent, too, of the
English music-hall ('I don't wish to know that'). The technique of repetition is closely similar to the recapitulations
and reprises of theatrical presentation:

'These hake are good!...'
'These grey mullet are delicious!...'
'These soles are excellent!...'
'These bass are superb!...'
'These whole anchovies are delightful!...'
As you can imagine, the hake, the grey mullet, the soles, the bass
and the anchovies all went...into the vat...[23]

This type of (double) repetition reminds one of the pantomime, where words are repeated to be learnt and chorused
out loud by the audience. Frequently in *Pinocchio* the dialogue is so dynamic and so structured as to provoke the
active participation of a child being read to. The puppet's
own several rambling and garbled recapitulations of what
has happened to him are a brilliant device for reminding
the readers of the first serial version, without pedantry,
about the 'story so far', but they are also a satire upon the
laborious theatrical, perhaps farcical, convention—as well
as illustrating the real behaviour of children.

Many different types of theatre are reflected in Collodi's
dialogue, including tragedy and the opera which he greatly
loved. There are several semi-quotations or pastiches of
opera, including the high-flown, unrustic language of the
peasant whose hen-house is robbed by the beech martens.[24]
At the puppet-theatre, Harlequin, parodying the tragic-

---

[22] Ch. II.   [23] Ch. XXVIII.   [24] Ch. XXII.

operatic genres, exclaims on seeing Pinocchio in the audience, 'Divine Providence! Do I dream or do I wake?...'[25] Dialogue of many kinds, both naturalistic and parodic, dominates to such an extent in *Pinocchio* that normal narrative is often minimal, while description throughout the story is almost non-existent.

Is there then no equivalent to stage scenery or stage effects? One can argue that there is, but the stage instructions are the basic ones for travelling companies of players: a white cottage, the Great Oak, a cave by the sea-shore. Indeed Geppetto/Joe has his own bit of painted scenery; unable to afford a real fire, he has the comforting illusion of a bright blaze painted on the wall (perhaps a nod by Collodi at the complexities of reality and artifice, fact and fiction). In the tragi-comedy of *Pinocchio*, however, it is the lighting and the props which create more dramatic impact than the scenery.

As if using the resources of the stage, there is great play with light and dark. Pinocchio acts as a guard-dog at night, twice lingers in town streets after dark, once to be drenched by a bucketful of water, and once getting his foot stuck in a hole in the door. Both times it is raining and both times the action can be visualized as stage business. There are two *tour de force* night scenes. As Pinocchio emerges from the Red Lobster Inn, we are plunged into total darkness which makes his fear palpable as he is brushed by the blundering night-owls and is silently pursued by the black-draped thugs (alias Cat and Fox). Later, he waits with Candle-Wick in the slowly gathering gloom, trying to tear himself away and go home 'by nightfall'. At last a tiny light is seen in the dark, and there comes the faint sound

[25] Ch. X. Whether intentionally or not, this sets up all sorts of reverberations, not only theatrical, ranging from Shakespeare (*Hamlet*) to Keats ('Ode to a nightingale').

of harness bells and a coach-horn, when the fateful carriage drawn by donkeys arrives in a *coup de théâtre*. Then there are the murky, watery depths of the Shark's belly, in which a faint little light is seen glimmering, and from which Pinocchio and his 'father' emerge into a night lit by moon and stars. Lights often punctuate the dark for dramatic or pictorial effect, and they can be mysterious, reassuring, or sinister, but in the case of the Snail with a candle on her head, the light serves the purposes of humour (and, incidentally, education), for there is a play on words between 'lumaca' (snail) and 'lume' (light).

Collodi's humour is ever-present, multi-faceted, both theatrical and political in inspiration. Sometimes it is broad physical humour, often with a painful edge, and the reader may experience the *Schadenfreude* that can delight a theatre, circus, or cinema audience witnessing pantomime, clowns, or Charlie Chaplin: the bucket of water is a case in point, as is the policeman's grabbing Pinocchio by his long nose. Physical incongruity is the source of more subtle mirth: the sight and sound of the wooden puppet racing along town streets, his feet clattering; the conjunction of the 'free' puppet with his dependent 'brothers' hanging from strings; the puppet made to imitate a guard-dog, sitting in a stale kennel with a spiked collar around his neck and barking ferociously; the Green Fisherman slowly turning the puppet about among the fish caught in his net, puzzled as to his species, and finally flouring him thoroughly for the pot.

There are some major set-pieces where a whole episode is to be savoured at different levels of understanding, including the satirical. One of these is the courtroom scene, analogous in its dual purpose and dual effect to the trial in *Alice's Adventures in Wonderland*. In both cases, this solemn occasion is 'peopled' by a combination of grotesque animals and normally inanimate objects. Just as Carroll's

Kings and Queens are petulant and trivial, so Collodi's representatives of authority are pompous and ineffectual or illogical. Both writers indicate the absurdity and injustice of the real processes of law. In Collodi's post-Darwinian courtroom the Judge is a great ape, described with a truly Carrollian *non sequitur*: for years he had been obliged to wear gold-rimmed glasses without lenses, because of inflammation of the eyes. The particulars of the social satire would be just as appropriate today, for the Judge is respected for his advanced age, the crime turns out to be *allowing* oneself to be robbed, and the victim is sent to gaol; later he is set free only after 'confessing' his criminality. In this episode, the policemen are mastiffs. At the beginning of *Pinocchio*, the human 'carabiniere' who catches the running puppet was equally fallible; hearing the bystanders gossiping about how Old Joe will certainly be cruel to Pinocchio, he takes their word for it and imprisons the old man, letting the childish miscreant run off into the night.

The medical profession is also lampooned. When the hanged Pinocchio has been rescued by the Fairy and is lying prone in bed, she sends for three doctors, represented by a Crow, an Owl, and a Cricket. She wants the finest advice as to whether the puppet is alive or dead. Naturally, the doctors with a great air of authority contradict each other in elegantly wrought, satirical dialogue. When the Cricket's common sense makes the puppet sob, the doctors remain immovable from their hypotheses and their opposition; the fact that the corpse weeps means that he is recovering, according to one expert, but according to the other it is a sign that he is sad at dying. All this is couched in imperturbed, professional flourishes ('my illustrious friend and colleague'), which are all the more funny because hypocritical. Thus the well-placed professionals and officials, as well as the mystique of their working practices, are the butt of satire in *Pinocchio*.

Dialogue is one vehicle *par excellence* for Collodi's humour, ranging from the simple woodworkers' knockabout repartee (followed by comic fisticuffs) to the pretentious, half-educated nonsense pronounced grandiloquently by the Ringmaster and to the over-educated hocus-pocus of the professionals. Whether it is in the form of dialogue or narration, it is above all the potential of words themselves in which Collodi and his readers rejoice (another similarity with Carroll). *Pinocchio* is full of puns and plays on words; these are not devised for empty cleverness, but for the pleasure inherent in words and for the added value in layers of meaning. While Pinocchio is being mistaken for a fish, he is described as 'squirming like an eel'. Thanking the dog which saves him, Pinocchio says that he would have been 'fried' by now, or 'in the soup' in the nearest English colloquial expression, which is both literally and metaphorically true. Double entendres are thickly woven into the texture of the style. The distinctive quality of the humour which resided so much in Collodi's use of language was recognized immediately. An early advertisement quoted a critic, writing in the *Corriere del Mattino* newspaper of 14 February 1883, who had said that in this novel Italian good sense was grafted onto a whole-hearted humour which could no longer be considered as solely English. This sounds like an acknowledgement of the kinship in the zany zest for words between Carroll and the 'nonsense' school in England and Collodi in Italy.

The potential of words for humour is often combined in *Pinocchio* with their potential for beauty, for poetry; in turn, these are frequently associated with patterning and symmetry. The puppet engages in a fateful conversation with the ghost of the Talking Cricket (who appears on a tree-trunk, glowing like a nightlight):

'But I want to go on.'
'It's very late . . .'

'I want to go on.'
'It's a very dark night . . .'
'I want to go on.'
'The path is dangerous . . .'
'I want to go on.'[26]

After this the light of the Cricket is 'extinguished'.

Even Collodi's use of language, which is stylish by any
literary standards, also has social and political overtones.
First, there are some Tuscanisms which, on the one hand,
establish the authentic and demotic nature of the speech in
the book; on the other, paradoxically, they assert the cultural primacy of Florence. Then, there is a form of democracy in the very naturalness of much of Collodi's diction.
His characters' conversations are full of idioms, colloqui-
alisms, proverbial expressions, popular parlance, and excla-
mations. This truth to life is significant evidence of Collodi's
originality, in terms of both literature and children's literature. It does not, however, entail diffuseness or lack of
direction. On the contrary, the language is taut and con-
trolled; this very lack of ornament was new and forward-
looking.

Pinocchio was begun just as the greatest work employing
the literary theory of *Verismo* was published: Verga's novel
I Malavoglia (1881) ('The House by the Medlar Tree', 1950)
was intended to be a faithful and objective record of the
reality of life in a simple, Sicilian fishing village. *Pinocchio*
has much in common with it, in spite of the personal point
of view expressed satirically and ironically by Collodi. In
both novels one finds the sympathetic depiction of the poor,
in both there is an abundance of dialogue, little narration,
and almost no description, both echo the natural cadences of
conversation (and especially the use of proverbs and conventional sayings); most striking is the use of theatre tech-
niques by both writers. To convey the life of a community,

---

[26] Ch. XIII.

Verga deploys his villagers as a kind of Greek chorus, gossiping the narration of events to each other and commenting on what occurs; the village square is like a stage and the reader 'watches' the action unfold and 'hears' the actors reveal the story. (Interestingly, from 1865 the Sicilian writer had spent some years working in Florence, where he had become deeply immersed in theatre.)

Whether coincidence was at work, or whether Collodi consciously adopted some of the ideas of Verga's *Verismo*, there are two passages in *Pinocchio* where it appears that he parodies *I Malavoglia*, though with serious intentions. In both cases, he was writing about fishermen. Surprisingly, the sea plays an important part in *Pinocchio*. When it is first introduced, Pinocchio is trying to save his drowning father; the fishermen shake their heads and quietly chorus their fears. Later, a fisherman in his hut by the shore provides a naked Pinocchio with an empty sack, meant for lupin seeds, to wear; the Malavoglia family lost their fishing-boat when it went down with a cargo of lupin seeds.

While Verga intended detachment, Collodi's writing, by contrast, has a strongly personal inflection. One of his most individual methods for conveying his point of view is his use of irony. Yet more important than his social satire on the contemporary world was his commentary on universal human nature. Some of his caricaturing is Dickensian in its delineation of failings, and hypocrisy receives the full sardonic force of his ironic genius. The Cat kills the White Blackbird to teach it not to interfere in future in other people's conversations. At the Red Lobster Inn none of the party has any appetite: 'The poor Cat, . . . seriously indisposed with stomach trouble, could only manage thirty-five mullet with tomato sauce and four portions of tripe and onions . . .' Likewise, the 'Fox would have gladly nibbled at a little something too, but as the doctor had prescribed an extremely strict diet, he had to make do with a simple jugged hare . . .'.[27] This is not set out as dialogue, and yet one can hear the insinuating, two-faced conversation of this pair of tricksters, who left their victim to pay the bill. (Food is another recurring theme. Collodi clearly loved food himself, and recognized its importance in children's lives.) The dissembling double act, with the Cat invariably echoing the last words of the Fox, is a creation of genius, both funny and shiveringly threatening. Hypocrisy is also proper to the sinister Little Man with the coach and donkeys, and irony is as usual Collodi's weapon for identifying the viciousness. When one of the donkeys is recalcitrant, the Little Man, unlike the children, does not laugh; instead he 'felt so affectionate towards that restless little ass that, with a kiss, he took the top half of the other ear clean off'.[28]

In *Pinocchio*, the emphasis is on comedy, yet tragedy is present to a significant degree. These adventures entail danger, fear, loss, and grief, and there is a great deal of death in the book. Pinocchio kills the Talking Cricket who later appears as a ghost; he finds a child who pronounces herself to be dead and awaiting her bier; he is nearly killed himself and a bier is brought for him; he finds the tombstone of the Fairy, supposedly dead of grief at his neglect; his 'father' is thought to have drowned; a schoolmate seems to have died in a fight on the beach; donkey Pinocchio nearly drowns; donkey Candle-Wick does die of overwork; Old Joe seems at death's door, and the Fairy is said to be gravely ill in hospital. A century ago death was a commonplace of everyday life; Collodi had ample experience of it himself, especially among his siblings and through the early death of his father. Perhaps the deaths and griefs in *Pinocchio* were a way of confronting children's worst fears. Although shocking and unpalatable to modern taste, they have an important function in the balance of the narrative: the joy is

---

[27] Ch. XIII.   [28] Ch. XXXI.

more joyous because of survival through the experience of sorrow, and conversely the story is constantly pulled back from shallow frivolity by the depth of serious emotion evoked.

Pinocchio's entertaining series of adventures can be read just for the thrills and the amusement. The extraordinary and vivid nature of the fantastic adventures is liberating from the confines of the norm and Collodi's emphasis on exuberant imagination represented a leap forward in the history of children's literature. At a deeper level the sequence of journeys equates to youthful flights from reality, but is simultaneously the story of a quest or a rite of passage, one which everyone experiences with greater or lesser difficulty: Pinocchio's eventual desire to be a real boy (not voiced until Chapter XXV) is everyone's desire for a place in adult society, the need to move beyond a phase felt to be incomplete and provisional. *Pinocchio* is about growing up, as are, to some extent, the *Alice* books; all three are about finding one's way in a mystifying, dangerous, illogical, and unattractive adult world, while at the same time wanting to do things (*Pinocchio*) or wanting to know things (*Alice*). Collodi addresses the development of the child's emotions, morality, and responsibility, as well as education. Hence the presence of a wide range of stimuli provoking strong responses, including horror, anxiety, and sorrow. He understands the discomforts of childhood, and the frightening nature of the physical world and of some grown-ups. Certain passages in both *Pinocchio* and *Alice* can be terrifying to the child reader: notably perhaps, in *Pinocchio*, the chase culminating in the hanging. There are also moments of gratuitous cruelty (as perceived a hundred years on), by way of teaching the puppet a lesson, like his kind 'mother' sending him imitation food to eat. We frequently read that Pinocchio has a kind heart, yet he can seem detestably cruel to his devoted 'father' and 'mother'. The message here is that what one does in life has consequences for other people; we have to learn how to make choices (until the end Pinocchio makes all the wrong ones), and how to take into account the effects of our decisions on others. At first the juvenile Pinocchio wants to do what will please himself; by the end, what he wants most is to look after the needs of others. He has matured morally and emotionally; selfishness has been replaced by generosity. The point of the story is that difficulty is confronted and, with good will on all sides, is overcome. (Alice's waking from a nightmare is not so secure a resolution as earning maturity and release from childish tribulations.)

Pinocchio also places great emphasis on nurturing the mind. It might be supposed that Collodi's teaching about the importance of education is all overt and literal and even somewhat unsubtle. In fact there are subliminal indications, too. Pinocchio is impeded and embarrassed by being unable to read properly. One occasion is directly after he has chosen not to go to school to learn to read. He still retains the possibility in the shape of his alphabet book, which he then decides to sell in exchange for entertainment. When the boys fight on the seashore, and throw their books (by well-meaning educators like Collodi himself) into the sea, it appears that the author is just making a pleasant joke against himself; but he is also raising the question of the suitability of (the best) books for children, which even the fishes reject for nutriment. The last chapter has profound theoretical and philosophical implications concerning the most effective form of education. Though assiduous for a time, Pinocchio rejected conventional education in favour of experience of the world. At first this was a negative dissipation of his energies in frivolity, with painful results.

Finding first his 'father' and then a new purpose and direction, Pinocchio starts to learn in new ways. He teaches himself how to control the physical world, rescuing his father and then caring for him by earning a living through physical exertion. Having learned through personal physical experience, he begins to want to inform his mind, and, through his own choice, he turns to such written matter as he can obtain, studying it to improve his intellectual abilities. The puppet is now learning because he wants to and not because he has to. For 'Pinocchio', read 'Émile': the puppet is putting into practice the educational theory of Rousseau, a process which, more recently, was to be explored again in fantastic fiction by Italo Calvino, an admirer of Collodi, in his novel *Il barone rampante (The Baron in the Trees).*[29] Pinocchio's educational progress was more apposite than a mere harking back to a great theorist of the past. Rousseau's ideas had greatly influenced the leading educational thinkers of the early nineteenth century, Froebel and Pestalozzi, and soon after Collodi's time they were to be given new vigour by the Italian educational reformer Maria Montessori. They have since been established by child psychologists such as Piaget as the correct basis for early education.

Pinocchio's difficult and dangerous journey through experience to knowledge has been compared to the *Odyssey* and to Dante's *Divine Comedy*. In Italy especially, as much has been written about it and as many interpretations put forward as for those great works of world literature. *Pinocchio* has been seen as a Catholic tract, with the Fairy as the Virgin Mary and Joe as Joseph. In this scenario, the wayward puppet makes for a somewhat shocking Christ-child, there is a colour mismatch between the indigo hair and the different blue of the Virgin's mantle, and a blind eye is turned to Collodi's rejection of the Church and wholly secular literary personality. Even so, conventional respect would almost certainly have caused him to regard such ideas as sacrilegious. There have been ideological,

---

[29] Jean-Jacques Rousseau, *Émile*, 1762. I. Calvino, *Il barone rampante* (Torino: Einaudi, 1957) (*The Baron in the Trees*, London, 1959; New York, 1977).

Marxist, philosophical, anthroposophical, psychoanalytical, and Freudian readings of *Pinocchio*. The Freudian explanation of Pinocchio's nose as phallic is largely ignored in Italy, unsurprisingly since it is derived from inadequate knowledge of Italian proverbial expressions linking lies and noses and unfamiliarity with Collodi's other work. It takes small episodes out of literary and social context and burdens them with a once fashionable, northern, Judaeo-Protestant preoccupation. Alice suffers a similar physical fright when she tries the 'Drink Me' bottle; once she shrinks and once she grows to fill the room. For both children, what is represented is the ordinary fear of being found out or of being trapped.

Many of these elaborate theories now seem outdated, but *parti pris* interpretations will continue to emerge following each new intellectual vogue. This is, indeed, one of the signs—and penalties—of greatness. Perhaps one of the most extraordinary qualities of *Pinocchio*, which makes it especially available to reinterpretation, is its essential ambiguity. The central character is, on the one hand, an inanimate puppet, and on the other a running, talking, thinking, headstrong child. Then there is the question of dependence and autonomy. A puppet is reliant for his every activity upon human agency; he has no freedom; his strings are pulled. Pinocchio, however, is a rebel; he seizes his freedom at the earliest opportunity, and continues repeatedly to assert it. What is more, he subversively upsets the existing order of things, and like Collodi he calls everything into question. In this there is a profound and progressive recognition of the processes of growing up, and of the value of a critical, independent, questioning mind. Finally, there is the pervasive ambivalence and interweaving of fantasy and reality. The gawky, wooden puppet whose running and speaking make him unreal is cherished as a son by a straightforward, believable old man. The magical and the picaresque are constantly brought down to earth by acerbic, sardonic, hard-headed Tuscan realism. Like Collodi's personality, his novel possesses a distinctive combination of formality and irreverence. The ambiguity, the diversity, the coexistence of imagination and intellect, make *Pinocchio* capable of meaning all things to all people; they make it universal.

NOTE ON THE TEXT AND TRANSLATION

This new translation of *The Adventures of Pinocchio* has been made from the text established by Ornella Castellani Pollidori for the critical edition which was published in Italy by the Fondazione Nazionale Carlo Collodi (Pescia, 1983) for the *Pinocchio* centenary in 1983. The first publication of *Pinocchio*, in children's newspaper serial form, appeared with substantial interruptions between 1881 and 1883. Like Dickens's novels, it had been composed in segments while serialization was in progress. The final part of the serial was contained in the issue of *Il Giornale per i bambini* of 25 January 1883. In February, Collodi's regular publisher, Felice Paggi of Florence, brought out the first book edition. Three more editions followed in 1886, 1887, and 1888; then the Paggi publishing house was sold and, under the new name of R. Bemporad e Figlio, continued both the distinguished tradition of the Paggi brothers and the frequent business of republishing *Pinocchio*. The first Bemporad edition, the fifth, came out soon after Collodi's death in 1890. It is this fifth edition which forms the basis of the 1983 critical edition.

The nature of the original publication, the speedy issuing of new editions, Collodi's sometimes casual approach to proof-correction, as well as many imperfections in typesetting, all conspired to produce a large number of errors and subsequent emendations (not all of them truly corrections) in all the early stages. Ornella Castellani Pollidori believes that Collodi supervised the editorial work until his death; however, since, in his lifetime, his writings were frequently revised for book publication by other hands, there are arguments for privileging the first, or another earlier, book edition of *Pinocchio* rather than the fifth in seeking to arrive

at a definitive version. A further modern edition prompted
by the centenary year was that of Fernando Tempesti (Milan,
1983), in which he advances the arguments for the altern-
ative procedure. Nevertheless a translation which itself
aims to be scholarly cannot but be taken from the text of
the critical edition, itself a work of detailed and impressive
scholarship.

Translating Collodi is not, as one might suppose, child's
play. He was a writer of great culture, of great wit, style,
and sophistication. Yet his humble and poverty-stricken
origins nurtured in him a sympathetic, and acute, ear for
the (dialectal) language and cadences of the people. Both
his dialogue and his narration are full of everyday idiom
and proverbial expression. He employed a uniquely personal brand of irony as part of a whole armoury of comic,
and polemical, skills. He relished the texture and the pattern
of cultural and etymological connections between words,
and this gives rise to highly entertaining word-play. He is
a teasing stylist, and, at the same time, apparently artlessly
'natural'.

How to capture all these subtleties in a translation? Of
course, it is not possible. No translation of *Pinocchio* can be
more than an approximation. One might even say that it is
a logical impossibility, since the single word upon which the
whole story is founded and, more importantly, on which
the central concept is constructed is not fully translatable.
The original title and subsequent subtitle is [*La*] *storia di
un burattino*, the story of a puppet. 'Burattino', in addition
to meaning 'puppet' or 'marionette', can be used figuratively
to describe a fidgety child. So, the word itself has that
ambiguity, between the animate and the inanimate, that
Pinocchio has. Then again, because of the importance of
the puppet-theatre and related theatrical forms in Italy, not
only historically but still in some regions today, the words
for 'puppet', and a range of connected terminology, have
quite different cultural resonances in Italian from those

prompted in English-speaking contexts. For a hint of likely
different responses, consider the transmogrification over
the centuries of Pulcinella, played by a live actor wearing
a mask in the improvised plays of the Commedia dell'Arte,
into Punch, the archetypal, stereotyped, knockabout
(often glove-)puppet of the seaside esplanade, now all but
defunct. Or, consider the life-size, armour-clad 'pupi', which
in Sicily, after half a millennium, are still acting out the
chivalric struggles between Christian and Saracen.

Albeit acknowledging the losing battle, I have tried to fill
my version as full of meaning and suggestion as is possible
while, at the same time, attempting to keep the language
sprightly. The original serial, in their own weekly newspaper, was often likely to be read by children themselves, but
it is abundantly clear that much of *Pinocchio* was written
to be read aloud by an adult to children. Some of the words
are difficult for the young to tackle; at the same time the
sounds of the words are glorious, maybe gloriously funny,
or gloriously evocative. The·use of lists and repetitions and
prompt-words promotes the participation, out loud, of the
child listener, as well as providing for the joys of recognition. I hope I have adequately replicated the idiom and the
vivacity.

It is a byword of Italian criticism that *Pinocchio* is very
Tuscan, both in language and in the delineation of character or the creation of incident. It is equally a truism that
the book is now thoroughly international, so much so that
probably most of its readers worldwide have no awareness
at all of its Italian authorship. A translator, it seems to me,
faces a strategic decision at the outset, either to accentuate
the Italianness, or to universalize by translating—in the
broadest sense—*everything*. Much as I love Italy (or perhaps because I do), I decided against the former; I wanted
to avoid piling on local colour to the point of rendering
the text 'folksy', quaint, olde worlde. I wanted it to live and
have direct meaning, now, for English-speaking readers,

for whom, perhaps, the differences between traditional pasta recipes, or between the educational writers of Italy in the 1870s, might be somewhat mysterious. The translation, like the original, still had to speak of a real world. So I have turned 'tortellini' into steak and kidney pudding and *Giannettino* into *Alice*. I may have fallen between two stools, since it is not possible always to be wholly consistent. But these—and a desire to get away from the awful, denaturing 'cuteness' of the Walt Disney school of thought—are the explanations for my having translated the names, including that of Geppetto; the exception is Pinocchio himself, since his name now has universal currency, and 'Pine-nut' or 'Pine-kernel' might sound a trifle odd.

Mine may seem an oblique way to achieve it, but none the less authenticity is the objective and the guiding watchword of this translation. Precise equivalence has always been sought, but where it is not possible, truth to the spirit of the original is the aim. Most translations of *Pinocchio* are to a greater or lesser extent adaptations, usually with modern children in mind. This edition is not specifically or exclusively for children. My hope is to convey the reality of Collodi's writing, without any more approximations or concessions than are strictly necessary; to this end some idiosyncrasies of punctuation have been retained. While the book is still vigorously alive, it is simultaneously a period piece; so *Giannettino* is replaced by *Alice*, not by *Just William*, and the vocabulary chosen sometimes has a nineteenth-century rather than a late twentieth-century ring. This is a literary translation, in which it is no more appropriate to update the expressions used than it would be to modernize the language and style of Charles Dickens. Collodi did not talk down to the young, as we almost automatically do today; he expected children to make deductions, ask questions, and look words up, and so this sophistication is reflected in the language of the translation.

Illustrations, at any rate, do not need to be translated.

Or do they? We are all too familiar with the saccharine-sweet, roly-poly Disney Pinocchio, hardly a puppet at all. Yet in Italy, in spite of the reinterpretations of more than 150 illustrators, the mental image that dominates, still, is the one created by the illustrator of the first book edition (and the fifth) more than a hundred years ago, Enrico Mazzanti. These are reproduced again in this volume and may, perhaps, help to establish the essentially unsentimental character of Collodi's masterpiece.

SELECT BIBLIOGRAPHY

Note: Although Collodi is the subject of a veritable academic industry in Italy, very little of substance has been written on *Pinocchio* in Britain. Most of the material in English has been published in the USA. In the main, Italian sources have been used for this book; therefore a few of the fundamental titles are included here for readers of Italian. For more detailed Collodi bibliographies in Italian, see *Schedario*, no. 4, Florence, April–June 1954, and Marchetti, Pancrazi, Traversetti, and Volpicelli below.

Biography and Criticism

Bacon, M., 'Puppet's Progress: Pinocchio', in Virginia Haviland (ed.), *Children and Literature: Views and Reviews* (Glenview, Ill., and Brighton, UK, 1973), 71–7.

Baldacci, V., and Rauch, A., *Pinocchio e la sua immagine* (Firenze, 1981) (catalogue for exhibition of Pinocchio illustrations).

Bertacchini, R., *Collodi narratore* (Pisa: Nistri-Lischi, 1961).

Cambon, G., 'Pinocchio and the Problem of Children's Literature', in *The Great Excluded, Journal of the Modern Language Association Seminar on Children's Literature*, 2 (1973), 50–60.

Gannon, S., 'A Note on Collodi and Lucian', in *Children's Literature*, 8 (1980), 98–102.

—— 'Pinocchio: The First Hundred Years', in *Children's Literature Association Quarterly*, 6 (1981–2), 1, 5–7.

Génot, G., *Analyse structurelle de Pinocchio* (Pescia/Firenze: ITF, 1970).

Gilbert, A., 'The Sea-Monster in Ariosto's *Cinque Canti* and in *Pinocchio*', in *Italica*, 32, no. 4 (December 1956), 260–3.

Heins, P., 'A Second Look: *The Adventures of Pinocchio*', in *Horn Book Magazine*, 58, no. 2 (April 1982), 200–4.

Heisig, F. J., 'Pinocchio: Archetype of the Motherless Child', in *Children's Literature*, 3 (1974), 23–35.

Kuznets, L. R., *When Toys Come Alive* (New Haven and London: Yale University Press, 1994).

Marchetti, I., *Carlo Collodi* (Firenze: Le Monnier, 1959) (includes biography/bibliography).

Michanczyk, M., 'The Puppet Immortals of Children's Literature', in *Children's Literature*, 2 (1973), 159–64.

Morrissey, T. J., 'Alive and well but not unscathed. A reply to Susan R. Gannon's *Pinocchio at 100*', in *Children's Literature Association Quarterly*, 7, no. 2 (1982), 37–9.

—— 'A *Pinocchio* for All Ages', in *Children's Literature Association Quarterly*, 13, no. 1 (1988), 90–1.

—— and Wunderlich, R., 'Death and Rebirth in *Pinocchio*', in *Children's Literature*, Annual of Modern Language Association, Division on Children's Literature, and the Children's Literature Association, vol. 2 (New Haven, 1983), 64–75.

Pancrazi, P., *Venti uomini, un satiro e un burattino* (Firenze: Vallecchi, 1923).

—— (ed.), *Tutto Collodi per i piccoli e per i grandi* (Firenze: Le Monnier, 1948) (collected works of Collodi with a biography).

Perella, N. J., 'An Essay on *Pinocchio*', in Carlo Collodi, *Le Avventure di Pinocchio—The Adventures of Pinocchio* (Berkeley, Los Angeles, and London: University of California Press, 1986).

Russell, D. L., 'Pinocchio and the Child-Hero's Quest', in *Children's Literature in Education*, 20, no. 4 (1989), 203–13.

Sachse, N. D., *Pinocchio in USA*, Fondazione Nazionale Carlo Collodi (Pescia, 1981).

Santucci, L., *Collodi* (Brescia: La Scuola, 1961).

Stych, F. S., 'Anglosaxon Attitudes to Collodi in the Seventies', in *Studi Collodiani*, Fondazione Nazionale Carlo Collodi (Pescia, 1976), 581–5.

—— *Pinocchio in Gran Bretagna e Irlanda* (Pescia, 1971).

Tempesti, F. (ed.), C. Collodi, *Le avventure di Pinocchio* (Milan: Mondadori, 1983) (includes updated version of L. Volpicelli's Bibliography).

—— C. Collodi, *Pinocchio* (Milan: Feltrinelli, 1972) (includes 2 essays on Collodi and composition of *Pinocchio*: 'Chi era il Collodi'; 'Com'è fatto *Pinocchio*').

Traversetti, B., *Introduzione a Collodi* (Bari: Laterza, 1993) (includes bibliography).

Volpicelli, L., *La verità su Pinocchio* (Roma: Avio, 1954) (includes bibliography).

—— *Bibliografia collodiana (1883–1980)*, Quaderni della Fondazione Nazionale Carlo Collodi, no. 13 (Pescia/Bologna, 1981).

Wunderlich, R., and Morrissey, T. J., 'Carlo Collodi's *The Adventures of Pinocchio*: A Classic Book of Choices', in *Touchstones: Reflections on the Best in Children's Literature*, vol. 1, ed. Perry Nodelman (West Lafayette: Children's Literature Association, 1985).

—— —— 'The Desecration of *Pinocchio* in the United States', in *Horn Book Magazine*, 58, no. 2 (April 1982), 205–11.

—— —— 'Pinocchio before 1920: The Popular and Pedagogical Traditions', in *Italian Quarterly*, 23, no. 88 (Spring 1982), 61–72.

General

Ariès, P., *Centuries of Childhood: A Social History of Family Life*, transl. R. Baldick (New York, 1962).

Batey, M., *The Adventures of Alice* (London, 1991).

Bertoni Jovine, D., *Storia dell'educazione popolare in Italia* (Bari, 1965).

Bettelheim, B., *The Uses of Enchantment: The Meaning and Importance of Fairy Tales* (New York, 1976).

Bingham, J. M. (ed.), *Writers for Children: Critical Studies of Major Authors since the 17th Century* (New York, 1988).

Butts, D. (ed.), *Stories and Society: Children's Literature in its Social Context* (London, 1992).

Carpenter, H., and Prichard, M. (eds.), *The Oxford Companion to Children's Literature* (Oxford and New York, 1984).

Dusinberre, J., *Alice to the Lighthouse: Children's Books and Radical Experiments in Art* (London, 1987).

Fiedler, L., 'An Eye to Innocence: Some Notes on the Role of the Child in Literature', in *The Collected Essays of Leslie Fielder* (New York, 1971), vol. 1, 471–511.

Fisher, M., *Who's Who in Children's Books: A Treasury of the Familiar Characters of Childhood* (London, 1975).

Hazard, P., *Les Livres, les enfants, les hommes* (Paris, 1932, 1949); *Books, Children, and Men*, transl. M. Mitchell (Boston, 1960) (see also for Perrault).

Hearder, H., *Italy in the Age of the Risorgimento, 1790–1870* (London and New York, 1983).

Hunt, P., *An Introduction to Children's Literature* (Oxford, 1994).

—— (ed.), *Children's Literature: An Illustrated History* (Oxford and New York, 1995).

Hurlimann, B., *Three Centuries of Children's Books in Europe* (London, 1967).

Jan, I., *On Children's Literature*, transl. C. Storr (London, 1973).

Lugli, A., *Storia della letteratura per l'infanzia* (Firenze, 1961).

Lurie, A., *Don't tell the Grown-ups* (Boston, 1990).

Lüthi, M., *Once Upon a Time: On the Nature of Fairy Tales* (Bloomington, 1976).

Meigs, C. (ed.), *A Critical History of Children's Literature* (New York, 1953).

Nodelman, P. (ed.), *Touchstones: Reflections on the Best in Children's Literature* (West Lafayette, Ind., 3 vols., 1985–9).

Santucci, L., *La letteratura infantile* (Milano, 1958).

Tatar, M., *Off With Their Heads! Fairy Tales and the Culture of Childhood* (Princeton, NJ, 1992).

Valeri, M., and Monaci, E., *Storia della letteratura per i fanciulli* (Bologna, 1961).

Warner, M., *From the Beast to the Blonde. On fairy tales and their tellers* (London, 1994).

A CHRONOLOGY OF CARLO COLLODI

1826 Carlo Lorenzini born in Florence in the independent Duchy of Tuscany on 24 November.

1837 Publication of L. A. Parravicini's *Giannetto*, regarded as Italy's first 'popular' book for children.
CL sent to seminary at expense of Marquis Ginori, his father's employer.

1842 CL leaves the seminary; his education is continued in Florence until 1844.

1844 CL joins the staff of Piatti bookshop in Florence.

1848 YEAR OF REVOLUTIONS IN ITALY AND EUROPE: FIRST WAR OF INDEPENDENCE IN FUTURE ITALY.
CL's father dies.
CL volunteers for the campaign against Austria in Lombardy. Fights at Montanara and Curtatone, 29 May.
13 July, on return to Florence, CL founds and edits *Il Lampione*, a politico-satirical paper.
2 August, CL becomes a civil servant when appointed Secretary to the Tuscan Senate.

1849 JANUARY, GRAND DUKE LEOPOLD II OF TUSCANY FLEES FLORENCE.
CL briefly promoted Secretary (First Class) to provisional government, but Austrian army provokes political reaction.
Il Lampione forced to close on 11 April.
CL dismissed from public service, but reinstated 1 June.
JULY, LEOPOLD II RETURNS.

1850s Throughout 1850s CL very active as freelance journalist.

1853 The theatrical paper *Lo Scaramuccia* is launched, with CL as editor from 1853 to 1855.
Writes play, *Gli amici di casa* ('Family friends').
Pietro Thouar, the 'father of Italian children's literature', active in Florence.

1855 *The Boy's Own Magazine* launched in Britain.

1856   Definitive edition in Germany of the Fairy Tales of the Brothers Grimm.
CL first uses pseudonym 'Carlo Collodi'.

1857   CL publishes first novel, *I misteri di Firenze* ('The mysteries of Florence').

1858–9 CL works for a short time for a publisher in Milan.

1859   SECOND WAR OF INDEPENDENCE. PIEDMONT, SUPPORTED BY FRANCE, AT WAR WITH AUSTRIA; LOMBARDY CEDED BY AUSTRIA TO PIEDMONT.
10 April, CL enlists as a volunteer in a regular army light cavalry unit, witnessing disastrous battle at Novara.

1859–60 LEOPOLD II LEAVES FLORENCE FOR GOOD. TUSCANY VOTES FOR FUSION WITH PIEDMONT.

1860   GARIBALDI AND HIS 'THOUSAND' TAKE SICILY AND THE SOUTH. UNIFICATION OF ITALY COMPLETE BUT FOR ROME AND VENETIA.
February, in Florence CL appointed to the Commission for Theatre Censorship, a position he holds until 1881.
March, commissioned by new government, CL publishes a polemical pamphlet, *Il signor Albèri ha ragione* ('Mr A. is right'), attacking an apologist for the old regime.
15 May, *Il Lampione* relaunched, after 11 years; CL editor.

1861   VICTOR EMMANUEL BECOMES KING OF ITALY: PARLIAMENT CALLED IN TURIN, FIRST CAPITAL.
The 'Casati Law' (public education act) of 1859 extended to all Italy.
La manifattura delle porcellane di Doccia, pseudonymous publication by 'C.L.' of booklet on Ginori porcelain. (Brother, Paolo, Director-General.)

1862   Jules Verne's *Le Tour du monde en 80 jours* ('Around the world in 80 days') published. (Italian translation 1874.)

1865   FLORENCE BECOMES CAPITAL OF THE KINGDOM OF ITALY.
Lewis Carroll's *Alice's Adventures in Wonderland* published. (Italian translation published in England 1872; first in Italy 1912.)

1866   ITALY AT WAR WITH AUSTRIA; VENICE AND VENETO CEDED TO ITALY.

1867   CL briefly visits France.

1868   October, CL invited to contribute to major new dictionary.

1870   FRANCO-PRUSSIAN WAR; ITALIAN TROOPS OCCUPY ROME: UNIFICATION OF ITALY COMPLETE.

1871   ROME BECOMES CAPITAL.

1872   CL's play *L'onore del marito* ('The husband's honour') staged in Florence.

1873   CL appointed Secretary (First Class) to the Prefecture of Florence.

1875   Collodi's first work for children appears: a translation of French fairy tales, commissioned by the publisher Paggi.

1876   Mark Twain's *The Adventures of Tom Sawyer* published.

1877   Collodi's didactic *Giannettino* published, taking the central character's name from Parravicini's *Giannetto* of 1837, and launching CL's new career as innovative writer of educational books.

1878   Collodi's *Minuzzolo*, another didactic work, published. CL made 'Knight of the Crown of Italy'.

1879   Two more 'Giannettino' books appear, on geography and grammar.

1880   Giannettino's journey through Italy begins: first of three 'unifying' textbooks for the children of the new nation.

1881   After 33 years, CL takes early retirement from the civil service, to write full-time.
        7 July, the first version of *Pinocchio*, entitled *La storia di un burattino* ('The story of a puppet'), begins to appear as a serial in the first issue of an early and distinguished children's newspaper, *Il Giornale per i bambini*, published weekly in Rome. The serial initially comes to a tragic conclusion on 27 October 1881.

1882   16 February, Collodi's serial resumes under the title *Le avventure di Pinocchio* ('The adventures of P.'). With another break between June and November the story finally ends on 25 January 1883.
First publication of R. L. Stevenson's *Treasure Island* as a serial in *Young Folks*; published as a book in 1886.

1883   February, *Le avventure di Pinocchio* first appears as a volume, illustrated by Enrico Mazzanti and published by Felice Paggi, Florence; further editions appear in 1886, 1887, and 1888.

1884   Mark Twain's *The Adventures of Huckleberry Finn* published (Italian translation 1915).

1886   Edmondo De Amicis' novel for children, *Cuore* ('A Boy's Heart'), published.
CL's mother dies.

1889   CL publishes a primary-school reading book.

1890   *La lanterna magica di Giannettino* ('G.'s magic lantern'), the last of the Giannettino books, comes out.
26 October, while working on a sequel to *Pinocchio*, Carlo Collodi (Carlo Lorenzini) dies at the house in Florence of his brother, Paolo, and sister-in-law, with whom he has lived.
A new edition (the fifth) of *Pinocchio* published by Bemporad, Florence.

1892   First English edition of *Pinocchio*, translated by Mary E. Murray, published London.

CHAPTER I

*How maestro Cherry, a carpenter, found
a piece of wood which laughed and
cried like a child.*

Once upon a time there was . . .

'A king!' my little readers will say straight away. No, children, you are mistaken. Once upon a time there was a piece of wood.*

It was not expensive wood, but just a bit of firewood, like the ones that people use to light a fire in the stove or on the hearth to warm their rooms in winter.

I don't know how it happened, but the fact is that one fine day this piece of wood appeared in the workshop of an old carpenter whose name was Master Anthony, except that everyone called him *maestro* Cherry because of the end of his nose, which was always shiny and purple, just like a ripe cherry.*

When he saw that piece of wood, *maestro* Cherry was overjoyed and, rubbing his hands together in delight, he muttered to himself, 'This wood has turned up at the right time; I'll use it to make the leg for a little table.'

No sooner said than done. He picked up his honed axe at once to start taking the bark off and thinning it down; but when he was about to make the first cut with the axe, his arm stopped in mid-air, for he could hear a little, tiny voice saying pleadingly, 'Don't hit me too hard!'

You can imagine the feelings of that good old man, *maestro* Cherry!

In astonishment, he looked all round the room to see where on earth that little voice could have come from, but he couldn't see anybody. He looked under his bench, but there was no one there; he looked inside a cupboard which was always kept shut, but there was no one there; he looked

into the basket full of shavings and sawdust, but there was no one there; he even opened his workshop door to glance up and down the street, but there was no one there. Well then? ...

'I see,' he said, laughing and scratching his wig,* 'it's clear that I must have imagined that little voice. Let's get back to work then.'

And picking up the axe again, he struck a mighty blow against the piece of wood.

'Ouch! you hurt me!' cried the same little voice plaintively.

This time *maestro* Cherry was thunderstruck, his eyes popping out of his head with terror, his jaw dropping and his tongue hanging out of his mouth right down to his chin, so that he looked just like a stone gargoyle.*

When he was able to speak again, he began to say, shaking and stammering with fright, 'Wherever did that little voice come from that said "Ouch"? ... After all, there isn't a living soul here. Could it be this piece of wood, by any chance, that has learned to cry and complain like a child? I can't believe that. Here's the stick; it's a bit of firewood like any other. Chucked on the fire, it would heat up a bean stew nicely ... Well then? Could somebody be hidden inside? If someone's hiding in there, so much the worse for him. I'll soon take care of him!'

As he said this, he took hold of that poor piece of wood with both hands, and he set about beating it mercilessly against the walls of the room.

Then he stopped to listen, to find out whether there was any little voice complaining. He waited for two minutes and heard nothing; then for five minutes and heard nothing; then for ten minutes and heard nothing!

'I see,' he said, forcing himself to laugh and ruffling his wig, 'it's clear that I must have imagined the little voice that said "Ouch!"'! Let's get back to work then.'

And because a terrible fear had taken hold of him, he tried to hum a tune to keep his spirits up.

Meanwhile, putting his axe on one side, he picked up the plane, so as to plane and polish the piece of wood; but while he planed it up and down, he heard the same little voice laughing and saying, 'Stop it! you're tickling me all over!'

This time poor *maestro* Cherry fell over as if he had been struck by lightning. When he opened his eyes again, he found himself sitting on the floor.

His face looked transformed, and even the end of his nose, instead of its usual purple colour, had turned blue from fright.

CHAPTER II

How maestro Cherry gives the piece of wood
to his friend, Old Joe,* who wants to make
it into a wonderful puppet able to dance,
fence and do somersaults.

At that moment there was a knock at the door.

'Please come in,' said the carpenter, who hadn't the strength to get up.

A sprightly old man came into the workshop. His name

was Old Joe, but when the children of the neighbourhood wanted to make him really lose his temper, they called him by his nickname, Semolina, chosen on account of his yellow wig which looked just like a semolina pudding.*

Old Joe had a very short temper. Woe betide anyone who called him Semolina! He'd go wild on the spot and there'd be no holding him back.

'Good morning, Master Anthony,' said Old Joe. 'What are you doing there on the floor?'

'I'm teaching the ants their numbers.'

'Much good may it do you.'

'What brought you here, my friend?'

'My legs. Well, in fact, Master Anthony, I came to see you to ask you a favour.'

'And here I am, at your service,' replied the carpenter, getting up onto his knees.

'This morning a bright idea came into my head.'

'Let's hear it then.'

'I decided to make myself a fine wooden puppet, a wonderful puppet, that would be able to dance and fence and do somersaults. I'm going to see the world with my puppet; it'll earn me a crust and a glass of wine. What do you think?'*

'Good old Semolina!' cried the same little voice, but you couldn't tell where it was coming from.

Hearing himself called Semolina, neighbour Joe turned as scarlet as a red pepper with rage. Facing the carpenter he said furiously, 'Why are you insulting me?'

'Who's insulting you?'

'You called me Semolina! . . .'

'It wasn't me.'

'You're not going to tell me it was me! I say it was you.'

'It was not.'

'It was.'

'It was not.'

'It was.'

As they got more and more heated, their words became actions and they grabbed each other by the hair, scratching, biting and mauling each other.

After the fight, Master Anthony found he had Old Joe's yellow wig in his hands, and Joe realized that the carpenter's grizzled wig was in his mouth.

'Give me back my wig!' shouted Master Anthony.

'You give me back mine, and let's make peace.'

The two old men handed over each other's wigs, shook hands and swore to stay good friends for ever and ever.

'So, neighbour Joe,' said the carpenter as a peace offering, 'what is the favour that you want of me?'

'I should like a bit of wood to make my puppet with. Can you help?'

Master Anthony was delighted and went straight to his bench to fetch the piece of wood that had given him such a fright. But as he was on the point of giving it to his friend, the piece of wood shook violently and jerked out of his hands, hitting poor Old Joe hard on his skinny shins.

'Ow! do you always give your things away so courteously, Master Anthony? You nearly lamed me! . . .'

'I swear it wasn't me!'

'So it must have been me, must it? . . .'

'It's this wood that's to blame . . .'

'I know it was the wood, but it was you who threw it at my legs!'

'I didn't throw it at you!'

'Liar!'

'Joe, don't insult me, or I'll call you Semolina! . . .'

'Ass!'

'Semolina!'

'Donkey!'

'Semolina!'

'Ugly brute!'

'Semolina!'

Blinded by anger on hearing himself called Semolina for

the third time, Old Joe hurled himself at the carpenter, and
they went for each other hammer and tongs.

After the battle, Master Anthony found two more
scratches on his nose, and his adversary had two fewer
buttons on his jacket. Upon this equitable settlement, they
shook hands and swore to stay good friends for ever and
ever.

Then Old Joe took his nice piece of wood and, thanking
Master Anthony, went limping home.

CHAPTER III

*How Old Joe, having reached home, begins at
once to make the puppet and gives him the
name Pinocchio. The puppet's first pranks.*

Old Joe lived in a basement room lit by a skylight under
the front steps.* The furniture could not have been more
simple: an awkward chair, an uncomfortable bed and a

broken table. On the back wall there was a hearth with a fire burning; but the fire was painted, and beside the fire there was a painted pot, boiling merrily, with a cloud of steam rising from it that looked just like real steam.

As soon as he got home, Joe collected his tools and settled himself to carve and create his puppet.

'What shall I call him?' he said to himself. 'I'd like to call him Pinocchio. It's a name that will bring him luck. I once knew a whole Pinocchio family: father Pinocchio, mother Pinocchia and the Pinocchi children, and they all did well for themselves. The richest was a beggar.'*

Having thought of a name for his puppet, he got down to work seriously and quickly shaped his hair, then his forehead, then his eyes.

Once the eyes were done, you can imagine his amazement when he noticed the eyes moving and staring straight at him.

Knowing he was being watched by those two wooden eyes, Joe took it somewhat amiss and said with feeling, 'Old wooden eyes, why are you looking at me?'

Nobody replied.

So from the eyes he went on to the nose. But no sooner

was the nose carved than it began to grow: it grew and grew and grew, and in a few minutes it became a nose that never seemed to end.

Poor Old Joe laboured to cut it back again; but the more he cut and shortened it, the more that impertinent nose grew longer.

From the nose he went on to the mouth.

The mouth was still not finished when it suddenly started to laugh and tease him.

'Stop your laughing!' said Joe, vexed; but it was like talking to the wall.

'Stop your laughing, do you hear!' he shouted threateningly.

Then the mouth stopped laughing, but stuck out its tongue all the way.

So as not to spoil his work, Old Joe pretended not to notice, and continued carving. From the mouth he went on to the chin, and then the neck, and then the shoulders, the stomach, the arms and the hands.

The moment the hands were finished, Old Joe felt his wig being snatched from his head. He looked up, and what did he see? He saw his yellow wig in the puppet's hand.

'Pinocchio! . . . give me back my wig at once!'

And Pinocchio, instead of returning his wig to him, placed it on his own head, disappearing, half swamped, under it.

Such an insolent and mocking manner made Old Joe feel gloomy and wretched as never before in his whole life, and turning towards Pinocchio, he said, 'You young scoundrel! I haven't finished making you, and you are already showing little respect for your father! That's bad, my lad, that's bad!'*

And he mopped up a tear.

He still had to make the legs and feet.

When the feet were finished, he felt a kick land on the end of his nose.

'I deserve it!' he said to himself. 'I ought to have thought of that first! Now it's too late!'

Then he took hold of the puppet under the arms and put him down on the floor of his room, so as to get him to walk.

Pinocchio's legs were stiff and he did not know how to move, and Old Joe led him by the hand to teach him how to take one step after another.

When Pinocchio had stretched his legs, he began to walk by himself and then to run around the room until, slipping through the front door, he hopped into the street and took to his heels.

And poor Old Joe went running after him but was unable to catch him up, for that young rascal leapt along like a hare and, with his wooden feet hammering on the pavement slabs, he made as much of a din as twenty pairs of peasants' clogs.

'Catch him! Catch him!' shouted Joe, but when the people in the street saw the wooden puppet racing along like an Arab stallion,* they stopped to watch, entranced, and they laughed and laughed and laughed, you can't imagine how much.

In the end, by good fortune, a policeman came along. Hearing all that uproar, and supposing it to be a young colt that had broken loose from its master, he courageously planted himself, feet apart, in the middle of the road, determined to halt it and prevent any greater disaster.

However, when Pinocchio saw the policeman in the distance and that he was blocking the whole street, he devised a ruse to get past him by running between his legs. But it all went wrong . . .

Without moving an inch, the policeman neatly caught him by the nose—for it was an enormous great nose, which looked as if it was specially made for policemen to catch hold of it—and placed him back in Old Joe's hands. As a punishment Joe wanted to give him a good box on the ears, but somehow he could not find them, and do you know why? Because, in his haste to carve him, he had forgotten to make any!

So he seized him by the nape of his neck and, while he was leading him back, he said, shaking his head sternly at him, 'We're going straight home. And make no mistake, you're going to pay for this when we get back!'

Seeing the lie of the land, Pinocchio threw himself to the ground and wouldn't walk any more. Meanwhile bystanders and loiterers began to pause and collect in a little knot around them.

They all said their say about it.

'Poor puppet!' some exclaimed, 'He's right not to want to go home! Who knows how hard that brute Joe might beat him! . . .'

And others added spitefully, 'That Joe looks decent, but he's a monster with children! If that poor puppet is left in his hands, he's quite capable of making matchwood of him! . . .'

All in all, they had so much to say about it that the

policeman set Pinocchio free again and put poor Old Joe in prison. Unable to find the words to defend himself on the spot, he cried like a baby, and walking towards the gaol he sobbed and stammered, 'Wretched child! Just think of all the trouble I've taken to make him into a good puppet! But it's my fault! I should have thought about it before! . . .'

What happened next is a story so strange that it is hard to believe it, and I shall tell it to you in the following chapters.

CHAPTER IV

The story of Pinocchio and the Talking Cricket, which shows that naughty boys get bored with being corrected by those who know more than they do.

So, children, I must tell you that while poor Old Joe was taken off to prison—though he had done no wrong—that scallywag, Pinocchio, set free from the clutches of the policeman, took to his heels down across the fields, so as to get home more quickly. In his furious haste, he leapt over steep embankments, and blackthorn hedges, and ditches full of water, just as a kid or a young hare might have done with the huntsmen after him.

At the house he found the front door ajar. He pushed it, went inside and, the minute he had bolted the door, he flung himself down to sit on the ground, letting out a great sigh of pleasure.

But that pleasure did not last long, because somewhere in the room he could hear a voice saying, 'Cree—cree—cree!'

'Who's that calling me?' said Pinocchio all afraid.

'I am!'

Pinocchio turned round and saw a big cricket very slowly climbing up the wall.

'Tell me, Cricket, who are you?'

'I am the Talking Cricket* and I have lived in this room for more than a hundred years.'

'But now this room is mine,' said the puppet, 'and if you wouldn't mind doing me a big favour, go away this minute, without even turning round.'

'I shall not leave here,' replied the Cricket, 'without first telling you a big home truth.'

'Say it and hurry up about it.'

'Woe betide those children who rebel against their parents and who take it into their heads to run away from home. They will never do well in this world, and sooner or later they will bitterly regret what they did.'

'Croak away, Cricket mine, if it pleases you. All I know is that at dawn tomorrow I shall be leaving, because if I stay here what happens to all other children will happen to me, and that's to say they will send me to school and, like it or not, I'll have to study. As for me, and I tell you this in confidence, I haven't the slightest desire to study, because I have more fun chasing after butterflies and climbing trees to take the baby birds from their nests.'

'You poor little silly! Don't you know that, if you do that, you'll be a great big ass when you grow up, and everyone will make jokes about you?'*

'Silence, you ill-omened creature!' shouted Pinocchio.

But the Cricket, who was patient and philosophical, instead of taking offence at such impertinence, went on in the same tone of voice, 'And if you don't care for the idea of going to school, why don't you at least learn a trade, so as to earn yourself an honest crust?'

'Do you want me to tell you?' replied Pinocchio, who was beginning to lose patience. 'Out of all the trades in the world there's only one that really suits me.'

'And what trade would that be?'

'Eating, drinking, sleeping, and enjoying myself from morn till night, and living the life of Riley.'

'For your guidance,' said the Talking Cricket with his usual tranquillity, 'those who take up that career generally all finish up in the workhouse or in prison.'*

'Look, you ill-omened creature! . . . if I should get a tantrum, just beware! . . .'

'Poor Pinocchio! I feel really sorry for you! . . .'

'Why do you feel sorry for me?'

'Because you're a puppet and, what's worse, because you've got a wooden head.'

At these last words, Pinocchio jumped up in a fury and, snatching a wooden mallet from the bench, hurled it at the Talking Cricket.

Perhaps he never meant to hit him, but unluckily he caught him right on the head, so that the poor Cricket barely had breath for a '*Cree—cree—cree*' before he was stuck to the wall stone dead.

CHAPTER V

*How Pinocchio gets hungry and looks for
an egg to scramble; but how, when least
expected, the scrambled egg flies away through
the window.* *

By now it was getting dark, and Pinocchio, remembering that he had eaten nothing, felt his tummy rumbling in a manner that much resembled having an appetite.

But in youngsters appetite soon takes great strides and, indeed after a few minutes, that appetite became hunger and, in the twinkling of an eye, the hunger turned into a ravenous hunger, a craving that you could cut with a knife.

Poor Pinocchio ran to the hearth where there was the

pot on the boil, and made as if to lift its lid to see what was inside; but the pot was only painted on the wall. You can imagine how he felt. His nose, which was already long, grew at least another four inches.

So he set about darting around the room, rummaging in all the drawers and in every nook and cranny in his search for a bit of bread, even a bit of dry bread, a little crust, a bone left by the dog, a spot of mouldy pasta,* a fish bone, a cherry stone, in other words, something to chew. But he found nothing, nothing at all, really and truly nothing.

And all the while his hunger was growing, growing all the time, and poor Pinocchio had no relief other than to yawn, and he gave such great, long yawns that sometimes his mouth reached right round to his ears. And after yawning, he would spit, and felt as if his stomach was collapsing.

Then weeping and in despair, he said, 'The Talking Cricket was right. It was a mistake to rebel against my papa and run away from home ... If my pa was here, I wouldn't be dying of yawning now! Oh, what a terrible disease hunger is!'*

Then, lo and behold, he thought he saw something round and white in the heap of rubbish, something that looked exactly like a hen's egg. He was across the room, bending over it, in a second. It really was an egg.

It is impossible to describe the puppet's joy: you will just have to imagine it for yourselves. Thinking it might be a dream after all, he turned the egg over and over in his hands, and touched it and kissed it, and while he was kissing it he said, 'And now how shall I cook it? I'll scramble it! ... No, it's better to bake it! ... Or wouldn't it be more tasty to do it in a frying-pan? ... Or why don't I cook a beaten egg? No, the quickest of all is to fry it or bake it; I'm so longing to eat it!'*

No sooner said than done: he put a little pan on a brazier full of glowing embers; into the pan, instead of oil or butter,

he put some water, and when the water began to steam, pop! . . . he broke the eggshell, and made as if to pour it in.

But instead of the white and the yolk, out came a chick all chirpy and courteous who made a deep bow and said, 'Very many thanks, Mr Pinocchio, for having saved me the trouble of breaking my shell! *Au revoir*, keep well and all good wishes to the family!'

So saying, he spread his wings and flew through the open window, disappearing into the distance.

The poor puppet stood there as if mesmerized, his eyes staring, his mouth open, and with the bits of eggshell in his hands. All the same, having recovered from the first shock, he began to cry and scream and bang his feet on the ground in desperation. Weeping, he said out loud, 'So the Talking Cricket was right! If I hadn't run away from home and if my papa was here, I wouldn't be dying of hunger now! Oh, what a terrible disease hunger is! . . .'*

And because his tummy went on rumbling more than

ever, and he did not know how to quieten it, he thought he'd better go out and take a look around the little village nearby, in the hope that he might find some kind person who would give him a bit of bread out of charity.

CHAPTER VI

How Pinocchio falls asleep with his feet on the brazier, and the following morning wakes up to find his feet burnt to bits.

As it happened it was a terrible, hellish night. The thunder-claps were as loud as can be, the lightning seemed to set the sky on fire, and a cold and buffeting wind, which whistled angrily and raised a huge cloud of dust, made all the trees of the countryside creak and groan.

Pinocchio was very frightened of thunder and lightning but, because his hunger was stronger than his fear, he set the door ajar and, going full-pelt, in a hundred hops and leaps he reached the village, panting loudly and with his tongue hanging out, just like a fox-hound.

But everywhere was dark and deserted. The shops were shut; the doors of the houses were shut; and, in the street, there wasn't even a dog to be seen. It looked like the land of the dead.

So Pinocchio, driven by desperation and hunger, pressed a door-bell and kept on ringing it, saying to himself, 'Some-one will come.'

In fact a little old man, wearing his night-cap, peered out of a window and called out irritably, 'What do you want at this hour of the night?'

'Would you do me the favour of giving me a piece of bread?'

'Wait there and I'll be back in just a moment,' said the old man, thinking he was dealing with one of those daredevil lads who amuse themselves at night by ringing people's door-bells in order to annoy decent folk who are trying to get a night's sleep.

After a moment the window opened again, and the same old man's voice called out to Pinocchio, 'Come underneath and hold out your hat.'

Pinocchio promptly took off his hat, such as it was. But while he was stretching it out, he felt a huge bucketful of water pour down on him, drenching him from head to foot as if he was a pot of dried-up geraniums.

He went home as wet as a drowned duck* and worn out with hunger and fatigue, and, because he no longer had the strength to stand, he sat down, resting his soaked and muddy feet on the brazier full of glowing embers.

There he fell asleep and, while he slept, his wooden feet caught alight, and little by little they burned away and turned to ashes.

Pinocchio went on sleeping and snoring, as if his feet belonged to someone else. At last, at daybreak, he awoke, because someone had knocked at the door.

'Who is it?' he asked, yawning and rubbing his eyes.

'It's me!' replied a voice.

That voice was the voice of Old Joe.

CHAPTER VII

*How Old Joe comes home, and gives the
puppet the breakfast that the poor man had
brought for himself.*

Poor Pinocchio, whose eyes were still only half open, had
not yet noticed that his feet were burnt to bits; so the
minute he heard his father's voice, he jumped down from
the stool to run and pull back the bolt. But instead, after
staggering a couple of paces, all of a sudden he fell flat on
his face on the floor.

As he hit the ground he made exactly the same noise as
if he had been a sack of wooden spoons dropped from the
fifth floor.

'Open the door!' shouted Old Joe from the street.

'Papa, I can't,' replied the puppet, weeping and rolling
around the floor.

'Why can't you?'

'Because they've gobbled up my feet.'

'Who gobbled them up then?'

'The cat,' said Pinocchio, who had caught sight of the cat
with its claws out, playing at making the wood-shavings
jump.

'Come along, open the door!' repeated Old Joe. 'Otherwise, when I get in, I'll set the cat on you all right!'

'I can't stand up, you must believe me. Oh poor me!
poor me, fated to walk on my knees all my life! . . .'

Old Joe, imagining that all these whimperings of the
puppet were just another prank, thought he would put a
stop to it all and, climbing up the wall, he got into the
house through the window.

At first he was going to teach him a lesson; but then,
when he saw his Pinocchio lying on the floor and really
without any feet, his heart was touched, and taking him in

his arms he kissed him and cuddled him and lavished endearments on him. Then, the tear-drops cascading down his cheeks, he said sobbing, 'My poor little Pinocchio! However did you burn your feet off?'

'I don't know, Papa, but believe me, it was a diabolical night which I shall remember as long as I live. It was thundering and the lightning flashed and I was famished, and then the Talking Cricket said to me, "There you are: you have been naughty, and you deserve it", and I said to him, "Watch out, Cricket! ...", and he said to me, "You're a puppet and you have a wooden head", and I threw the handle of a hammer at him, and he died, but it was his fault, because I didn't want to kill him, and the proof is that I put a little pan on the glowing embers in the brazier, but the baby chick flew out and said, "*Au revoir* ... and all good wishes to the family." And I was getting hungrier all the time, which is the reason why that old man in the night-cap who came to his window said to me, "Come under here and hold out your hat", and there I was drenched in a bucketful of water, because there's no harm in asking for a bit of bread, is there? and I came straight back home, and because I was still famished, I put my feet on the brazier to dry them, and then you came back, and I discovered they were all burnt, and I've still got my hunger but I haven't got my feet any more! Boo! . . . hoo! . . . hoo! . . . hoo!'*

And poor Pinocchio began to cry and screech so loud that he could be heard five miles away.*

In all that tangled tale Old Joe had understood one thing only and that was that the puppet was dying of hunger, so he drew three pears out of his pocket and offered them to Pinocchio, saying, 'These three pears were going to be my breakfast, but I'll gladly give them to you. Eat them up; they'll do you good.'

'If you'd like me to eat them, would you kindly peel them for me?'

'Peel them?' responded Joe in amazement. 'Well, my lad, I would never have believed that you would be so finicky and so fussy about food. That's bad! In this world, even children have to get used to eating anything and not having fads, because you never know what might happen to you. Anything can happen! . . .'

'I'm sure you're right,' affirmed Pinocchio, 'but I'll never eat a fruit that hasn't been peeled. Skin I can't abide!'

So good Old Joe, reaching for a little knife and arming himself with the patience of a saint, peeled the three pears and placed all the peel on a corner of the table.

When Pinocchio had downed the first pear in a couple of swallows, he was about to throw away the core, but Joe stayed his arm, saying, 'Don't throw it away; everything in this world can come in useful.'

'But I'm never going to eat the core! . . .', shouted the puppet, whipping round like a viper.

'Who knows! Anything can happen! . . .' repeated Joe, without getting heated about it.

And in fact the three cores, instead of being thrown out

of the window, were placed on the corner of the table next to the peelings.

After he had eaten, or rather devoured, the three pears, Pinocchio gave a long yawn and said tearfully, 'I'm still hungry!'

'But my lad, I have nothing more to give you.'

'What? Really, really nothing?'

'That's to say, I only have these pear skins and cores.'

'Oh well!' said Pinocchio, 'if that's all there is, I'll eat a piece of peel.'

So he began to chew. At first he wrinkled up his face a bit, but, one after the other, he dispatched all three skins in a trice, and after the skins down went the cores; when he had eaten everything up, he patted his hands contentedly on his stomach, and said chuckling, 'There! Now I feel better!'

'So you see,' said Old Joe, 'I was right when I told you that we mustn't get too sophisticated or too delicate in our tastes. Dear boy, you never know what will happen in this world. Anything can happen!! . . .'

CHAPTER VIII

How Old Joe makes new feet for Pinocchio,
and sells his own cape to buy him
an alphabet book.

As soon as his hunger had vanished, the puppet promptly began to grumble and cry because he wanted a new pair of feet.

But Old Joe, to punish him for his naughtiness, left him to cry and mope for half the day. Then he said to him, 'Well now, why should I make your feet all over again? Just to have you run away from home once more?'

'I promise you,' the puppet sobbed, 'from now on I'll be good ...'

'All children say that', replied Old Joe, 'when they want something.'

'I promise I shall go to school, I shall study and I shall get good marks ...'

'All children make those promises, when they want something.'

'But I'm not like other children! I'm good, much more than the others, and I always tell the truth. Papa, I promise that I'll learn a skill, and I shall comfort and support you in your old age.'

Although he had put on a stern face, Old Joe's eyes were brimming with tears and his heart was beating with emotion at the sight of his little Pinocchio in that sorry state. He said nothing more but, taking up the tools of his trade and two pieces of seasoned wood, he set to work with great concentration.

In less than an hour the feet were well and truly ready: a pair of agile, slender, vigorous feet, as if modelled by an artist of genius.

Then Joe said to the puppet, 'Close your eyes and go to sleep.'

So Pinocchio closed his eyes and pretended to go to sleep. While he was pretending to be asleep, Joe softened some glue in an eggshell and fixed the feet into place, and he fixed them so well that you couldn't even see where they were attached.

As soon as he realized that he now had feet, the puppet jumped down from the table where he had been lying, and started to gambol and caper all over the place, as if he was crazed with happiness.

'To repay you for all you have done for me,' said Pinocchio to his father, 'I want to go to school straight away.'

'Good boy.'

'But if I go to school I'll have to have some clothes.'

Old Joe was poor and didn't have so much as a half-penny in his pocket, so he made him a little suit of flowered paper, a pair of shoes of tree-bark and a cap fashioned out of bread dough.

Pinocchio immediately ran to look at himself in a bucket of water and was so pleased with himself that he said, showing off his finery, 'I look just like a fine gentleman!'

'Yes, you do,' replied Old Joe, 'but just remember, it's not fine clothes that make a gentleman, but rather clean clothes.'

'By the way,' the puppet went on, 'if I go to school, there's something else I need; in fact the most important thing.'

'And what's that?'

'I need an alphabet book.'

'Quite right; but how can we get one?'

'Easy as can be; we go to a bookshop and buy one.'

'And what about the money?'

'I haven't got any.'

'Nor have I,' said the good old man, looking wretched.

And, though he was a thoroughly cheerful boy, Pinocchio looked gloomy too. For poverty, when it's real poverty, is something that everybody understands, even children.

'Never mind!' cried Joe, suddenly getting up, and putting on his old fustian cape,* which was patched and mended all over, he rushed out of the house.

He was back before long, and on his return he was carrying the alphabet book for his little boy, but he was no longer wearing his cape. The poor man was in his shirt-sleeves, and outside it was snowing.

'Papa, where's your cape?'

'I sold it.'

'Why did you sell it?'

'Because it was making me hot.'

Pinocchio understood instantly and, prompted by his good nature, he leapt impetuously into Old Joe's arms and proceeded to kiss him again and again.

CHAPTER IX

How Pinocchio sells his alphabet book to go and see a puppet play.

Once the snow had stopped falling, Pinocchio set out along the road that led to the school, with his fine new alphabet book under his arm, and he went along thinking great thoughts in his little head and imagining all manner of castles in Spain, each one more glorious than the last.

All alone and talking to himself, he said, 'At school to-day I want to learn to read straight away; tomorrow I'll learn to write, and the day after tomorrow I'll learn to count. I'm clever, so then I'll earn lots of money and with my very first pay I want to get a lovely cape, made of cloth, for my dad. I don't mean cloth. I'll get him one all made of silver and gold, with diamond buttons. The poor old man truly deserves it. After all, to buy me books and get me educated, he left himself in his shirt-sleeves... and in this cold weather! Only fathers are capable of such sacrifices!...'

While he was saying all this and feeling a bit sad, he thought he could hear far away the sound of pipes playing and the banging of a big bass drum: fi-fi-fi, fi-fi-fi, tum, tum, tum.

He stopped to listen. The sounds came from the end of a very long side-road, which led to a little village beside the sea.

'What can that music be? What a pity I have to go to school; otherwise . . .'

And he stood there puzzled. Somehow he had to make up his mind: to go to school or to hear the pipes.

'Today I shall go to hear the pipes, and tomorrow I shall go to school. There's always time to go to school,' that scamp said at last, shrugging his shoulders.

No sooner said than done; he turned off into the side-road and started to run. The more he ran, the more clearly he heard the playing of the pipes and the beating of the big bass drum: fi-fi-fi, fi-fi-fi, fi-fi-fi, tum, tum, tum.

Then suddenly he found himself in the middle of a square full of people, who were thronging around a big tent made of wood and gaily painted canvas.

'What is that tent?' asked Pinocchio, turning round to a village lad standing there.

'Read what's written on the poster and then you'll know.'

'I would gladly read it, but as it happens today I don't know how to read.'

'Well done, blockhead! All right, I'll read it to you. You may be interested to know that, written in flame-red letters on that poster, it says: GRAND PUPPET THEATRE . . .'

'Did the play start long ago?'

'It's starting now.'

'And how much is it to go in?'

'Fourpence.'

Pinocchio was overcome with curiosity and, losing all reserve, he said without embarrassment to the other lad, 'Would you give me fourpence until tomorrow?'

'I would gladly give it to you,' he replied, making fun of Pinocchio, 'but today, as it happens, I am unable to.'

'For fourpence I'll sell you my jacket,' said the puppet.

'What do you expect me to do with a jacket of flowered paper? If it gets rained on, it'll never come off.'

'Do you want to buy my shoes?'

'They're only fit to light the fire with.'

'How much would you give me for my cap?'

'A good bargain that would be! A cap made of bread dough! I bet the rats would come and eat it off my head!'

Pinocchio was on pins. He was on the point of making him one last offer, but he didn't have the heart to. He hesitated and wavered and agonized. In the end he said, 'Would you give me fourpence for this new alphabet book?'

'I'm only a boy and I don't buy anything from other boys,' replied his young companion, who had more judgement than he did.

'I'll buy the book for fourpence,' shouted a dealer in second-hand clothes, who had overheard the conversation.

So the book was sold then and there. And just think how that poor man, Joe, was trembling with cold at home, in nothing but his shirt-sleeves, because he had been determined to buy the alphabet book for his little boy!

CHAPTER X

How the puppets recognize Pinocchio as their brother, and make a great fuss of him; but how the puppeteer, Swallowfire, appears in the middle of it all and Pinocchio is in danger of coming to grief.

When Pinocchio entered the puppet theatre something happened which nearly started a revolution.

By now the curtain had been raised and the play had begun.

Harlequin and Punchinello were on stage,* quarrelling with each other and, as usual, they were threatening to come to blows and beatings at any moment.

The members of the audience were utterly absorbed, and

laughed till it hurt to hear those two marionettes bickering, while, true to life, they gesticulated and made use of all manner of abuse, just as if they were both thinking beings, two real live people.

When all of a sudden, out of the blue, Harlequin stopped acting and, turning towards the spectators and pointing at someone in the back row, he began to declaim in dramatic tones, 'Divine Providence! Do I dream or do I wake? Yet over yonder that is surely Pinocchio! . . .'

'Yes, it's really Pinocchio!' shouted Punchinello.

'Yes, it's him all right!' screamed Signora Rosalba, peeping out from behind the scenery.

'It's Pinocchio! It's Pinocchio!' shouted all the puppets in chorus, leaping out from the wings. 'It's Pinocchio! It's our brother Pinocchio! Long live Pinocchio! . . .'

'Pinocchio, come up here with me!' called Harlequin, 'Come and embrace your wooden brothers and sisters!'

At this affectionate invitation Pinocchio jumped up, and from the back row of the stalls he reached the expensive seats, and from the expensive seats he climbed onto the head of the conductor of the orchestra, and from there he darted onto the stage. You just cannot imagine all the expressions of real, heartfelt brotherliness—the embraces, the bear-hugs, the friendly pinches, the slaps on the back— that Pinocchio received amidst all that commotion from the actors and actresses of that Wooden Drama Company.

One has to admit it was a moving spectacle; but the audience became impatient because the play was at a halt and they began to shout, 'We want the play! We want the play!'

It was all a waste of breath because, instead of proceeding with the performance, the puppets made even more din and disturbance and, hoisting Pinocchio onto their shoulders, they carried him in triumph up to the footlights.

So then the puppeteer came out, and he was such a huge, ugly brute that it was terrifying just looking at him. His beard was as black as a blot of ink, and it was so long that

it reached from his chin right down to the floor; needless to say, as he walked along, he kept treading on it. His mouth was as wide as a kitchen stove, his eyes looked like two lanterns with the flame burning behind red glass; with his hands he cracked a thick whip, made out of snakes and foxes' tails twisted together.

At the unexpected arrival of the puppet-master, everyone fell silent; no one breathed. You could have heard a fly passing. Those poor puppets, male and female alike, were trembling like leaves.

'Why did you come to cause chaos in my theatre?' the puppeteer asked Pinocchio, his enormous voice like that of an ogre with a serious cold in the nose.

'Believe me, Excellency, it wasn't my fault! ...'

'Enough of that! Tonight you will pay your debts.'

In point of fact, after the play was over the puppeteer went to the kitchen where a fine ram was being cooked for his supper. It was slowly turning on the spit, but there wasn't enough wood to finish the cooking and give it a proper roasting, so he called Harlequin and Punchinello and said to them, 'Fetch me that puppet; you'll find him hanging on the hook. It looks to me as if he's a puppet made of very dry wood, and I'm sure that when I throw him on the fire he'll give a lovely, bright flame for the roast.'

At first Punchinello and Harlequin hesitated; but, terrified by a harsh glance from their master, they obeyed, and soon after they returned to the kitchen, carrying poor Pinocchio in their arms. Slipping from their grasp like an eel out of water, he shrieked desperately, 'Papa, Papa, save me! I don't want to die. No, no, I don't want to die! ...'

CHAPTER XI

How Swallowfire sneezes and forgives
Pinocchio, who then saves his friend
Harlequin from death.

The puppet-master Swallowfire (for this was his name) appeared to be a terrifying man, I don't deny it, especially with that horrid black beard of his, which covered the whole of his chest and the whole of his legs, in the manner of an apron; but deep down he wasn't a bad man. And the proof is that when he saw poor Pinocchio being brought before him, struggling frantically and yelling 'I don't want to die, I don't want to die', he straight away began to feel concerned and sorry for him. Having held back a while, in the end he could contain himself no longer, and sent forth a resounding sneeze.

At that sneeze, Harlequin, who thus far had been grieving and bowed as a weeping willow, became visibly altogether more cheerful and, bending over Pinocchio, softly whispered in his ear, 'Good news, brother! The puppet-master sneezed, and that's the sign that he has been moved to pity for you and now you're safe.'

Because, you see, although everyone else who feels sorry for another person either weeps or at least pretends to wipe away a tear, Swallowfire on the contrary had a habit of sneezing every time that he really took pity on someone. It was as good a way as any other to let people know about the softness of his heart.

After his sneeze the puppeteer, maintaining his gruffness, called out to Pinocchio: 'Stop your crying! Your howls have given me a nagging feeling in the pit of my stomach ... it's a sort of pang, which very nearly ... Achoo! Achoo!' and he sneezed again, twice.

'Bless you!' said Pinocchio.

'Thanks. And your mama and papa are still alive?' asked Swallowfire.

'My papa is, yes, but I never knew my mama.'

'I dare say it might cause your old father some sorrow if I was to go and throw you in among those burning coals! Poor old man! I feel sorry for him! ... Achoo! Achoo! Achoo!' and he sneezed three more times.

'Bless you!' said Pinocchio.

'Thanks. Anyway, you must be sorry for me too, because, as you see, I have no more wood to finish cooking that roast ram,* and, to tell the truth, you could have been a great help to me with this problem. But now I'm sorry for you and so never mind. Instead of you, I'll use one or other of the puppets of my Company to burn up under the spit. Hey, constables!'*

At this command there instantly appeared two wooden

constables, both very tall, both very gaunt, wearing their
three-cornered hats and carrying their sabres unsheathed.

Then the puppet-master said to them in a gasping voice,
'Pick up Harlequin over there, tie him up well, and throw
him on the fire to burn. I want my ram well roasted!'

You can imagine how poor Harlequin felt! His fright
was so great that his legs buckled under him and he fell flat
on his face on the ground.

At the sight of that heart-rending spectacle, Pinocchio
flung himself at the puppeteer's feet; weeping torrents and
wetting all the hairs of his vast beard with his tears, he
began in an entreating voice to say, 'Have pity, Mr Swallowfire! . . .'

'There are no misters here!' the puppeteer replied harshly.

'Have pity, Sir! . . .'

'There are no sirs here!'

'Have pity, My Lord! . . .'

'There are no lords here!'

'Have pity, Excellency! . . .'*

Hearing the word 'Excellency', the puppet-master at once
pouted prettily, and suddenly becoming more human and

approachable, he said to Pinocchio, 'Oh, all right, what do you want of me?'

'I beg you have mercy on poor Harlequin...'

'There's no room for mercy here. As I spared you, I've got to put him on the fire, because I want my ram to be properly roasted.'

'In that case,' cried Pinocchio gallantly, getting up and throwing aside his cap of bread dough, 'in that case, I know what my duty is. Come forward, sir constable! Tie me up and throw me into the middle of those flames. No, no! It's not right that poor Harlequin, my true friend, should die for me!'

These words, declaimed in a loud voice and in heroic accents, made all the puppets present at the scene weep. Even the constables, although they were wooden, cried like new-born lambs.

At first Swallowfire remained as hard and immovable as a lump of ice, but then, little by little, even he began to be touched and to sneeze. And after four or five sneezes he affectionately spread wide his arms and told Pinocchio: 'You are a good boy! Come here and give me a kiss.'

Pinocchio ran straight to him and, climbing like a squirrel up the puppeteer's beard, he planted a great big kiss on the end of his nose.

'So has clemency been granted?' asked poor Harlequin in a wisp of a voice that could hardly be heard.

'Clemency has been granted!' responded Swallowfire; then he added, sighing and shaking his head, 'Never mind! For tonight I'll resign myself to eating the ram half raw. But next time the unlucky one had better watch out...'

When the news spread that the puppet had been spared, all the others rushed onto the stage and, lighting the footlights and the chandeliers as if for a gala evening, they all began to skip about and dance. They were still dancing at dawn.

CHAPTER XII

*How the puppet-master, Swallowfire, gives five
gold coins to Pinocchio to take to his papa,
Old Joe; and how, instead, Pinocchio allows
himself to be swindled by the Fox and the Cat
and goes off with them.*

The next day Swallowfire took Pinocchio to one side and
asked him, 'What is your father's name?'

'Old Joe.'

'And what's his trade?'

'Poor man.'

'Does he earn much?'

'He earns just the right amount for never having a half-
penny in his pocket. You know, in order to buy me the
alphabet book for school he had to sell the only cape he
had, one with so many darns and patches that it was in a
sorry state.'

'Poor fellow! I feel almost sorry for him. Look, here are
five gold coins. Take them straight back to him and give
him my best wishes.'

As you can well imagine, Pinocchio thanked the puppeteer over and over again; one by one he embraced all the
puppets of the company, even the constables; then, beside
himself with joy, he set out for home.

But he hadn't gone half a mile before he encountered
along the way a Fox who was lame in one leg and a Cat
who was blind in both eyes, who were trudging along
helping each other, as good companions in adversity. The
Fox who was lame leaned on the Cat while walking, and
the Cat who was blind was guided by the Fox.*

'Good morning, Pinocchio,' the Fox greeted him
courteously.

'How do you know my name?' asked the puppet.

'I know your father well.'

'Where did you see him?'

'Yesterday I saw him at his front door.'

'And what was he doing?'

'He was in his shirt-sleeves trembling with cold.'

'Poor papa! But, God willing,* from now on he won't have to tremble any more . . .'

'Why?'

'Because I've joined the gentry.'

'The gentry? You?' said the Fox, and began to laugh in a disagreeable, mocking way, and the Cat laughed too but, so as to disguise it, he combed his whiskers with his paws up in front.

'There's nothing to laugh about,' cried Pinocchio, vexed. 'I'm very sorry indeed to have to make your mouths water, but these things here, just in case you're not connoisseurs, are five rather nice gold coins.'

And he pulled out the coins given to him by Swallowfire.

At the pleasing sound of that money, the Fox made an involuntary movement, stretching out the leg that appeared to be paralysed, and the Cat opened wide both his eyes like two green lamps; but he hastened to close them again, so much so that Pinocchio did not notice a thing.

'And now,' the Fox asked him, 'what are you going to do with these coins?'

'First of all,' replied the puppet, 'I want to buy a lovely new cape for my papa, all made of gold and silver and with diamond buttons; then I want to buy an alphabet book for myself.'

'For yourself?'

'Of course, because I want to go to school and start studying hard.'

'Take a look at me!' said the Fox. 'Because of my ridiculous desire to study, I lost a leg.'

'Take a look at me!' said the Cat. 'Because of my ridiculous desire to study, I lost the sight of both eyes.'

At that moment a white Blackbird, which was perching on the hedge at the roadside, sang his usual song and said, 'Pinocchio, don't listen to the advice of those bad characters, otherwise you'll be sorry!'

Poor Blackbird, if only he had never said it! In one great bound, the Cat struck him down, and without giving him time to say *Ah*, ate him in one gulp, feathers and all.*

Having finished his meal and wiped his whiskers, he closed his eyes once more and pretended to be blind as before.

'Poor Blackbird!' said Pinocchio to the Cat. 'Why did you treat him so badly?'

'I did it to teach him a lesson. That way next time he'll know not to interrupt other people's conversations.'

They had got more than halfway when the Fox, stopping abruptly, said to the puppet, 'Do you want to double your money?'

'Meaning?'

'Do you wish to turn your pathetic five florins* into a hundred, or a thousand, or two thousand?'

'Rather! How?'

'Extremely easily. Instead of going home, you ought to come with us.'

'And where will you take me?'

'To the land of Boobies.'*

Pinocchio thought about it for a moment, and then said resolutely, 'No, I don't want to come. I'm near home now, and I want to go home where my papa is waiting. Poor old man, who knows how grieved he must have been yesterday, when I didn't return. I'm sorry to say that I have been a bad boy, and the Talking Cricket was right to say that "disobedient children will not fare well in this world". And I've proved it to my cost, because such great misfortune has befallen me, including last night at Swallowfire's house where I got into danger . . . Brrr! It gives me goose-pimples just to think of it!'

'I see,' said the Fox, 'you really want to go home, do you? Well then, go, and so much the worse for you!'

'So much the worse for you!' repeated the Cat.

'Think about it carefully, Pinocchio, because you're looking a gift-horse in the mouth.'

'In the mouth!' repeated the Cat.

'Your five florins would have grown to two thousand overnight.'

'Two thousand!' repeated the Cat.

'But however is it possible that they could grow so much?' asked Pinocchio, whose jaw had dropped in amazement.

'Let me explain,' said the Fox. 'You see, in the land of Boobies, there is some sacred ground, which everyone calls the Field of Miracles.* In this place you make a little hole in the ground and you put into it, for example, a golden florin. Then you cover the hole with a bit of earth; you water it with two buckets of spring water, you scatter on it a pinch of salt, and in the evening you go and have a good sleep. Then, during the night, the florin germinates and prospers, and the next morning, as soon as you're up, you go back to the field, and what do you find? You find a handsome tree covered in as many golden florins as a fine ear of corn has grains in June.'

'In that case,' said Pinocchio, who was getting more and more dumbfounded, 'if I buried my five florins in that ground, how many florins would I find the next day?'

'That's a very easy sum,' replied the Fox, 'so easy that you can do it on your fingers. Suppose that each florin makes you a cluster of five hundred florins; multiply the five hundred by five, and there you are next day with two thousand five hundred ringing gold shiners in your pocket.'*

'Oh, how lovely!' exclaimed Pinocchio, dancing for joy. 'As soon as I've harvested all those florins, I'll take two thousand for myself and the other five hundred left over I shall give to you two as a present.'

'A present for us?' cried the Fox, refusing, and making himself out to be insulted. 'Heaven forbid!'

'Forbid!' repeated the Cat.

'We', the Fox continued, 'do not work for base self-interest; we labour solely to enrich others.'

'Others,' repeated the Cat.

'What good people!' Pinocchio thought to himself, and then and there he forgot all about his papa, the new cape, the alphabet book and all his good intentions, and he said to the Fox and the Cat, 'Let's set off at once; I'm coming with you.'

CHAPTER XIII

At the Red Lobster Inn

They walked and walked and walked. At last, towards evening, they arrived dead tired at the Red Lobster Inn.

'Let's stop here for a while,' said the Fox. 'We'll have a

bite to eat and rest up for a few hours. We shall set off again at midnight in order to reach the Field of Miracles tomorrow at dawn.'

Inside the inn, they all three sat down to table; but none of them had any appetite.

The poor Cat, who was feeling seriously indisposed with stomach trouble, could only manage thirty-five mullet with tomato sauce and four portions of tripe and onions, and, because he thought the tripe insufficiently seasoned, he treated himself three times over to more butter and grated cheese!*

The Fox would have gladly nibbled at a little something too, but as the doctor had prescribed an extremely strict diet, he had to make do with a simple jugged hare* with a very light garnish of plump pullets and tender poussins. As an appetizer after the hare he ordered a little hotch-potch of game-birds, partridge, rabbit, frog, lizard and green grapes;* then he wanted nothing more. Food made him feel so ill, he said, that he really could not lift a thing to his mouth.

The one who ate least of all was Pinocchio. He asked for a lobe of walnut and the heel of a loaf, and left it all on his plate untouched. Poor boy, his thoughts were so concentrated upon the Field of Miracles that he had succumbed already to indigestion from an expected surfeit of gold coins.

When they had dined, the Fox said to the landlord, 'I require two good rooms, one for Mr Pinocchio and the other for me and my companion. Before going on our way we shall take forty winks. But remember that we wish to be woken at midnight to continue our journey.'

'Yes, sir,' replied the landlord, and winked at the Fox and the Cat, as if to say, 'I've taken the hint and understand you perfectly . . .'

No sooner had Pinocchio climbed into bed than he fell sound asleep and began to dream. In his dream he seemed to be in a field, and this field was full of little trees laden

with bunches of fruit, and these bunches were laden with gold florins; swayed by the wind, they went *ting ting ting* as if they wanted to say 'whoever wishes, may come and take us'. But when Pinocchio reached the best part, that's to say, when he stretched out to take handfuls of all those lovely coins and put them in his pocket, he was suddenly woken up by three resounding bangs on his bedroom door.

It was the landlord who had come to tell him that it was midnight.

'And are my companions ready?' the puppet asked.

'Ready? I'll say! They left two hours ago.'

'Why in such a hurry?'

'Because the Cat received a message that his eldest kitten, who is suffering from chilblains on the feet, is dangerously ill.'

'And did they pay for supper?'

'What do you imagine? They are persons of too refined an upbringing to offer such an affront to gentry such as yourself.'

'What a pity! It's an affront that would have pleased me greatly!' said Pinocchio, scratching his head. Then he asked, 'And where did my good friends say they would meet me?'

'At the Field of Miracles, tomorrow morning at daybreak.'

Pinocchio paid a florin for his supper and that of his two companions, and then departed.

But it has to be said that he set off groping his way, for outside the Inn the darkness was so dark that you could not see an inch. In the countryside round about you could have heard a leaf drop. Only from time to time some blundering nocturnal birds, flying across the lane from hedge to hedge, would beat their wings against Pinocchio's nose, and jumping back a step in fright he would shout 'Who goes there?', and the echo of the surrounding hills repeated in the distance, 'Who goes there? Who goes there? Who goes there?'*

Then, while he was walking along, he observed on a tree-trunk a little creature that shone with a pale, opaque light, just like a night-light inside a transparent porcelain lamp.

'Who are you?' Pinocchio asked him.*

'I'm the ghost of the Talking Cricket,' answered the little creature in a very faint voice that sounded as if it came from the other world.

'What do you want of me?' the puppet said.

'I want to give you some advice. Turn back and take the four florins that you have left to your poor papa, who is grief-stricken and desperate because he hasn't set eyes on you again.'

'Tomorrow my papa will be a grand gentleman because these four florins are going to turn into two thousand.'

'My boy, never trust those who promise to make you rich between lunch and supper. Usually they are either madmen or cheats! Listen to my advice and go back.'

'But I want to go on.'

'It's very late! . . .'

'I want to go on.'

'It's a very dark night...'

'I want to go on.'

'The path is dangerous...'

'I want to go on.'*

'Remember that boys who want to follow their whims and do things their way sooner or later regret it.'

'The same old story. Good night, Cricket.'

'Good night, Pinocchio, and may heaven protect you from moonshine and murderers.'

The moment he had spoken these last words, the Talking Cricket was suddenly extinguished, the way a candle is extinguished when you blow on it, and the path became darker than ever.

CHAPTER XIV

How Pinocchio, because he has not heeded the good advice of the Talking Cricket, encounters the murderers.

'Really,' the puppet said to himself as he started off again, 'we poor children, how unlucky we are! Everybody tells us off, everybody admonishes us, everybody gives us advice. If you let them have their way, they'd all take it upon themselves to be our fathers and our teachers: all of them, including Talking Crickets. There you are, just because I didn't pay any attention to that tiresome Cricket, who knows how many mishaps are going to happen to me, according to him! I'm even likely to meet murderers! It's just as well that I don't believe in murderers, and never have done. As far as I'm concerned, murderers were invented on purpose by fathers so as to frighten children who want to go out at night. And anyway, supposing I met

some here on this path, would they make me feel uneasy? Not in a million years! I'd go right up to them, shouting, "Mr Murderers, what do you want of me? Let me remind you that no one plays games with me! Kindly take yourselves off and mind your own affairs." If I was to make this little speech to them in earnest, those poor murderers would be off like the wind, I can see it all now. If by any chance they were so badly brought up as not to run away, then I'd run off, and that would be the end of it...'*

But Pinocchio was unable to finish his deliberations, for at that moment he thought he heard a very slight rustling of leaves.

He turned round to look, and in the dark he saw two awful black figures, all enveloped in coal-sacks, who were bounding along after him on tiptoe, like a pair of ghosts.

'They're really here!' he said to himself, and not knowing where to hide the four florins, he put them in his mouth, tucking them under his tongue.

Then he tried to escape. But before he had taken a step, he felt himself seized by the arms and heard two horrible, cavernous voices which said, 'Your money or your life!'

Pinocchio was unable to reply with words because of the coins in his mouth, so he bowed deeply over and over again and play-acted a whole pantomime to those two hooded beings, of whom only the eyes showed through holes in the sacks, so that they should understand that he was only a poor puppet who didn't have so much as a brass farthing in his pocket.

'Get on with it! Less prattling and hand over the money!' shouted the two brigands threateningly.

So the puppet made a gesture with his head and his hands as if to say, 'I haven't got any.'

'Hand over the money or you're dead,' said the taller murderer.

'Dead!' repeated the other one.

'And after we've killed you, we shall kill your father too!'

'Father too!'

'No, no, no, not my poor papa!' cried Pinocchio in desperate tones, but as he cried out the florins jingled in his mouth.

'Ah, you scoundrel! So you hid the money under your tongue? Spit it out at once!'

But Pinocchio stood firm!

'Ho, ho, so you're pretending to be deaf? Just you wait, we have ways of making you spit!'

Indeed, one of them caught hold of the puppet by the end of his nose and the other held his chin, and they began to pull roughly, one upwards and the other downwards, so as to force him to open his mouth; but there was no way of doing it. The puppet's mouth might have been nailed and riveted together.

Then the smaller murderer got out a wicked knife and tried to thrust it between Pinocchio's lips to act as a lever and a chisel; but quick as lightning, Pinocchio sank his teeth into the hand, bit it clean off, and spat it out, and you can imagine his amazement when, instead of a hand, he noticed that he had spat a cat's paw onto the ground.

Encouraged by this first victory, he tore himself out of the grasp of the murderers' claws, and, jumping the hedge, he began to flee across the fields. The two murderers ran after him, like a brace of hounds after a hare, and the one who had lost a paw ran with only one leg, though no one could ever imagine how.

After running fifteen miles, Pinocchio was at the end of his strength. So, believing himself defeated, he climbed up the trunk of a very tall pine tree and sat down among the branches at the top. The murderers tried to climb up there too, but half-way up they slipped, and falling back to earth they skinned their hands and feet.

Not that they gave up because of that; on the contrary, they gathered a bundle of dry wood at the foot of the pine and set fire to it. In less than no time the pine began to burn and flare up like a candle blown by the wind. Seeing the flames leaping and not wanting to end his days like a roast pigeon, Pinocchio made a huge jump from the tree-top, and once again ran away across the fields and vine-yards. And the murderers followed behind, ever present, never tiring.

Now day was beginning to break and they were still running after him, when suddenly Pinocchio found his path barred by a wide, deep ditch, full of dirty stagnant water the colour of milky coffee. What was to be done? 'One, two, three!' cried the puppet and, taking a tremendous run at it to launch himself, he leapt to the other side. The

murderers jumped, too, but not having judged the distance properly, *splish! splosh!* . . . they fell right into the middle of the ditch. Hearing the splash and the spray of water, Pinocchio, laughing and continuing to run, yelled out, 'Have a good swim, Mr Murderers!'

He was already imagining that they were well and truly drowned when, instead, glancing around, he saw that they were still running after him, the pair of them still wrapped up in their sacks, and both oozing water like two broken baskets.

CHAPTER XV

How the murderers follow Pinocchio, and having caught up with him, hang him on a branch of the Great Oak.

Losing heart, the puppet was on the point of throwing himself on the ground and giving up, when, gazing around, he saw amidst all the dark green of the trees, shining bright in the distance, a cottage as white as snow.

'If I had enough breath to reach that house, perhaps I would be safe!' he said to himself.

Without hesitating for a moment, he began again to run headlong through the wood. With the murderers still running behind.

After a frantic run of almost two hours, he at last arrived, utterly out of breath, at the door of the cottage, on which he knocked.

No one answered.

He knocked again, louder, for he could hear the approach of the footfalls and the heavy panting of his persecutors. Still silence.

Finding that knocking bore no result, in desperation he

went on to kick and butt the door with his head. Then there appeared at the window a beautiful Little Girl, with indigo hair and a face as white as a wax image. Her eyes were closed and her hands were crossed over her breast and, without moving her lips, she said in a faint voice that seemed to come from the other world,* 'There is no one here. They are all dead.'

'Please open the door yourself!' implored Pinocchio, weeping.

'I am dead too.'

'Dead? So what are you doing up there at the window?'

'I'm waiting for the bier to come and take me away.'

As soon as she had said this, the Little Girl vanished, and the window closed soundlessly.

'Oh, beautiful Little Girl with indigo hair,' called Pinocchio, 'have mercy and open the door! Take pity on a poor boy pursued by murd—'

But he could not complete the word, because he felt himself seized by the neck, and the same two harsh voices were muttering threats to him, 'You won't get away from us again!'

With the thought of death flashing through his mind, the puppet was overcome by such a severe bout of trembling that the joints in his wooden legs rattled and so did the four florins that he was keeping hidden under his tongue.

'Well then?' demanded the murderers, 'are you going to open your mouth, yes or no? Aha! You're not answering? . . . Leave it to us, we'll make you open it this time! . . .'

And bringing out two horrible great long knives as sharp as razors, *pow, pow*, they dealt him a couple of blows in the small of the back.

Luckily for the puppet he was made of extremely hard wood, which was the reason why the blades broke and shattered into a thousand splinters, leaving the murderers holding only the handle of each knife, and staring at each other in astonishment.

'Very well,' said one of them, 'we shall have to hang him! Let's hang him!'

'Let's hang him!' repeated the other.

Without further ado, they bound his hands behind his back and tying a slip-knot around his throat, they strung him up to dangle from a branch of a big tree known as the Great Oak.

Then they sat down on the grass, waiting for the puppet to kick the air for the last time. But, after three hours, the puppet still had his eyes open, his mouth shut and was more alive and kicking than ever.

Finally, getting tired of waiting, they looked up at Pinocchio and laughing sarcastically they said, 'Goodbye until tomorrow. When we come back tomorrow, we hope you will be courteous enough to be good and dead, with your mouth wide open.'

And off they went.

In the meantime a strong north wind had blown up and,

howling and roaring violently, it buffeted the poor hanging puppet hither and thither, making him swing about furiously like the clapper of a celebratory bell. The swinging caused him severe pain and the noose, growing tighter around his neck all the time, was choking him.

Little by little his eyes grew dim, and although he could feel death approaching, he kept hoping that at any moment some good soul would happen by to help him. He waited and waited, and when he realized that no one, but no one, was coming, his thoughts at last turned to his poor father ... and, half-dead, he murmured, 'Oh, my dear pa! if only you were here ...'

He had no breath left to say anything else. He closed his eyes, opened his mouth, straightened his legs and, giving a great shudder, hung there as if frozen stiff.*

CHAPTER XVI

How the beautiful Little Girl with indigo hair has the puppet taken down, and puts him to bed, and calls three doctors to see whether he is alive or dead.

Poor Pinocchio, hanged by the murderers on a branch of the Great Oak, by now seemed more dead than alive. Meanwhile, the beautiful Little Girl with indigo hair came to the window once more and, filled with pity at the sight of that unfortunate dangling by his neck and dancing the tarantella in the gusts of north wind, thrice clapped her hands and tapped thrice.

At this signal there was a rushing sound of wings flying fast, and a great Hawk came to rest on the windowsill.

'What is your command, oh gracious Fairy?' said the

Hawk, lowering his beak as a gesture of respect. (Because, you see, the Girl with indigo hair was really none other than a very good fairy,* who had lived beside that wood for more than a thousand years.)

'Can you see that puppet dangling from a branch of the Great Oak?'

'I see him.'

'Very well: fly straight there and with your strong beak undo the knot that is holding him high in the air, and lay him down gently on the grass at the foot of the Oak.'

The Hawk flew away and in two minutes he was back, and said, 'Your commands have been performed.'

'And how was he? Alive or dead?'

'He looked quite dead, and yet he is evidently not thoroughly dead, for when I loosened the slip-knot tied tight around his neck, he let out a sigh and muttered in a whisper, "Now I feel better . . .".'

Next the Fairy clapped her hands together and tapped twice, when in came a magnificent Poodle-dog who walked upright on his back legs, just like a man.

The Poodle-dog had the appearance of a coachman in full-dress livery. He wore a three-cornered tricorn hat on his head, trimmed with gold braid, with a white curly wig which fell to his collar, a chocolate-coloured jacket with

diamond buttons and two deep pockets to keep the bones
in that his mistress gave him at dinner, a pair of knee-
breeches made of crimson velvet, silk hose, court shoes,
and behind he had a sort of umbrella cover, all of indigo
satin, where he would put his tail if the weather turned to
rain.*

'Come here, good boy Medoro!'* said the Fairy to the
Poodle-dog. 'Harness up the finest carriage in my stables
without delay and take the road to the wood. When you
reach the Great Oak, you will find lying on the grass a
poor half-dead puppet. Lift him up with care, and lay him
very gently on the cushions in the carriage and bring him
here to me. Is that understood?'

The Poodle-dog, to show that he had understood, wagged
the indigo satin cover that he wore behind three or four
times, and hared away like an Arab charger.

Not long after, a splendid sky-blue carriage could be seen
emerging from the stables, all upholstered with canary-

feather cushions and lined inside with whipped cream and wafers and custard. The coach was drawn by a hundred pairs of white mice,* and the Poodle-dog, sitting up on the box, cracked his whip to right and left, like a cabby when he's afraid of being late.

In less than a quarter of an hour the little carriage returned, and the Fairy, who had been waiting at the cottage door, took the poor puppet up in her arms and, having carried him to a bedroom which had walls of mother-of-pearl, she sent for all the most famous doctors of the district.

The doctors arrived without delay, one after another, and that's to say there came a Crow, a Little Owl, and a Talking Cricket.*

'I should like to know from you gentlemen,' said the Fairy addressing the three doctors gathered around Pinocchio's bed, 'I should like to know from you gentlemen whether this unfortunate puppet is alive or dead...'

At this invitation, the Crow, moving forward first, felt Pinocchio's pulse, then he felt his nose and then his little toe. When he had felt them thoroughly, he solemnly pronounced these words, 'In my belief the puppet is quite dead; but if by some mischance he is not dead, that would be a sure sign that he is still alive!'

'I regret', said the Little Owl, 'to have to contradict my illustrious friend and colleague, the Crow. In my view, on the contrary, the puppet is still alive; but if by some mischance he is not alive, that would be a sign that he is really dead.'

'Are you not saying anything?' asked the Fairy of the Talking Cricket.

'I say that for the wise doctor who doesn't know what to say, the best thing to do is to stay silent. Besides, that puppet is no stranger to me; I've known him for some time.'

Up to that moment Pinocchio had been as immobile as

a real lump of wood, but then he gave a sort of convulsive shudder, that made the whole bed shake.

'That puppet', went on the Talking Cricket, 'is a first-class rascal . . .'

Pinocchio opened his eyes and closed them again at once.

'He is an out-and-out rogue, a lazybones, a good-for-nothing . . .'

Pinocchio hid his head under the sheets.

'That puppet is a disobedient son, who will be the death of his poor, broken-hearted father! . . .'

At this point the bedroom was filled with a suffocated sound of sobbing and weeping. You can imagine the scene when, after lifting up the sheets a little, they observed that the sobbing and weeping came from Pinocchio.

'When a corpse weeps, it's a sign that he is beginning to recover,' the Crow said solemnly.

'I regret to have to contradict my illustrious friend and colleague,' remarked the Little Owl, 'but in my opinion, when a corpse weeps, it's a sign that he is sorry to die.'

CHAPTER XVII

How Pinocchio eats the sugar but refuses
to take his medicine; but when he sees the
grave-diggers coming to take him away, then
he decides to swallow it. Further, how he tells
a lie and as a punishment his nose grows long.

As soon as the three doctors had left the room, the Fairy drew near to Pinocchio, and stroking his forehead she realized that he was suffering from an indescribably high fever.

So she dissolved a certain white powder in half a glass of water, and offering it to the puppet, said to him fondly, 'Drink it, and in a few days you'll feel better.'

Pinocchio looked at the glass, made a face, and asked in a whining voice, 'Is it sweet or sour?'

'It's sour, but it will do you good.'

'If it's sour, I don't want it.'

'Do what I say and drink it.'

'I don't like sour things.'

'Drink it, and when you have, I'll give you a sugar-lump to make your mouth sweet again.'

'Where is the sugar-lump?'

'Here it is,' said the Fairy, taking one out of a golden sugar-bowl.

'I want the sugar-lump first, and then I'll drink that nasty bitter stuff...'

'Do you promise me?'

'Yes...'

The Fairy gave him the sugar-lump, and when he had munched and swallowed it in an instant he said, licking his lips, 'Wouldn't it be nice if sugar was a medicine too!... I'd take it every day.'

'Now keep your promise and drink these few drops of water, which will do you good.'

Pinocchio reluctantly took the glass and stuck the end of his nose in it. Then he put it to his mouth; then he stuck the end of his nose into it again. Finally he said, 'It's too sour! too sour! I can't drink it.'

'How can you be so sure, if you haven't even tasted it?'

'I can imagine it. I've smelled its smell. First I want another sugar-lump . . . then I'll drink it!'

So the Fairy, with all the patience of a good mother, put in his mouth another bit of sugar, and then offered him the glass again.

'I can't drink it like this!' said the puppet, grimacing over and over again.

'Why?'

'Because that pillow on my feet is bothering me.'

The Fairy removed the pillow.

'It's no good! I can't drink it like this either.'

'What else is bothering you?'

'The bedroom door bothers me because it's half open.'

The Fairy went and closed the bedroom door.

'Anyway,' shouted Pinocchio, bursting into tears, 'I'm not going to drink this nasty stuff, no, no, no! . . .'

'You'll regret it, my lad . . .'

'I don't care . . .'

'You're seriously ill . . .'

'I don't care . . .'

'Your fever will carry you off to the next world in only a few hours . . .'

'I don't care . . .'

'Aren't you afraid of dying?'

'I'm not afraid at all! . . . I'd rather die than drink that nasty medicine.'

At that moment, the bedroom door flew open, and in came four rabbits as black as ink, carrying on their shoulders a small coffin.

'What do you want of me?' shouted Pinocchio, sitting up in bed in terror.

'We have come to take you away,' said the fattest rabbit.
'To take me away? . . . But I'm not dead yet! . . .'

'Not yet, no, but you have only got another few minutes
of life, as you have refused to take your medicine, which
would have cured you of the fever! . . .'

'Oh my dear Fairy, dear Fairy!' the puppet began to
shriek, 'Quick, hand me the glass . . . Hurry up, for mercy's
sake;* I don't want to die, no, no . . . I don't want to die.'

Taking the glass in both his hands, he emptied it in one
draught.

'Never mind!' said the rabbits. 'This time we've made
the trip free.' And once again hoisting the little coffin on
their shoulders, they left the room grumbling and muttering through their teeth.

At all events, a few minutes later Pinocchio jumped out
of bed thoroughly well again. For, you see, wooden puppets

have the privilege of falling ill rarely and of getting better speedily.

Seeing him run and romp around the room, as sprightly and chirpy as a spring chicken, the Fairy said, 'So my medicine really did you good?'

'Never mind good! It brought me back to life . . .'

'So why ever did I have to beg you to take it?'

'It's like this. We boys are all the same! We're more afraid of medicines than of wickedness.'

'Shame on you! Children should learn that a good medicine taken in good time can save them from a serious illness or even from death . . .'

'Well, next time I won't need persuading! I shall remember those black rabbits, with the coffin on their shoulders . . . then I'll quickly grasp the glass and swallow! . . .'

'Now come over here to me, and tell me how it was that you fell into the hands of the murderers.'

'It happened that the puppet-master, Swallowfire, gave me five gold coins, and said to me, "Here you are, take these to your papa!", and instead, along the way I met a Fox and a Cat, two very respectable people, who said to me, "Would you like these coins to turn into a thousand or two thousand? Come with us, and we'll take you to the Field of Miracles." And I said, "Come on then", and they said, "Let's stop here at the Red Lobster Inn, and at midnight we'll set off again." Then when I woke up, they weren't there any more because they'd already left. Then I went off into the night, which was dark as dark, so that on the way I met two murderers wearing coal-sacks, who said to me, "Hand over your money!" and I said, "I haven't got any", because I had hidden my gold coins in my mouth, and one of the murderers tried to get his hands in my mouth, and with one bite I severed his hand and spat it out, but instead of a hand I spat out a cat's paw. And the murderers ran after me, and I ran and ran, until they reached me, and in this wood they tied me to a tree by my neck, saying, "We'll come back tomorrow, and then you'll be dead with your mouth open, and so we'll be able to take away the gold coins you hid under your tongue."'

'And where have you put the four coins now?' asked the Fairy.

'I've lost them!' replied Pinocchio; but he was telling a lie, because they were in his pocket.

As he told the lie, his nose, which had always been long, suddenly grew two inches more.

'And where did you lose them?'

'In the wood near here.'

At this second lie, his nose grew some more.

'If you lost them in the nearby wood,' said the Fairy, 'we'll hunt for them and find them, because everything that's lost in this wood always gets found.'

'Oh! now I remember properly,' answered the puppet, getting in a muddle, 'I didn't lose the four coins, but without noticing I swallowed them when I was taking your medicine.'

At this third lie, Pinocchio's nose lengthened in such an extraordinary manner that he could no longer turn around. If he moved in this direction, he banged his nose on the bed or on the window-panes, if he moved in that direction, he banged it on the bedroom walls or on the door, and if he raised his head a little, he ran the risk of poking it in the Fairy's eye.

The Fairy was watching him and laughing.

'Why are you laughing?' asked the puppet, embarrassed and anxious about that nose of his which was growing before his very eyes.

'I'm laughing about that lie you told.'

'How do you know I told a lie?'

'Lies are quickly recognized, my lad, because there are two kinds: there are those with short legs (with which the truth soon catches up) and there are those with long noses (which stare you straight in the face); as it happens, yours is the long-nosed sort.'*

Wanting to hide himself in shame, Pinocchio tried to run out of the room, but he didn't succeed. His nose had grown so much that it would no longer go through the door.

CHAPTER XVIII

How Pinocchio meets the Fox and the Cat again, and goes with them to sow the four coins in the Field of Miracles.

As you can imagine, the Fairy let the puppet cry and howl for a good half-hour on account of that nose of his that would no longer go through the door, and she did that to teach him a hard lesson, so that he would learn for himself not to indulge in the nasty habit of telling lies, the worst vice that a child can have. But when she saw that he looked transformed, with his eyes popping out of his head from misery, she felt sorry for him and clapped her hands. At that signal there flew into the room through the window a thousand big birds called *Woodpeckers*, who all landed on Pinocchio's nose and began to peck at it and drill it, so that in a few minutes that enormous and ridiculous nose was reduced to its normal size.

'How good you are to me, dear Fairy,' said the puppet, drying his eyes, 'and I do love you so!'

'I love you too,' replied the Fairy, 'and if you want to stay here with me, you shall be my little brother and I shall be your good little sister . . .'

'I'd like to stay very much . . . but what about my poor papa?'

'I've thought of everything. Your papa has already received a message, and he'll be here before dark.'

'Truly?' cried Pinocchio, jumping for joy. 'In that case, dear little Fairy, if you will allow me, I should like to go and meet him! I can't wait to give that poor old man a kiss, who has suffered so much on my account!'

'Off you go then, but be sure that you don't get lost. Take the path through the wood and then you're bound to meet him.'

Pinocchio started out, and no sooner had he set foot in the wood than he began to frolic like a kid. But when he got to a certain place, almost in front of the Great Oak, he stopped because he thought he heard people among the bushes. Indeed, coming along the path, he saw, guess who? ... the Fox and the Cat, none other than the travelling companions with whom he had supped at the Red Lobster Inn.

'Here is our dear Pinocchio!' cried the Fox, embracing and kissing him. 'What brings you here?'

'What brings you here?' repeated the Cat.

'It's a long story,' said the puppet, 'which I'll tell you sometime. But you ought to know that the other night when you left me on my own at the Inn, I ran into murderers on the journey...'

'Murderers?... Oh, my poor friend! What did they want?'

'They wanted to steal my gold coins.'

'Disgraceful!' said the Fox.

'Most disgraceful!' repeated the Cat.

'But I managed to escape,' the puppet went on, 'with them behind me all the time, until they caught me up and hanged me from a branch of that oak-tree...'

And Pinocchio pointed to the Great Oak hard by.

'Can you imagine anything worse!' said the Fox. 'What is the world coming to? Is there nowhere safe for respectable gentlefolk like us?'

While they were talking together like this, Pinocchio noticed that the Cat was lame in the right-hand front leg, because the whole paw with its claws was missing, so he asked, 'What happened to your paw?'

The Cat began to say something, but got muddled up. So the Fox replied quickly, 'My friend is too modest, which is what prevents him from responding. I'll answer for him. It's like this: an hour ago we met an old wolf by the way-side, who was fainting from hunger and who begged for charity from us. As we hadn't even a bean to give him, do you know what my friend did, who really has a heart of gold? He cut off one of his front paws with his own teeth and threw it to that poor beast, to give him a bite to eat.'

And so saying the Fox wiped away a tear.

Pinocchio was touched by the story too, and drawing close to the Cat, he whispered in his ear, 'If only all cats were like you, what luck the rats would have! . . .'

'And you, what are you doing in these parts?' the Fox asked the puppet.

'I'm waiting for my papa, who should be arriving at any moment.'

'And what about your gold coins?'

'I've still got them in my pocket, minus the one I spent at the Red Lobster Inn.'

'And just think that you might have had a thousand or two by tomorrow, instead of just four! Why don't you take my advice? Why not go and sow them in the Field of Miracles?'

'I can't today, but I'll go another day.'

'Another day will be too late!' said the Fox.

'Why?'

'Because that field has been bought by a great landowner, and from tomorrow no one will be permitted to sow money there.'

'How far is the Field of Miracles from here?'

'Barely two miles. Do you want to come with us? In half

an hour we'll be there; you can sow your four coins straight away; after a few minutes you'll be able to pick up two thousand, and this evening you'll be back with your pockets full. Are you coming with us?'

Pinocchio hesitated a moment before replying, for he remembered the good Fairy, Old Joe, and the warnings of the Talking Cricket. Then he ended by doing what all those children do who haven't a scrap of sense or a scrap of feeling; that's to say, he ended by tossing his head and saying to the Fox and the Cat, 'Let's set off then; I'm coming with you.'

And off they went.

After walking for half the day they came to a town called Sillybillytrap. On entering, Pinocchio observed that all the streets were populated with bald dogs yawning with hunger, fleeced lambs trembling with cold, poultry relieved of both comb and wattles and begging in the street for one grain of maize, big flightless butterflies, who had sold their lovely colourful wings, tail-less peacocks, ashamed to be

seen like that, and pheasants strutting in silence, mourning the loss of their shining gold and silver feathers, now gone for ever.*

Every so often, in the midst of this crowd of poor beggars and black sheep, there passed a noble carriage with some Fox, or Thieving Magpie, or bird of prey* inside.

'And whereabouts is the Field of Miracles?' asked Pinocchio.

'It's just nearby.'

They hastened to cross the town and, once beyond its walls, they stopped at a lonely field which looked very much like any other field.

'Here we are!' said the Fox to the puppet. 'Now bend down, scrape out a little hole in the earth with your hands, and place your gold coins inside it.'

Pinocchio obeyed. He made the hole, put in the four coins which he had left, and then covered the hole with a little earth.

'Now then,' said the Fox, 'go to the pond over there, fill a bucket with water, and water the earth where you sowed the coins.'

Pinocchio went to the pond, and because just then he didn't have a bucket, he took off one of his shoes, filled it with water, and watered the earth covering the hole. Then he asked, 'Is there anything else to be done?'

'Nothing else,' answered the Fox. 'Now we can go away. In about twenty minutes you can come back, and you will find that the little tree has already grown out of the ground and has branches loaded with coins.'

Off his head with delight, the poor puppet thanked the Fox and the Cat a thousand times, and promised them a lovely present.

'We do not ask for presents,' replied those two blackguards. 'It suffices us to have taught you how to get rich without working, so we are as pleased as Punch.'

So saying, they took their leave of Pinocchio, and wishing him a bumper harvest, they went off on their own business.

CHAPTER XIX

How Pinocchio is robbed of his gold coins, and
as a punishment gets four months in gaol.

Back in the town the puppet began to count the minutes one by one, and when it seemed to him that the time was right, he retraced his steps towards the Field of Miracles.

While he was walking along with hurried steps, his heart beat hard, going tick, tock, tick, tock, like a drawing-room clock that's really going strong. Meanwhile he was thinking to himself, 'Say instead of a thousand coins, I found two thousand on the branches of the tree? . . . What if instead of two thousand I found five thousand? or instead of five thousand I found a hundred thousand? Oh what a fine gentleman I'd be then! . . . I'd like to have a fine mansion, a thousand wooden ponies and a thousand stables, so that I could play with them, a cellar for cordials and liqueurs, and a bookcase packed full of candied fruits and gateaux and fruit-breads and nougat and ice-cream cornets.'

While he was imagining all this, he drew near the field, and stopped to see whether by any chance he could espy a tree with its branches covered in money; but he could see nothing. He walked another hundred paces, and still nothing; he went into the field . . . and proceeded right up to the little hole where he had buried his florins, and there was nothing there. Then he fell to thinking and, forgetting all the rules of polite society and good breeding, he pulled his fist out of his pocket and at great length scratched his head.

As he did this, he heard screeching in his ears a great guffaw of laughter, and looking up he saw a big Parrot in a tree, preening the few feathers it had left.

'What are you laughing for?' asked Pinocchio irritably.

'I'm laughing because, while I was preening, I tickled myself under my wings.'

The puppet did not answer. He went to the pond and filled the same shoe with water and started to water the soil again over the place where the gold coins were.

All of a sudden another laugh, even more impertinent than the first, rang out in the silence and solitude of that field.

'Look here,' yelled Pinocchio, getting angry, 'would you care to tell me, you rude Parrot, why you're laughing?'

'I'm laughing about all those boobies who believe in any

nonsense they are told and let themselves get trapped by those more cunning than themselves.'

'Do you mean me, by any chance?'

'Yes, poor Pinocchio, I mean you, you who are so silly as to believe that money can be sowed and reaped in the fields, like you sow beans and pumpkins. Once upon a time I believed it too, and now I'm paying the price. Now it's too late, but I have had to realize that to put a bit of money together honestly, you have to know how to earn it, either by the labour of your own hands or by the intelligence of your own brain.'

'I don't understand you,' said the puppet, who was already beginning to tremble with fear.

'Never mind! I'll explain myself more clearly,' the Parrot continued. 'You see, while you were in town, the Fox and the Cat came back to this field; they took the buried gold coins, and ran off like the wind. You'd have to be clever to catch them now!'

Pinocchio's jaw had dropped, and not wanting to believe the Parrot's words, he began to dig with his hands and fingernails in the soil that he had watered. He dug and dug and dug and made such a deep hole that you could have stood a haystack in it. But the coins were no longer there.

Seized with despair, he raced back to the town and went directly to the courtroom, so as to make a deposition to the judge about the two ruffians who had robbed him. The judge was a great ape of the Gorilla species; he was an aged great ape who was respected for his advanced years, for his white beard and especially for his gold-rimmed spectacles, without lenses, which he was obliged to wear continually as a result of an inflammation of the eyes which had been troubling him for many years.*

In the presence of the judge, he recounted in every particular the iniquitous fraud of which he had been the victim; he gave the forename and surname and a detailed description of the robbers, and he ended by demanding justice.

The judge heard him out with much kindliness; he took a lively part in the narration: he was moved to pity, he grew upset, and when the puppet had nothing further to say, he stretched out a hand and rang a bell.

In answer to the ringing, two mastiffs immediately appeared, dressed as police constables.

Indicating Pinocchio, the judge then said to the constables, 'This poor fellow has been robbed of four gold coins; seize him, therefore, and cast him into prison at once.'

Hearing himself sentenced like this out of the blue, the puppet was flabbergasted and wanted to protest. However, the constables, to avoid a useless waste of time, stopped his mouth and led him down to the dungeons.

And there he had to stay for four months, four very long months, and he would have had to stay even longer had it not been for a very lucky chance. You see, the young Emperor who reigned over the town of Sillybillytrap, having won a fine victory over his enemies, gave the order for great public festivities, illuminations, fireworks, horse and bicycle races, and as a sign of the greatest exultation he decided to open all the prisons and release all the miscreants.

'If all the others are leaving prison, I want to leave too,' said Pinocchio to the gaoler.

'Not you, no,' replied the gaoler, 'because you're not one of the chosen few . . .'

'I beg your pardon,' retorted Pinocchio, 'I'm a miscreant too.'

'In that case you have every reason,' said the gaoler, lifting his cap in respect and, giving him a good-day, he opened the gates of the prison and let him escape.

CHAPTER XX

How, freed from prison, Pinocchio sets out to return to the Fairy's house; but on the journey he meets a terrible Serpent, and later gets caught in a gin-trap.

You can imagine Pinocchio's joy at being freed. Without any humming and hawing he made haste to leave the town and once more took the road towards the Fairy's Cottage.

Because of the rainy weather, the road had turned into a morass and was knee-deep in mud. But the puppet took no notice. Urged on by his longing to see his father and his little sister with the indigo hair, he went along by leaps and bounds like a greyhound, and as he ran the splashes of mud stuck to him right up to his cap. He went along, saying to himself, 'What a lot of misfortunes have befallen me . . . And I deserve it! For I'm a stubborn and peevish puppet . . . and I always want my own way, and never listen to the people who love me and who have a hundred times more sense than I have! . . . But from this point onwards I plan to change my ways and become a well-behaved, obedient boy . . . In any case, I've well and truly seen that when children are naughty, they pay for it, and nothing ever turns out right for them. I wonder if my papa still wants me back? . . . Will he be at the Fairy's house?

Poor old man, it's so long since I saw him, and I'm dying to hug him hundreds of times and smother him with kisses! And will the Fairy forgive me for my bad behaviour to her? . . . And when I remember how much goodness and kindness she lavished on me . . . and to think that I owe my life to her! . . . Could there ever be a more ungrateful and heartless boy than me? . . .'

While he was saying this, he suddenly stopped and took four steps backwards.

What had he seen?

He had seen a huge Serpent lying across the road, with green skin, fiery eyes and a pointed tail which smoked like a chimney.

It is hard to imagine the fright this gave the puppet, whereupon he retreated more than half a mile and sat down on a heap of stones to wait for the Serpent to go about its own affairs, once and for all, and leave the way clear for passers-by.

He waited an hour, two hours, three hours, but the Serpent was still there and even from afar one could see the glowing of his fiery eyes and the column of smoke that rose from the tip of his tail.

So Pinocchio, wanting to be brave, went quite close, and putting on a gentle, ingratiating, soft voice, said to the Serpent, 'Excuse me, Mr Serpent, but would you be so kind as to move just a little to one side, to let me pass?'

It was like talking to a brick wall. Nobody moved.

So he began again in the same little voice, 'You see, Mr Serpent, I'm going home where my papa is waiting for me and it's such a long time since I saw him! . . . Would you please permit me to continue on my way?'

He awaited some sort of reply to his question, but the reply didn't come. On the contrary, the Serpent, which up till then had appeared vigorous and full of life, became immobile and almost stiff. His eyes closed and his tail stopped smoking.

'What if he's really dead?' said Pinocchio, rubbing his hands together with such pleasure; and without wasting more time, he made as if to clamber over him so as to walk on down the road. But he had hardly lifted his foot when the Serpent suddenly reared up like a released spring and, drawing back, the startled puppet stumbled and fell over.

In fact he fell so badly that he landed with his head stuck in the mud on the road and with his legs up in the air.

At the sight of that upside-down puppet kicking his legs about at an incredible rate, the Serpent was seized with such convulsive laughter—laugh, laugh, laugh, he went— that in the end, what with the strain of too much laughing, a blood vessel in his chest burst. And this time he really did die.

After that Pinocchio began to run again so as to arrive at the Fairy's house before it got dark. But on the way, no longer able to resist the agonizing pangs of hunger, he hopped into a field, intending to pick a few clusters of muscat grapes. If only he hadn't done it!

The minute he got to the vines, *snap* . . . he felt his legs

gripped by two sharp irons, which made him see all the stars in the firmament.

The poor puppet had been caught in a gin-trap placed there by some peasants to nab certain fat beech martens, which were the scourge of all the hen-coops of the neighbourhood.

CHAPTER XXI

*How Pinocchio is caught by a peasant,
who makes him take the place of the
guard-dog for his hen-house.*

As you can imagine, Pinocchio began to cry and shriek and implore; but his tears and cries were useless, for thereabouts there were no houses to be seen and not a living soul was going along the road.

Meanwhile it was getting dark.

Partly because of the pain from the gin-trap which was cutting into his shins, and partly because he was frightened at finding himself alone in the dark in the middle of those fields, the puppet was nearly fainting.* Then, suddenly, he saw a firefly above his head, and he called out: 'Dear little Firefly, please take pity on me and free me from this torture! . . .'

'Poor little boy!' answered the Firefly, feeling sorry for him and stopping to look. 'However did you get your legs clamped between these sharp teeth?'

'I came into the field to pick a couple of bunches of these muscat grapes, and . . .'

'But did the grapes belong to you?'

'No . . .'

'So who taught you to take other people's belongings? . . .'

'I was hungry . . .'

'Hunger, my lad, is no good reason to steal things that don't belong to us . . .'

'That's true! That's true!' exclaimed Pinocchio, weeping, 'but I won't do it again.'

At this point the conversation was interrupted by the faintest sound of footsteps coming closer. It was the owner of the field, arriving to see if one of those beech martens —which had been eating his chickens by night—had been snared in his trap.

And great was his amazement when he pulled out his lamp from beneath his overcoat and discovered that, instead of a beech marten, the trap had caught a boy.

'Aha, you little thief!' said the peasant angrily, 'So you're the one who's been carrying off my hens!'

'It wasn't me, it wasn't me!' cried Pinocchio, sobbing. 'I only came into the field to take a couple of bunches of grapes!'

'Anyone who steals grapes is just as likely to steal chickens. You wait and see. I'll give you a lesson you won't forget.'

And opening the trap, he seized hold of the puppet by the nape of his neck and carried him dangling all the way home, as if he was carrying a new-born lamb.

Reaching the farmyard in front of his house, he flung him on the ground and, keeping a foot on his neck, he said, 'It's late and I want to go to bed. We'll settle our affairs tomorrow. But for the moment, as the dog that kept watch for me at night died today, you can take his place right away. You can be my watchdog.'

No sooner said than done. Around his neck he placed a thick collar all covered in brass spikes, and tightened it so that he could not take it off by slipping his head out. There was a long iron chain attached to the collar, and the chain was fixed to the wall.

'Tonight,' said the peasant, 'if it happens to rain, you can go and lie down in that wooden kennel, where there's still the straw that my poor dog slept on for four years. And if

by ill-luck the thieves happen to come, remember to prick your ears and bark.'

Having given this final instruction, the peasant went into his house, securing his door with a great big chain, and poor Pinocchio stayed crouching in the farmyard, more dead than alive from cold, hunger and fear. Every so often, weeping and frantically pushing his hands inside the collar which was rubbing his neck, he would say, 'It serves me right! . . . More's the pity, it serves me right! I wanted to be a lazybones and a good-for-nothing . . . I was determined to heed bad company, and that's why I'm dogged by misfortune all the time. If only I had been a good boy like most boys, if only I had wanted to study and work, if only I had stayed at home with my poor papa, I wouldn't be here now acting as a guard-dog at a peasant's house in the middle of the country. Oh, if only I could be born all over again! . . . But now it's too late, so I'll have to put up with it . . .'

Having relieved his feelings a bit in this heartfelt speech, he went into the kennel and fell asleep.

CHAPTER XXII

*How Pinocchio exposes the thieves, and as a
reward for being trustworthy is given
his liberty.*

He had already been sleeping deeply for two hours and
more when, at about midnight, he was woken by a mur-
muring and a whispering of strange little voices which
seemed to come from the farmyard. Putting the tip of his
nose out of the hole of the kennel, he saw, gathered together in consultation, four small creatures with dark fur,
that looked to him like tiny cats. But they weren't cats;
they were beech martens, little carnivorous animals* with
a particular taste for eggs and baby chicks. One of these
martens left its companions and went to the entrance of the
kennel, saying softly, 'Good evening, Impala.'*

'My name is not Impala,' replied the puppet.

'Well, who are you then?'

'I'm Pinocchio.'

'And what are you doing here?'

'I'm a watchdog.'

'And where is Impala, then? Where's the old dog who
used to live in this kennel?'

'He died this morning.'

'Died? Poor thing! . . . He was such a good dog! . . . But
to judge by your looks, you seem to be a decent dog too.'

'I'm very sorry, but I'm not a dog! . . .'

'Who are you then?'

'I'm a puppet.'

'Acting as a watchdog?'

'Yes, unfortunately it's my punishment!'

'All right then, I can offer you the same contract as I had
with the late Impala; you'll be very happy with it.'

'And what would this contract be?'

'We shall arrive once per week, as in the past, to pay a visit to this hen-house, and we shall take away with us eight chickens. Of these chickens, seven will be eaten by ourselves and one will be presented to you, on condition, naturally, that you pretend to be asleep and that you never take it into your head to bark and wake the peasant.'

'And did Impala do all that?' asked Pinocchio.

'He did indeed, and we were always on good terms, him and us. So, have a nice, quiet sleep, and be assured that before we go, we shall deliver to your kennel a fine, plucked chicken for tomorrow's lunch. Is that understood?'

'All too well!' replied Pinocchio, and he shook his head in a menacing kind of way, as if he had wanted to say, 'Just wait and see! . . .'

When the four martens thought they were on safe ground they went straight to the hen-house, which in any case was very close to the dog-kennel. Opening the wooden door which barred the entrance by scrabbling with their teeth and claws, they all stole inside, one after the other. But they were hardly in before they heard the door slamming loudly shut behind them.

It had been closed by none other than Pinocchio who, not content with just closing it, placed a big stone against it to act as a prop for greater security.

Then he began to bark and, barking just like a watchdog, he raised his voice in a *woof-woof-woof-woof*.

At that barking, the peasant jumped out of bed, seized his gun and, leaning out of the window, he called, 'What's the matter?'

'The thieves are here!' replied Pinocchio.

'Where are they?'

'In the hen-house.'

'I'm coming down.'

And sure enough, in less than the twinkling of an eye, the peasant appeared. He ran to the hen-house where he caught hold of the four martens and put them inside a sack.

Then he said to them in tones of real pleasure, 'At last you
have fallen into my hands! Your chastisement is my due,
but I'll not stoop so low!* Instead, I'll content myself with
taking you to the village innkeeper tomorrow; he'll skin
you and cook you in the manner of jugged hare. It's an
honour which you don't deserve, but generous men like
me are not given to pettiness! . . .'

Then, turning to Pinocchio, he began to pat and stroke
him and, amongst other things, he asked him, 'How did
you manage to discover the plot of these four little robbers? And to think that Impala, my faithful Impala, never
noticed anything! . . .'

At that, the puppet could have recounted what he knew;
that's to say, he could have told about the shameful contract negotiated between the dog and the martens. But,
remembering that the dog was dead, he thought to himself
instead, 'What's the point of betraying the dead? . . . The
dead are dead, and the best thing one can do is to leave
them in peace . . .'

'When the martens came into the farmyard, were you
asleep or awake?' the peasant went on to ask.

'I was asleep,' said Pinocchio, 'but the martens woke me with their chattering, and one came right up to the kennel to say, "if you promise not to bark and not to wake your master, we'll give you a present of a freshly plucked pullet!..." Well! Just fancy having the effrontery to make me such an offer! Because, let's face it, I'm a puppet, after all, and I may have all the faults it's possible to have, but I'll never be guilty of standing guard for criminals or lending them a hand!'

'Good boy!' exclaimed the peasant, slapping him on the shoulder. 'These sentiments do you credit, and to prove my great satisfaction, I'm setting you free right now so that you can go home.'

And he took off the dog collar.

CHAPTER XXIII

*How Pinocchio grieves for the death of the
beautiful Little Girl with the indigo hair;
and how he then finds a Pigeon, that takes
him to the seashore, and how he throws
himself into the water to go to the aid of his
papa, Old Joe.*

No sooner did Pinocchio feel the lifting of that terribly heavy and humiliating weight of the collar around his neck, than he set about making his escape across the fields, and he didn't stop for a single minute until he had reached the highway, which would lead him back to the Fairy's Cottage.

Once he was on the highway, he turned to look down at the plain below, where he could clearly see with the naked eye the wood where he had had the misfortune to meet the Fox and the Cat. Among the trees he could see the top of

the Great Oak towering up, where he had been strung up
to dangle by the neck; but look as he might in all direc-
tions, he could not make out the cottage of the beautiful
Girl with the indigo hair.

Then he had a kind of grim presentiment, and, running
with all the strength left in his legs, in a few minutes he
found himself on the meadow where once the white Cottage had stood. But the white Cottage was no longer there.
Instead, there was a little marble tablet, with these painful
words engraved in capitals upon it:

HERE LIES

THE GIRL WITH THE INDIGO HAIR

WHO DIED OF GRIEF

HAVING BEEN ABANDONED BY HER

LITTLE BROTHER PINOCCHIO.

How the puppet felt on spelling out those words as best
he could, I leave to your imagination. He fell flat on his
face, and covering that gravestone with kisses by the hundred, he burst into a flood of tears. He cried all night, and
the following morning as day dawned he was still crying,
even though there were no tears left in his eyes, and his
wails and lamentations were so heart-rending and shrill
that all the hills around repeated the echoes.

And, weeping, he said, 'Oh dear little Fairy, why are you
dead? . . . why can't I be dead instead of you as I'm so bad
and you were so good? . . . And wherever can my papa be?
Oh dear Fairy, tell me where I can find him, for I want to

be with him always, and never, never, never leave him again! ... Oh dear Fairy, tell me it's not true that you are dead! ... If you really love me ... if you love your little brother, come back to life ... come alive like you were before! ... Aren't you sorry to see me all alone, abandoned by everybody? ... If the murderers come back, they'll hang me up on the tree branch all over again ... and then I'll die for good. How do you think I can manage all alone in the world? Now I've lost both you and my papa, who is going to give me something to eat? Where shall I go to sleep at night? Who will make me a new jacket? Oh! it would be better, a hundred times better, if I were to die too! Boo! hoo! hoo! ...'

While he was grieving like this, he made as if to tear his hair; but as his hair was all of wood, he could not even have the satisfaction of thrusting his fingers into it.

Just then a big Pigeon flew by above and, pausing with its wings spread wide, it called down to him from a great height, 'Tell me, little boy, what are you doing way down there?'

'Can't you see? I'm crying!' said Pinocchio, lifting his head towards the voice and rubbing his eyes with the sleeve of his jacket.

'Tell me,' the Pigeon then went on, 'you don't happen to know a puppet among your friends whose name is Pinocchio, do you?'

'Pinocchio? ... Did you say Pinocchio?' repeated the puppet, jumping to his feet at once. 'I'm Pinocchio!'

At this reply, the Pigeon plummeted down and came to rest on the ground. He was bigger than a turkey.

'So you must know Old Joe as well, then?' he asked the puppet.

'Do I know him? He's my poor father! Maybe he talked to you about me? Will you take me to him? Is he still alive then? Please, please tell me, is he still alive?'

'I left him three days ago on the seashore.'

'What was he doing?'

'He was building a little boat for himself, so as to cross the Ocean. That poor man has spent the last four months and more travelling all over in search of you; and as he couldn't find you, he took it into his head to look for you in the faraway lands of the New World.'

'How far is it from here to the seaside?' asked Pinocchio with breathless impatience.

'More than a thousand miles.'

'A thousand miles? Oh, for the wings of a dove! Dear Pigeon, if only . . .'

'If you want to come, I'll take you there myself.'

'How?'

'Astride my back. Ar you very heavy?'

'Heavy? Anything but! I'm as light as a feather.'

So, without more ado, Pinocchio leapt onto the Pigeon's back, and sitting with one leg on this side and one on the other, like a jockey, he called out happily, 'Gallop, gallop, little horse, for I must hasten fast! . . .'

The Pigeon took to the air and in a few minutes he had flown so high that he nearly touched the clouds. At that amazing height the puppet felt curious to look down, whereupon he was overwhelmed by such fright and such dizziness that, so as not to run the risk of falling off, he clung on very, very tight with his arms wrapped around the neck of his feathery mount.

They flew all day. Towards evening the Pigeon said, 'I'm very thirsty!'

'And I'm very hungry!' added Pinocchio.

'Let's stop for a few moments at this dovecote; then we'll set off again, so as to be at the seashore at dawn tomorrow.'

They went inside the deserted dovecote, where there was only a small bowl full of water and a little basket heaped with tares.

Never in his life had the puppet ever been able to abide tares; according to him they made him feel sick, they turned his stomach. But that evening he ate a bellyful, and when he had nearly finished them, he turned to the Pigeon and said, 'I would never have believed that tares could be so good!'*

'You have to realize, my lad,' replied the Pigeon, 'that when hunger is really in command and there's nothing else to eat, even tares become delicious! Hunger allows neither fads nor fancies!'

Having had their hasty snack, off they went again. The next morning they arrived at the seashore.

The Pigeon deposited Pinocchio on the ground and, not wanting the embarrassment of being thanked for having done a good deed, he immediately took flight again and disappeared.

The beach was full of people shouting and gesticulating as they looked towards the sea.

'What's happened?' Pinocchio asked an old woman.

'What's happened is that a poor father who has lost his son has got the idea of sailing away in a boat to look for him beyond the sea. The sea is very rough today and the little boat is about to go down...'

'Whereabouts is the boat?'

'There it is, down there, where my finger's pointing,' said the old woman indicating a skiff which, seen from that distance, looked like a walnut shell with a tiny, tiny, little man inside.

Pinocchio fixed his gaze in that direction, and after he had looked carefully he let out a piercing shriek, yelling, 'That's my papa! That's my papa!'

All this time the little boat, buffeted by the fury of the waves, kept disappearing between the great breakers and then reappearing to float on the surface. Pinocchio, standing on the tip of a high cliff, never ceased calling his father's name and signalling to him over and over again with his hands and his kerchief and even with the cap he had on his head.

And it looked as if Old Joe, although he was a long way from the shore, had recognized his little boy because he too raised his cap and waved to him and, by dint of gestures, made him understand that he would have gladly turned back, but the sea was so rough that it was preventing him from rowing and from approaching the land.

All of a sudden there came a terrible great wave, and the skiff vanished. They waited for the boat to rise to the surface, but it did not come up again.

'Poor fellow,' the fishermen said then, all gathered together on the beach, and, muttering a prayer under their breath, they moved away to go back to their houses.

When, lo and behold! they heard a desperate cry, and turning round they saw a little boy who was throwing him-

self into the sea from the top of a cliff, shouting, 'I want to save my papa!'

As he was entirely made of wood, Pinocchio floated easily and swam like a fish. Every so often he disappeared under the water, driven down by the power of the billows, then an arm or a leg would reappear above the water, far out to sea. In the end they lost sight of him and saw him no more.

'Poor lad!' the fishermen said then, all gathered together on the beach, and, muttering a prayer under their breath, they went off to their houses.*

CHAPTER XXIV

How Pinocchio arrives at the island of the 'Busy Bees' and finds the Fairy again.

Pinocchio, urged on by the hope of arriving in time to help his poor father, swam the whole night long.

And what a horrible night it was! It poured with rain, it

hailed, it thundered terrifyingly and as for the lightning, it made the night seem like day.

As dawn broke, he managed to sight, not far away, a long ribbon of land. It was an island in the middle of the sea.

So he did all in his power to reach that shore, but it was useless. The waves, chasing each other and breaking over each other, bundled him about between them, as if he were a twig or a bit of straw. In the end, fortunately for him, a wave came along which was so all-powerful and violent that it flung him bodily onto the sandy beach.

The blow was so strong that as he hit the ground all his ribs and all his joints rattled; but he consoled himself at once by saying, 'What luck! Another narrow escape!'

Meanwhile the sky was gradually clearing again; the sun came out in all its splendour, and the sea became as calm and gentle as oil.

So the puppet spread out his clothes to dry in the sun, and set about looking hither and thither just in case he might be able to discern on that vast, flat watery surface a little skiff with a tiny man inside. But having searched high and low, he could see nothing in front of him but sky, sea and a few ships' sails, but so very far away that they seemed like flies.

'If only I knew at least the name of this island!' he was saying to himself. 'If only I knew whether this island is inhabited by decent people, by which I mean people who are not in the habit of attaching young boys to the branches of trees! But whoever can I ask? Especially as there's no one here! . . .'

The thought of being all, all alone in the middle of that great uninhabited country filled him with such melancholy that he was on the point of crying then and there. But all of a sudden he saw a big fish passing, at little distance from the shore, quietly going about its own business, with its whole head out of the water.

Not knowing by what name to call him, the puppet

shouted at the top of his voice, so as to make himself heard, 'Hey, Mr Fish, would you allow me a word with you?'

'Two even,' replied the fish, which was a Dolphin* of such courtesy as to be a rarity in all the seas of the world.

'Would you be so kind as to tell me whether there are any villages on this island where one may eat, without running the risk of being eaten?'

'I am certain of it,' replied the Dolphin. 'Indeed, you will find one not far from here.'

'And how do I get there?'

'You need to take that little lane there, on the left, and walk straight on following your nose. You can't miss it.'

'Would you tell me another thing? As you travel all day and all night up and down the sea, you wouldn't by any chance have met a little tiny boat with my papa in it?'

'And who is your papa?'

'He's the best papa in all the world, just as I'm the worst son you could ever have.'

'What with the squall that blew up last night,' replied the Dolphin, 'the little boat must have sunk.'

'And what about my father?'

'By now he must have been swallowed by the dreaded shark, who has been here in our waters for several days now, spreading death and destruction.'

'Is he really very big, this shark?' asked Pinocchio, who was already beginning to tremble with fear.

'Big? I'll say!' answered the Dolphin. 'To give you some idea, I can tell you he's bigger than a five-storey building, and he has such an ugly, great wide mouth that a whole railway train with its furnace lit could easily run through it.'

'My golly!' cried the puppet terrified and, dressing fast and furiously, he turned to the Dolphin and said, 'Good day, Mr Fish. So sorry to have troubled you and many thanks for your kindness.'

Having said that, he immediately set out along the lane, walking at a swift pace, so swift that he almost seemed to be running. And at the slightest sound, he would turn at once to look behind him, for fear of being followed by that dreaded shark the size of a five-storey building with a railway train in its mouth.

After walking for half an hour or more, he came to a little village known as 'the village of the Busy Bees'. The streets, full of people scurrying here and there, seeing to their tasks, were a hive of activity: everyone was working, everyone had something to do. You might hunt high and low, but you could not find a lazybones or a good-for-nothing anywhere.

'I can see', that lazy Pinocchio said at once, 'that this village isn't for me! I wasn't born to work!'

All this time he was being tormented by hunger, for by now he had eaten nothing—not even a plate of tares—for twenty-four hours.

What was to be done?

There were only two ways for him to break his fast: he could either ask for some work, or he could beg for pennies or a crust.

He was ashamed to beg for charity, for his father had always instructed him that only the old and the infirm had a right to ask for charity. The real poor of this world, who do merit help and compassion, are limited to those who, by reason of age or illness, are prevented from earning their bread by the labour of their own hands. Everyone else has a duty to work, and if they don't work and they suffer from hunger, so much the worse for them.

At that moment, a man went along the street who was sweating and breathless because, with great difficulty and all by himself, he was dragging along two carts laden with coal.

Judging by his looks, Pinocchio thought he must be a good man and drew near him. Lowering his eyes in shame, he said to him beneath his breath, 'Would you do me the kindness of giving me a penny, because I'm dying of hunger?'

'Not just one penny,' replied the coalman, 'but I'll give you four, as long as you'll help me pull these two coal carts home.'

'You amaze me!' answered the puppet in offended tones. 'For your information, I've never been a beast of burden, and I've never pulled a cart!'

'Lucky you!' said the coalman. 'In that case, my boy, if you're really dying of hunger, you'd better eat two fine slices of your own pride, and watch out that you don't get indigestion.'

A few minutes later a bricklayer went along the road carrying a basket of mortar on his back.

'Please Sir, would you give a penny in charity to a poor boy who is aching with hunger?'

'Certainly; come with me to carry mortar,' replied the bricklayer, 'and instead of one, I'll give you five pennies.'

'But mortar is heavy,' responded Pinocchio, 'and I don't want to have to labour.'

'Well, if you don't want to labour, my boy, enjoy your aching, and much good may it do you.'

In less than half an hour another twenty people passed, and Pinocchio asked each one for a little charity, but they all replied, 'Aren't you ashamed? Instead of idling around the street, why don't you go and look for a bit of work instead, and learn to earn your bread!'

Finally a nice little woman went by, carrying two pitchers of water.

'Would you mind, dear lady, if I drank a sip of water from your pitcher?' said Pinocchio, whose throat was burning with thirst.

'Of course, have a drink, my boy!' said the little woman, resting her two pitchers on the ground.

When Pinocchio had drunk his fill like a sponge, he muttered in a low voice, while wiping his mouth, 'That's my thirst gone! If only I could get rid of my hunger...'

The good woman, hearing this, remarked at once, 'If you will help me carry one of these water pitchers home, I'll give you a nice piece of bread.'

Pinocchio looked at the pitcher and did not reply yes or no.

'And with the bread, I'll give you a lovely dish of cauliflower seasoned with oil and vinegar,' added the good woman.

Pinocchio gave another glance at the pitcher, and did not reply yes or no.

'And after the cauliflower, I'll give you a lovely sweetmeat filled with cordial.'

Won over by this last dainty morsel, Pinocchio could no longer resist, and taking his courage in both hands, he said, 'Well, never mind! I'll carry your pitcher home for you!'

The pitcher was very weighty, and the puppet hadn't the strength to carry it with his hands, so he made up his mind to carry it on his head.

At her house, the good woman sat Pinocchio down at a little table which was laid ready, and placed in front of him the bread, the seasoned cauliflower and the sweetmeat.

Pinocchio did not eat, he gobbled. His stomach felt like an empty dwelling that had been uninhabited for five months.

Little by little the violent pangs of hunger died down, and then he raised his head to thank his benefactress, but he had hardly begun gazing into her face when he let out a long *ohhhh!* of wonderment, and he stayed transfixed, his eyes wide, his fork in the air, and his mouth full of bread and cauliflower.

'Whatever is all this amazement for?' said the good woman, laughing.

'The fact is . . .' replied Pinocchio, stammering, 'the fact is . . . the fact is . . . that you look very like . . . you remind me of . . . yes, yes, yes, it's the same voice . . . the same eyes . . . the same hair . . . yes, yes, yes, . . . you even have indigo hair . . . like she does! . . . Oh my dear little Fairy! . . . oh my dear little Fairy? . . . tell me you're you, really and truly you! . . . Don't let me cry any more! If only you knew! I've wept so much and suffered so much! . . .'

So saying, Pinocchio wept a flood of tears, and throwing himself onto his knees on the floor, he hugged the knees of that mysterious lady.

CHAPTER XXV

*How Pinocchio promises the Fairy to be good
and to study, because he is tired of being a
puppet and wants to become a good boy.*

At first the good woman tried to say that she was not the
little Fairy with the indigo hair; but then, acknowledging
that she had been recognized and not wanting to play-act
any longer, in the end she made herself known and said to
Pinocchio, 'You young rascal of a puppet! However did
you realize it was me?'

'It was because of the great affection I feel for you; my
heart told me so.'

'So you remember, do you? When you left, I was a little
girl, and now you have found me again, I'm a woman; so
much so that I could almost be your mother.'

'I like that very much, because instead of calling you
little sister, I shall call you my mama. I've been longing to
have a mother like all the other boys for such a long time!
But how did you manage to grow so fast?'

'It's a secret.'

'Teach me the secret; I wish I could grow a bit too. Have
you noticed? I've always stayed knee-high to a cricket.'*

'But you can't grow,' replied the Fairy.

'Why not?'

'Because puppets don't ever grow. They are born puppets, live as puppets and die puppets.'

'Oh! I'm tired of being nothing but a puppet!' exclaimed
Pinocchio, giving himself a slap. 'It's time I too became a
man . . .'

'You will, if you learn to deserve it . . .'

'Truly? And what can I do to deserve it?'

'It's very easy: you have to learn to be a good boy.'

'But I am that now, aren't I?'

'Anything but! Good boys do what they're told, whereas you . . .'

'Whereas I never do what I'm told.'

'Good boys are devoted to their studies and their work, whereas you . . .'

'Whereas I'm a lazybones and a good-for-nothing all year round.'

'Good boys always tell the truth . . .'

'Whereas I always tell lies.'

'Good boys like going to school . . .'

'Whereas school gives me tummy-ache. But from now on I want to change my ways.'

'Do you promise me?'

'Yes, I promise. I want to be a good little boy, and I want to be my father's pride and joy . . . Wherever can my poor papa be now?'

'I don't know.'

'Will I ever be lucky enough to see him and hug him again?'

'I think so; in fact, I'm sure of it.'

At this reply Pinocchio's happiness was such that he took the Fairy's hands and began to kiss them with so much fervour that he seemed almost beside himself. Then raising his face and looking at her lovingly, he asked, 'Tell me, dear little mother: it's not true that you're dead then?'

'It would seem not,' the Fairy replied, smiling.

'If you only knew what sorrow I felt and how choked with tears I was when I read *Here lies* . . .'

'I do know: and that's the reason why I forgave you. The sincerity of your grief told me that you have a good heart, and with good-hearted children, even when they are naughty and a bit spoiled, there's always hope. That's to say, one can hope they will mend their ways. That's why I came all this way to find you. Now I'll be your Mama . . .'

'Oh, how lovely!' cried Pinocchio, jumping for joy.

'You will always be obedient and do what I tell you to.'

'Of course, of course, of course!'

'From tomorrow', the Fairy added, 'you'll begin by going to school.'

Pinocchio at once became a little less joyful.

'Then you can make your own choice of a skill or profession . . .'

Pinocchio turned serious.

'What are you muttering under your breath?' asked the Fairy sharply.

'I was saying . . .' mumbled the puppet in a faint voice, 'that by now it's a bit late for me to go to school . . .'

'Oh, no, it isn't! Just remember that it's never too late to learn or to be educated.'

'But I don't want to have any skills or professions . . .'

'Why not?'

'Because work seems tiring to me.'

'My boy,' the Fairy said, 'people who say that almost always end up either in prison or in the workhouse. Mark my words, whether rich or poor, human beings are duty-bound to do something in this life. They have to work and keep busy. Woe betide if you let sloth rule you! Sloth is a terrible disease and must be cured at once, in childhood; otherwise, when we grow up it can't be cured at all.'

These words touched Pinocchio deeply, and lifting his head briskly he said to the Fairy, 'I'll study and I'll work and I'll do everything you tell me to; after all, I've got bored with the life of a puppet, and I want to be a boy, come what may. You promised me, didn't you?'

'Yes, I promised, and now it's up to you.'

CHAPTER XXVI

*How Pinocchio goes with his school-friends to
the seashore, to see the ferocious Shark.*

The next day Pinocchio went to the local school.

You can imagine those schoolboy scamps when they saw
a puppet walk into their schoolroom! There was such a
roar of laughter that went on and on. Some played tricks
on him, some made jokes, some stole his cap, some tugged
at his jacket from behind, some tried to draw two big
moustaches under his nose with ink, and some even dared
to tie strings to his feet and hands, so as to make him
dance.

For a while Pinocchio adopted a casual manner and put
up with it all; but in the end, losing patience, he turned to
those who were goading him and poking fun at him most,
and said with composure, 'Look here, boys, I didn't come
here to play the clown for you. I respect others and want
to be respected myself.'

'Well done, Old Nick!* You talk just like a book!' yelled

all those urchins, falling about with howls of laughter, and one of them, who was more impertinent than the rest, reached out his hand intending to grab the puppet by the end of his nose.

But he didn't manage it in time, for Pinocchio stretched out a leg under the desk and delivered a good kick to his shins.

'Ouch! What hard feet!' shouted the boy, rubbing the bruise that the puppet had given him.

'And what elbows! . . . even harder than his feet!' said another boy who had earned himself an elbowing in the stomach for his shameless teasing.

The fact is that after that kick and that elbowing, Pinocchio was at once rewarded with the admiration and friendship of all the children in the school. They all lavished affection on him and were all devoted to him heart and soul.

And the schoolmaster was fond of him too, observing him to be attentive, studious, intelligent, always first to arrive, always the last to get up to go at the end of the day.

His only defect was to go around with too many friends, and among these were many rascals who were notorious for their unwillingness to study and to do well.

The schoolmaster warned him every day; nor did the good Fairy fail to tell him and to repeat on various occasions, 'Take care, Pinocchio! Sooner or later those wretched school-friends of yours will make you lose your love of learning, and, who knows, may even lead you into some terrible trouble.'

'There's no danger of that!' the puppet would reply, shrugging his shoulders and pressing his forefinger to the middle of his brow, as if to say, 'I'm too sensible for that!'

Now it happened that one fine day, while he was walking to school, he met a troop of his usual companions who came up to him and said, 'Have you heard the great news?'

'No.'

'Swimming in the sea near here there's a Shark as big as a mountain.'

'Honestly? . . . I wonder if it's the same Shark that was there when my poor papa drowned?'

'We're going to the beach to see it. Do you want to come?'

'No, I don't. I want to go to school.'

'What does school matter? We'll go to school tomorrow. One lesson more or one less makes no difference to us dunces.'

'And what will the teacher have to say?'

'The teacher? Let him talk! He's paid good money precisely to grumble all day.'

'And what about my Mama?'

'Mothers never know anything,' answered those villains.

'You know what I'll do?' said Pinocchio. 'I want to see this Shark for certain reasons of my own . . . but I shall go and see him after school.'

'Silly fool!' one of the troop responded. 'Do you imagine that a big fish like that is going to hang around for your convenience? As soon as he gets bored, he'll dart off somewhere else, and that's that.'

'How long does it take to get to the beach from here?' asked the puppet.

'We can easily get there and back within the hour.'

'Come on then, run!—and may the best man win!' shouted Pinocchio.

At this signal for the off, the troop of urchins, carrying their textbooks and exercise books under their arms, started to run across the fields, and Pinocchio was ahead of the rest all the way; he seemed to have wings on his feet.

Every so often he would turn around to poke fun at his friends trailing behind, and seeing them puffing and panting and covered in dust, with their tongues hanging out, he laughed heartily. The wretch, little did he know then what terrors and what frightful disasters he was on his way to meet!

CHAPTER XXVII

How a great battle takes place between
Pinocchio and his school-friends; and how,
when one of them is injured,
Pinocchio is arrested by the police.

When he arrived at the beach, Pinocchio immediately scanned the sea, but he could see no Shark. The sea was as smooth as a vast glass mirror.

'So where's the Shark?' he asked, turning to his companions.

'Maybe he's gone to have breakfast,' one of them replied, laughing.

'Or maybe he's tucked himself up to have a nap,' added another boy, laughing louder than ever.

From those rambling replies and from that foolish laughter, Pinocchio realized that his friends had played a nasty trick on him, making him believe something that was not true. Losing his temper, he said in an angry voice, 'Well then! What exactly was the point of making me believe the story of the Shark?'

'There was a point all right! . . .' all those urchins chorused together.

'Which is to say?'

'Making you miss school and come with us. It's a disgrace to appear at lessons so punctually and so diligently every day, isn't it? It's a disgrace to study so hard, the way you do.'

'And if I study, what does it matter to you?'

'It matters a lot to us, because you make us look silly with the teacher . . .'

'Why?'

'Because schoolboys who work hard always show up boys like us who have no desire to study. And we don't want to be shown up! Even we have our pride! . . .'

'So what do you want me to do to keep you happy?'

'You've got to dislike the school, the lessons, and the teacher as well: our three great enemies.'

'And if I wanted to continue studying?'

'We won't speak to you any more, and at the first opportunity you'll pay for it! . . .'

'Really, you make me laugh, you know,' said the puppet with a toss of his head.

'Hey, Pinocchio!' the biggest boy shouted, going up to speak face to face. 'Don't you come here to play the bully; don't you come here to be so cocky! . . . because if you're not afraid of us, nor are we afraid of you! Remember that you're on your own and there are seven of us.'

'Like the seven deadly sins,' said Pinocchio with a loud laugh.

'Did you hear that? He insulted us all! He called us the seven deadly sins! . . .'

'Pinocchio! Say you're sorry for that insult . . . or else, watch out . . .'

'Cuckoo!' called the puppet, tapping his forefinger on the end of his nose, as a teasing gesture.

'Pinocchio! There's going to be trouble . . .'

'Cuckoo!'

'You'll catch it, you ass! . . .'

'Cuckoo!'

'You'll go home with a broken nose! . . .'

'Cuckoo!'

'I'll give you cuckoo now!' shouted the boldest of those urchins. 'Take this instalment for the moment, and keep it for supper this evening.'

And saying this he landed a punch on his head.

But, as the saying goes, it was a case of tit for tat, because the puppet, as was to be expected, promptly responded with another punch, and in no time at all it became an all-out, furious battle.

Although Pinocchio was on his own, he defended himself valiantly. He struck out so keenly with those feet of his, made of such hard wood, that he kept his enemies at a respectful distance all the time. Where his feet managed to reach and touch, they always left a bruise as a reminder.

Therefore the boys, who were annoyed at not being able to fight with the puppet hand-to-hand, decided to use missiles. Untying their bundles of schoolbooks, they began to hurl at him their *Primers* and *Grammars*, their *Alices* and *Huckleberry Finns*, their *Lamb's Tales* and *Black Beauties*, as well as other schoolbooks. But the puppet, who had a quick eye and sharp wits, always ducked in time, so that the volumes, passing over his head, all fell into the sea.*

Just imagine the fishes! Believing that those books were eating matter, the fishes rushed in multitudes to the surface of the water; but having tasted a page or two or the occasional frontispiece, they spat it out at once, making a sort of grimace with their mouths, as if to say, 'That's not to our taste; we're used to dining on finer fare!'

All the while the battle raged more fiercely, when suddenly a big Crab, that had come out of the water to climb ever so slowly up the beach, called out in the harsh voice of a trombone with a cold, 'Give over! You're nothing but rascals! These fisticuff wars, boys versus boys, rarely end well. There's always some disaster! . . .'

Poor Crab! He might just as well have saved his breath to cool his porridge. Indeed, that scamp Pinocchio, turning round and scowling at him, said rudely, 'Shut up, boring old Crab! You'd do better to suck a couple of lichen lozenges to cure that sore throat. Or else go to bed and try to sweat! . . .'

Meanwhile the boys, who had now finished throwing their supply of books, were eyeing the puppet's bundle a short distance away, and in less than no time they had got hold of it.

Amongst these books there was a volume bound in thick board, with the spine and the corners made of parchment. It was a *Treatise on Arithmetic*. I'll leave you to consider whether it was very weighty!

One of those urchins grabbed hold of the volume and, taking aim at Pinocchio's head, he hurled it with as much force as his arms could muster; but instead of hitting the puppet, it struck one of the other boys on the head. He turned as white as a sheet, and uttered only these words: 'Oh dear, help me . . . I'm dying! . . .'

Then he fell spreadeagled on the sandy beach.

At the sight of his prone little body, the scared boys took to their heels, and moments later were nowhere to be seen.

But Pinocchio stayed there, and although he, too, was more dead than alive from grief and fright, nevertheless he ran to soak his handkerchief in sea-water and started to bathe the forehead of his poor school-friend. All the while he wept profusely and cried out loud, calling the boy by name and saying: 'Eugene! ... poor Eugene! ... open your eyes and look at me! ... Why don't you reply? It wasn't me, you know, who hurt you so badly! Believe me, it wasn't me! ... Open your eyes, Eugene ... If you keep your eyes closed, you'll make me die too ... Oh Lord! how can I ever go home now? How could I dare present myself to my dear, good Mama? What will become of me? ... Where shall I go? ... Where shall I hide? ... Oh dear, it would have been better, a thousand times better, to go to school! ... Why did I listen to those boys, who will be my ruination? ... My teacher told me so! ... and my Mama told me again and again, "Keep clear of bad company!" ... But I'm stubborn ... and self-willed ... I let everyone have their say, and then I always go off and do whatever I please! And afterwards I have to pay for it ... And so, there hasn't been a decent quarter-hour in all my life. Oh Lord! What will become of me, what will become of me, what will become of me?'

Pinocchio continued to cry and screech and pummel his head and call poor Eugene's name, when all of a sudden he heard the dull thud of steps approaching.

He looked round; it was two policemen.

'You there, what are you doing lying on the ground?' they asked Pinocchio.

'I'm looking after this school-friend of mine.'

'Is he ill?'

'It seems so! ...'

'I'll say!' said one of the policemen, bending down and looking at Eugene closely. 'This boy has been injured on the temple; who was it that injured him?'

'Not me!' stammered the puppet, gasping for breath.

'If it wasn't you, who was it that hurt him?'

'Not me!' said Pinocchio again.

'And what was it that caused the injury?'

'This book.' And the puppet lifted up the *Treatise on Arithmetic*, bound in card and parchment, to show it to the policeman.

'And whose book is this?'

'Mine.'

'That's enough; you've told us all we need to know. Stand up, and come with us.'

'But I . . .'

'Come along! . . .'

'But I'm innocent . . .'

'Come along! . . .'

Before leaving, the policemen summoned some fishermen, who happened to be sailing their boat close in to the shore at that time, and told them, 'We're leaving this boy with a head wound in your care. Take him home with you and look after him. We'll come back tomorrow to see him.'

Then they turned to Pinocchio and, standing one on either side of him, they instructed him in military tones: 'Forward and quick march! or else, so much the worse for you!'

Not waiting to hear it again, the puppet began to walk down the lane that led to the village. But the poor wretch scarcely knew where he was. He thought he must be dreaming, and what an awful dream it was! He was beside himself. His eyes saw everything double; his legs trembled; his tongue was stuck to the roof of his mouth and he could no longer utter a single word properly. Even so, in the midst of his stunned and bewildered state, he felt an agonizing aching in his heart, caused by the thought of having to walk between the two policemen past the windows of the good Fairy's house. He would rather have died.

As they arrived and were about to enter the village, a gust of rough wind snatched Pinocchio's cap from his head, carrying it ten paces or so away.

'Would you permit me,' said the puppet to the policemen, 'to go and fetch my cap?'

'Off you go, but be quick!'

The puppet went and picked up the cap . . . but instead of putting it on his head, he put it in his mouth between clenched teeth, and then he was off like a shot, running full-tilt towards the seashore.

The policemen, deciding it was too difficult to catch up with him, set a big mastiff on him*—one that had won first prize in all the dog races. Pinocchio ran, but the dog ran harder than he did. All the people hurried to their windows and crowded into the street, eager to see the result of such a ferocious chase. But their desires were not to be satisfied, because along the way Pinocchio and the mastiff raised such a cloud of dust that after a few minutes it was no longer possible to see anything at all.

CHAPTER XXVIII

How Pinocchio runs the risk of being fried in a frying-pan, like a fish.

In the middle of that desperate race there was one terrible moment, a moment when Pinocchio thought he was lost. You see, Mercury (for this was the mastiff's name),* by running furiously, had almost caught him up.

Suffice it to say that the puppet could hear at his back the laboured panting of the brute, and even feel the scorching heat of his breath.

Fortunately the beach was now close and the sea only a few steps away.

Once he was on the beach, the puppet gave a great leap, like a frog would have done, and landed plop in the water. Mercury, on the other hand, intended to stop; but, carried along by the impetus of his gallop, he found himself in the water, too. And the poor thing didn't know how to swim. Soon he began to splash around with his paws, blindly trying to keep himself afloat; yet the more he thrashed the more his head went under.

When he succeeded in lifting his head out of the water

again, the unhappy dog's eyes were terrified and staring wildly and, barking, he howled, 'I'm drowning! I'm drowning!'

'Go to blazes!' Pinocchio answered from afar, observing himself to be out of danger now.

'Help me, dear Pinocchio! ... save me from certain death! ...'

Hearing those heart-rending cries the puppet, who really was a kind soul, was moved to compassion, and facing the dog he told him, 'But if I help you to save yourself, will you promise me not to bother me any more and not to run after me?'

'I promise! I promise! Hurry up, for pity's sake; if you wait another half-minute, I'm as good as dead.'

Pinocchio hesitated slightly; but then remembering that his papa had told him many times that you never lose by doing a good deed, he swam towards Mercury and, holding him by the tail with both his hands, he pulled him safe and sound to the dry sand of the shore.

The poor dog could no longer stand upright. Without wanting to, he had drunk so much salt water that he had swelled up like a balloon. Nevertheless, the puppet, not wanting to be too trusting, considered it prudent to throw himself back into the sea, and swimming away from the beach he shouted out to his rescued friend, 'Bye bye, Mercury. Have a good journey and best wishes to all at home.'

'Goodbye, Pinocchio,' the dog replied, 'very many thanks for saving me from death. You've done me a great service, and in this life good deeds reap rewards. If the occasion arises, I'll be as good as my word ...'

Pinocchio went on swimming, keeping his course close to the land. At last he decided he had reached a safe place, and, glancing at the beach, he saw among the rocks some sort of cave, from which a long plume of smoke was emerging.

'In that cave', he said to himself, 'there must be a fire. So much the better! I'll go and dry myself and get warm, and then what? . . . and then we'll see what we shall see.'

Having made up his mind, he drew close to the cliff, but when he was about to climb up he felt something beneath him in the water, which was pushing him up, up, up and lifting him into the air. At once he tried to escape, but it was too late because, to his huge amazement, he found himself enclosed in a big net in the thick of a seething mass of fish of every size and shape, waggling their tails and struggling like so many lost souls.

At the selfsame moment he saw emerging from the cave a fisherman who was so ugly, so very ugly, that he looked more like a sea-monster. Instead of hair, on his head he had a dense bush of green grass; the skin of his body was green, his eyes were green, and green was the colour of his long, long beard reaching down to the ground. He looked like a huge green lizard standing on his hind legs.

When the fisherman had drawn his net right out of the sea, he exclaimed with pleasure, 'Providence is being kind to me! I shall be able to gorge on fish again today!'

'What a good thing that I'm not a fish!' Pinocchio said to himself, feeling more cheerful.

The net full of fish was carried inside the cave, a cave that was dark and smoky, in the middle of which a great frying-pan of oil was sizzling and emitting such an odour of candle-grease as to take your breath away.

'Now let's see what fish we have caught this time!' said the green fisherman and, thrusting into the net such a ridiculously huge hand that it might have been a baker's peel,* he pulled forth a handful of red mullet.

'These red mullet are good!' he said, gazing at them and sniffing them with satisfaction. Having sniffed them, he flung them into a vat without water.

He repeated the same process a number of times, and as

he went on extracting the other fish, his mouth watered and, chuckling, he kept saying:

'These hake are good! . . .'

'These grey mullet are delicious! . . .'

'These soles are excellent! . . .'

'These bass are superb! . . .'

'These whole anchovies are delightful! . . .'

As you can imagine, the hake, the grey mullet, the soles, the bass and the anchovies all went higgledy-piggledy into the vat to keep the red mullet company.

The last item in the net was Pinocchio.

As soon as the fisherman had hauled him out, his great green eyes opened wide in astonishment, and he shouted almost in fright, 'What kind of fish is this? I don't remember having ever eaten fishes of this shape!'

And he went on looking at him attentively, and having examined him all over, he said at last, 'I see; it must be a shore crab.'

Then Pinocchio, who was mortified at being mistaken for a crab, said in a peeved voice, 'What do you mean by calling me a crab? What a way to treat me! For your information, I'm a puppet.'

'A puppet?' replied the fisherman. 'I have to admit that the puppet fish is a new fish to me! So much the better! I'll be even more pleased to eat you.'

'Eat me? But can't you understand I'm not a fish? Or haven't you noticed that I speak and reason like you do?'

'That's very true,' the fisherman commented, 'and as I can see that you are a fish which has the good fortune to speak and reason as I do, therefore I shall certainly treat you with appropriate respect.'

'And what kind of respect might this be? . . .'

'As a mark of my friendship and particular esteem, I shall leave you to choose how you want to be cooked. Would you like to be fried in the frying-pan, or alternatively would you prefer to be cooked in the pot with tomato sauce?'

'To tell the truth,' Pinocchio replied, 'if I can choose, I would rather be set free so that I could go back home.'

'That's a joke! You don't really think I would miss the chance to taste such a rare fish? It's not every day that we get a puppet fish in these waters. Leave it to me; I'll fry you in the frying-pan along with all the other fishes, and you'll find it quite satisfactory. Being fried in company is always a consolation.'

The unfortunate Pinocchio, perceiving his drift, began to cry and screech and beg, and through his sobs he said, 'How much better it would have been if I'd gone to school . . . I fell in with my school-friends, and now I'm paying for it! Boo . . . hoo . . . hoo.'

And because he was wriggling like an eel and struggling with amazing strength to slide out of the clutches of the green fisherman, the latter took the outside of a long reed and, after tying him hand and foot like a sausage, threw him into the depths of the vat with the others.

Then, pulling out a great wooden board covered in flour, he set about flouring all those fish, and as he floured them, he threw them into the frying-pan to fry.

The poor hake were the first to leap about in the boiling oil; then it was the turn of the bass, then the grey mullet, then the soles and anchovies, and then it was Pinocchio's turn. Seeing himself so close to death—and what a terrible death!—he was seized with such a trembling and such a terror that he no longer had any voice or breath left to plead for mercy.

The poor lad was pleading with his eyes! But the green fisherman, taking not the slightest notice, covered him five or six times in flour, flouring him so thoroughly from head to foot that he looked as if he had become a plaster puppet.

Then he grabbed him by the head, and . . .

CHAPTER XXIX

*How he returns to the Fairy's house, and she
promises him that the next day he will no
longer be a puppet, but will become a boy.
Grand breakfast of coffee with milk to
celebrate this great event.*

Just as the fisherman was on the point of tossing Pinocchio
into the frying-pan, a large dog came into the cave, at-
tracted by the pungent smell and greedy for fried fish.

'Go away!' shouted the fisherman threateningly, while
still holding the floury puppet in his hands.

But the poor dog was hungry enough for four, and yelp-
ing and wagging his tail, he seemed to be saying, 'If you'll
give me a bite of fried fish, I'll leave you in peace.'

'Go away, I said!' the fisherman repeated, and stretched
out his leg to give him a kick.

Then the dog, who didn't let anybody get in his way
when he was really hungry, turned on the fisherman, snarl-
ing and showing his fearsome fangs.

At that moment a faint, tiny little voice was heard in the
cave, saying, 'Mercury, save me! If you don't save me, I'll
be in the soup! . . .'

The dog immediately recognized Pinocchio's voice, and
to his great astonishment he observed that the little cry had
come from that floury bundle that the fisherman was holding in his hand.

So what did he do? From where he stood he made a
great bound, seized the floury bundle in his mouth and,
holding it lightly between his teeth, he ran out of the cave,
and vanished like lightning!

Furious at seeing a fish that he was about to eat with
such pleasure snatched from his hand, the fisherman tried

to run after the dog; but after a few steps he was halted by a bout of coughing and had to go back.

Meanwhile Mercury stopped on reaching the lane that led back to the village, and gently deposited his friend Pinocchio on the ground.

'I'm so grateful to you!' said the puppet.

'There's no need to thank me,' replied the dog, 'you saved me, and one good turn deserves another. It's well known that in this life we all have to help each other.'

'But however did you land up in that cave?'

'I was still lying on the beach more dead than alive, when the wind wafted a lovely smell of fried food to me. That scent tickled my appetite so I went off to follow it. And if I'd arrived a minute later . . .'

'Don't say it!' shouted Pinocchio, who was still trembling with fear. 'Don't say it! If you'd arrived one minute later, by now I'd be well and truly in the soup, not to mention eaten and digested. Brrr! I get the shivers just thinking about it . . .'

Laughing, Mercury held out his right paw to the puppet, who shook it and shook it to show the warmth of his friendship, and then they parted from each other.

The dog took the path home, and Pinocchio, left alone, went to a cabin nearby and asked an old man, who was sitting sunning himself at the door, 'Please can you tell me,

sir, do you know anything about a poor boy called Eugene who had a head wound?'

'Some fishermen carried the boy to this cabin, and now . . .'

'Now he's dead!' interrupted Pinocchio, very sadly.

'No, he's alive, and he's already gone back to his home.'

'Really? . . . really? . . .' cried the puppet, jumping for joy. 'So the wound wasn't serious? . . .'

'But it might have been very serious and even fatal,' said the old man, 'because it was a big book bound in board that they threw at his head.'

'And who threw it at him?'

'One of his school-friends: someone called Pinocchio . . .'

'And who is this Pinocchio?' asked the puppet, feigning ignorance.

'They say he's a hooligan, an idler, a real dare-devil . . .'

'Lies! It's all lies!'

'Do you know this Pinocchio, then?'

'By sight!' the puppet replied.

'And what do you think of him, then?' asked the old man.

'I think he's a really good boy, who is devoted to his studies, obedient, fond of his father and family . . .'

While the puppet was unleashing this string of bare-faced lies, he touched his nose and found that his nose had grown longer by a hand's breadth. Frightened by this, he cried out, 'Please sir, take no notice of all the good things I said about him; actually I know Pinocchio well and I too can assure you that he really is a hooligan, and a wayward lazy-bones who, instead of going to school, goes off with his friends to play the street urchin!'

As soon as he had uttered these words, his nose shrank and went back to its natural size, just as before.

'And why are you white all over like that?' the old man asked suddenly.

'Let me explain . . . without noticing what I was doing,

I rubbed myself along a wall which had just been white-washed,' replied the puppet, feeling too embarrassed to recount how he had been taken for a fish and covered in flour so as to be fried in a frying-pan.

'And what have you done with your jacket and trousers, and your cap?'

'I met some thieves and they stripped me. You're a kind old gentleman; could you by any chance let me have a bit of clothing, so that I can go home?'

'Well, my lad, as far as clothes are concerned, all I've got is a little sack where I keep lupin seeds. If you'd like that, take it! It's over there.'

Pinocchio didn't wait to be told again; he promptly took the lupin sack, which was empty,* and, having made a little hole in the bottom and two holes at the sides with some scissors, he put it on like a smock. And dressed lightly like that, he went off towards the village.

But as he went along he was beset by worries; so much so that he would take one step forward and one step back and, talking to himself, he kept saying, 'However will I manage to show my face to my good Fairy? What will she say when she sees me? . . . Will she ever forgive me this second escapade? . . . I bet she won't forgive me! . . . Oh! she's not going to forgive me, I'm certain . . . And it serves me right: I'm a rascal who's always promising to improve, and I don't ever keep my promises! . . .'

By the time he got to the village, night had fallen and, because the weather was bad and it was raining buckets, he went straight to the Fairy's house with his mind made up to knock on the door and get himself let in.

But when he arrived he felt his courage fail him, and instead of knocking he ran away twenty paces down the road. Then he went back a second time to the door, and did nothing; then he went back a third time, and still did nothing; the fourth time, trembling, he took the iron knocker in his hand and knocked with a little tiny tap.

He waited and waited, and at last after half an hour a window on the top floor (for the house had four floors) opened, and Pinocchio saw a large snail looking out, with a glowing night-light on her head,* who said, 'Who is that at this hour?'

'Is the Fairy at home?' asked the puppet.

'The Fairy is asleep and doesn't want to be disturbed; but who are you?'

'It's me!'

'Who is me?'

'Pinocchio.'

'Who's Pinocchio?'

'The puppet who lives with the Fairy.'

'Oh! I see,' said the Snail, 'wait there for me, and I'll come down and let you in right away.'

'Hurry, for pity's sake; I'm dying of cold.'

'I'm a snail, my boy, and snails are never in a hurry.'

An hour passed, and then two went by, and the door still did not open. So Pinocchio, who was shaking from cold, from fright, and from the soaking rain, took courage and knocked a second time, this time more loudly.

This second time a window opened on the floor below and the same snail looked out.

'Lovely little snail,' called Pinocchio from the street, 'I've been waiting two hours now! And two hours on a horrible evening like this seem longer than two years! Hurry, for pity's sake.'

'Dear boy,' that wholly tranquil, wholly stolid little creature replied from the window, 'dear boy, I'm a snail and snails are never in a hurry.'

And the window closed once more.

A little later it struck midnight, and then one, then two in the morning, and the door was still shut.

Then Pinocchio, losing patience, angrily seized the door-knocker so as to make a bang that would have rattled the whole building. But the iron knocker all at once turned into a live eel which slid out of his grasp and disappeared along a gutter that ran along the middle of the street.

'Oh, yes?' shouted Pinocchio, more and more blinded by anger. 'If the knocker disappears, I'll still go on banging by kicking the door.'

And drawing back a little, he let fly a ferocious kick on the house-door. The blow was so strong that his foot made a hole half-way through the wood, and when the puppet wanted to pull it out again it was useless to try, for his foot stayed stuck inside, like a riveted nail.

You can just imagine poor Pinocchio! He had to pass all the rest of the night with one foot on the ground and one stuck up in the air.

Next morning, at daybreak, the door opened at last. To come down from the fourth floor to the street-door that good little creature, the Snail, had only taken nine hours. It has to be admitted that she had really rushed.

'What are you doing with this foot jammed in the front door?' she asked the puppet, laughing.

'It was an accident. Have a little look, lovely little Snail, to see whether you can release me from this torture.'

'Dear boy, such as this requires a joiner and I've never done joinery.'

'Please ask the Fairy for me! . . .'

'The Fairy is asleep and does not wish to be disturbed.'

'But what am I to do, do you suppose, stuck to this door all day?'

'Amuse yourself by counting all the ants* walking along the street.'

'At least bring me something to eat: I feel famished.'

'At once!' said the Snail.

In fact after three and a half hours, Pinocchio saw her return with a silver tray on her head. On the tray there was a loaf, a roast chicken and four ripe apricots.

'The Fairy has sent you this meal,' said the Snail.

At the sight of that bounty, the puppet felt thoroughly consoled. But how great was his disappointment when he began to eat and discovered that the bread was made of plaster, the chicken of cardboard and the four apricots of alabaster, all coloured to look real.

He wanted to cry; he felt driven to despair; he was tempted to throw away the tray and everything on it. Instead, whether as a result of his great misery or his great hollowness of stomach, the fact is he fainted away.

When he came to, he found himself lying on a sofa with the Fairy standing beside him.

'I have forgiven you this time as well,' said the Fairy, 'but woe betide if you play me up again . . .'

Pinocchio promised and swore that he would study hard, and that he'd always be good. And he kept his word for the whole of the rest of the year. Indeed, in the annual examinations he had the distinction of being the best pupil in the school. Also his conduct in general was judged to be so satisfactory and commendable that the delighted Fairy said to him, 'Tomorrow, at last, your wish will be granted!'

'What's that?'

'Tomorrow you will cease to be a wooden puppet, and you'll become a real, good boy.'

Anyone who did not witness Pinocchio's joy at this longed-for news will never be able to imagine it for himself. All his friends and classmates were to be invited for a grand meal the next day at the Fairy's house, to celebrate together the great event, and the Fairy had prepared two hundred cups of coffee with milk and four hundred rolls buttered inside and out. That day promised to be full of joy and gaiety; but . . .

Unfortunately, in a puppet's life there are always *buts*, which spoil everything.*

CHAPTER XXX

*How, instead of becoming a boy,
Pinocchio secretly goes away with his friend
Candle-Wick to the 'Land of Toys'.*

As was only natural, Pinocchio promptly asked the Fairy for permission to go round the village inviting the guests.

The Fairy said to him, 'Certainly you may go to invite your classmates for the meal tomorrow, but remember to come home before it gets dark. Do you understand?'

'I promise to be well and truly back within the hour,' replied the puppet.

'Be careful, Pinocchio! Children are quick to make promises but, more often than not, they are slow to keep them.'

'But I'm not like the others; when I give my word, I keep it.'

'We shall see. Just suppose you were to disobey, it would be the worse for you.'

'Why?'

'Because children who don't listen to the advice of those who know more than they do always finish up in some sort of trouble.'

'Which I've proved myself!' said Pinocchio. 'But I'm not going to fall into the trap again!'

'We shall see if you really mean it.'

Without adding anything further, the puppet said good-bye to his good Fairy, who was a kind of mother to him, and singing and dancing he left the house.

In little more than an hour all his friends had been invited. Some of them enthusiastically accepted on the spot; some of them had to be persuaded at first but, when they learnt that the rolls for dunking in the coffee with milk would be buttered on the outside as well, they all ended by saying, 'We'll come too, just to please you.'

Now you must know that, among his friends and classmates, Pinocchio had one very close and favourite friend, whose name was Romeo, but everyone called him by the nickname of *Candle-Wick*, because of his slender figure which was wiry, lean and tall, just like the new wick of a night-light.*

Candle-Wick was the laziest and most rascally boy in the school; but Pinocchio was devoted to him. Of course he went immediately to see him at his home to invite him to the meal, but he was out. He went back a second time, and Candle-Wick was not there; he went back a third time, and made the journey in vain.

Where would he dig him out? After hunting here and hunting there, he found him hiding under the porch of the house of some peasants.

'What are you doing there?' asked Pinocchio, walking up to him.

'I'm waiting to leave . . .'

'Where are you going?'

'Far, far, far away!'

'I've been to your house three times looking for you! . . .'

'What did you want me for?'

'Don't you know about the great occasion? Don't you know about my good luck?'

'What's that?'

'Tomorrow I shan't be a puppet any more; I'm going to be a boy like you and all the others.'

'Much good may it do you.'

'So tomorrow you're invited to breakfast at my house.'

'What if I'm leaving this evening?'

'At what time?'

'Soon.'

'And where are you going?'

'I'm going to live in a country which is the most beautiful country on earth, a land of pleasure and plenty! . . .'*

'And what's it called?'

'It's called the "Land of Toys". Why don't you come too?'

'Me? Oh no!'

'You're making a mistake, Pinocchio! Believe me, if you don't come you'll regret it. Where would you look for a healthier place for us children to live? There are no schools there; there are no teachers there; there are no books there. In that blessed country no one ever studies. There's no school on Thursdays, and every week is composed of six Thursdays and one Sunday.* Just think: the summer holidays begin on the first day of January and end on the last day of December. That's a country that I could really like! That's the way all civilized countries ought to be! . . .'

'But how do you spend the time in the "Land of Toys"?'

'You spend it playing games and having fun from morning to night. In the evening you go to bed, and the following morning you start all over again. What do you reckon to that?'

'Uhm . . .' Pinocchio said, and nodded his head slightly, as if to say, 'That's a life I'd gladly live myself.'

'So, do you want to come away with me? Yes or no? Make up your mind.'

'Oh no, no, no and again no. I've promised my good Fairy to become a good boy now, and I intend to keep my promise. What's more, as I see the sun's going down I'll leave you and be on my way. So goodbye and have a good journey.'

'Where are you going in such a hurry?'

'Home. My good Fairy wants me to be home before dark.'

'Stay another couple of minutes.'

'I'll be late.'

'Only a couple of minutes.'

'And what if the Fairy tells me off?'

'Let her. After she's told you off good and proper, then she'll be quiet,' said that rascally Candle-Wick.

'So what are you doing? Are you going alone or with other people?'

'Alone? No, there'll be more than a hundred children.'

'And are you walking there?'

'Soon the waggon will be here to collect me and take me into that happy land.'

'What wouldn't I give for the waggon to arrive now . . .'

'Why?'

'To see you all leave together.'

'Stay a little while longer and you'll see us.'

'No, no; I want to go home.'

'Wait another couple of minutes.'

'I've stayed out too long already. The Fairy will be worried about me.'

'Poor Fairy! Maybe she's afraid the bats will eat you!'

'So then,' Pinocchio went on, 'are you really sure that there are no schools at all in that country? . . .'

'Not a whisper of one.'

'And no teachers?'

'Not a single one.'

'So you are never obliged to study?'

'Never, never, never.'

'What a nice place!' said Pinocchio, with his mouth beginning to water. 'What a nice place!* I've never been there, but I can just imagine it!'

'Why don't you come too?'

'It's no use trying to tempt me! I've given my word to my good Fairy to be a sensible boy now, and I don't want to break my promise.'

'Goodbye then, and give my best wishes to all the high schools . . . and all the grammar schools, if you happen to meet any.'

'Goodbye, Candle-Wick; have a good journey, enjoy yourself and remember your friends sometimes.'

Having said that, the puppet took a couple of steps in the direction of home. Then stopping and turning towards his friend, he asked, 'But are you really sure that there every week is composed of six Thursdays and a Sunday?'

'Quite sure.'

'But are you certain that the holidays begin on the first day of January and end on the last day of December?'

'Quite certain!'

'What a nice place!' Pinocchio said again, spluttering at such a superabundance of pleasure. Then, with great determination, he added hurriedly, 'Well, it's really goodbye then, and have a good journey.'

'Goodbye.'

'When do you leave?'

'Very soon.'

'I might almost wait, maybe.'

'What about the Fairy? . . .'

'I'm late already! . . . and if I go home an hour early or an hour late, it hardly matters.'

'Poor Pinocchio! And what if the Fairy tells you off?'

'Too bad! I'll let her. After she's told me off good and proper, then she'll be quiet.'

Meanwhile night had fallen and it was very dark; then, all at once in the distance, they saw a little light moving ... and they heard the sound of harness bells and a bugle call, but so quiet and muffled that it sounded like the whisper of a mosquito!

'There it is!' exclaimed Candle-Wick, standing up.

'Who is it?' asked Pinocchio under his breath.

'It's the waggon coming to collect me. So, do you want to come, yes or no?'

'Well, is it really true', asked the puppet, 'that in that country children are never obliged to study?'

'Never, never, never!'

'What a nice place! ... what a nice place! ... what a nice place!'

CHAPTER XXXI

How, after five months in the land of pleasure and plenty, to his great astonishment Pinocchio finds he is growing a fine pair of ass's ears, and he becomes a donkey, tail and all.

At last the waggon arrived, and it arrived without making the slightest sound because its wheels were wrapped in tow and rags.

Twelve pairs of donkeys were pulling it, all of the same size but with coats of different colours.

Some were grey, others white, others speckled pepper and salt style, and yet others were striped with big bands of yellow and indigo.

But the strangest thing was this: those twelve pairs, or twenty-four donkeys, instead of being shod like all other

draught animals or beasts of burden, had on their feet men's ankle-boots made of white leather.

And where was the waggon-driver . . .?

Try to conjure up a little man who was wider than he was tall, as soft and unctuous as a pat of butter, with a little red-apple face, an ever-smiling little mouth, and a sweet and gentle voice, like that of a cat winning over the tender-hearted mistress of the house.*

As soon as they saw him, children always fell in love with him and competed with each other to climb up onto his waggon and be taken by him to that land of pleasure, known on the map by the seductive name: 'The Land of Toys'.

Indeed, the waggon was already crammed with little children from eight to twelve years old, piled up on top of each other like so many anchovies in brine. They were uncomfortable, they were crushed together, they almost could not breathe; but no one said *ouch!* and no one complained. The satisfaction of knowing that in a few hours' time they would arrive in a land where there were no books, no schools, and no teachers, made them so happy and patient that they did not even feel the discomfort, the fatigue, the hunger, the thirst or the sleepiness.

As soon as the waggon stopped, the Little Man turned towards Candle-Wick and, with many wheedling smiles and mincing ways, he sweetly enquired of him, 'Tell me, my fine lad, do you want to come to the happy land too?'

'Of course I want to come.'

'But I must warn you, dear boy, that there's no room left in the waggon. As you see, it's all full! . . .'

'Never mind!' responded Candle-Wick, 'if there's no room inside, I'll manage to sit on the waggon shafts.'

And with one bound, he climbed astride the shaft.

'And you, my darling,' said the Little Man, turning towards Pinocchio flatteringly, 'what do you intend to do? Are you coming with us, or are you staying? . . .'

'I'm staying,' replied Pinocchio. 'I want to go home; I want to study and I want to do well at school, like all good boys do.'

'Much good may it do you!'

'Pinocchio!' said Candle-Wick. 'Listen to me; come with us, and we'll all have fun together.'

'No, no, no!'

'Come with us, and we'll have fun together,' cried four other voices from the waggon.

'Come with us, and we'll have fun together,' yelled a hundred voices in unison.

'And if I come with you, what will my good Fairy say?' said the puppet, beginning to weaken and waver in his resolve.

'Don't fret your head with so many worries. Remember that we're going to a country where we'll be our own masters and allowed to make a din from morn till night!'

Pinocchio did not reply, but sighed. Then he sighed again; then he sighed a third time. At last he said, 'Make a bit of room for me; I want to come too! . . .'

'All the seats are full,' replied the Little Man, 'but to show you how welcome you are, I'll give you my place on the box . . .'

'And what about you? . . .'

'I'll make the journey on foot.'

'No really, I can't let you do that. I'd rather ride on the back of one of these donkeys!' called Pinocchio.

No sooner said than done. He went up to the right-hand donkey of the first pair, and made as if to mount him, but the animal, turning unexpectedly, nuzzled him roughly in the stomach and sent him flying.

You can imagine the unruly and immoderate laughter of all those children watching.

But the Little Man did not laugh. Exuding kindliness, he drew near the rebellious donkey and, pretending to give it a kiss, he clean bit off half its right ear.

Meantime Pinocchio, picking himself up angrily, took one leap up onto the back of that poor animal. And his leap was so fine that the children, ceasing to laugh, began to shout: 'Bravo, Pinocchio!', and to applaud loud and long.

Then lo and behold! the donkey unexpectedly kicked up both its back legs and, bucking vigorously, it flung the poor puppet into the middle of the road on top of a mound of gravel.

So there was much mirth as before; but the Little Man,

instead of laughing, felt so affectionate towards that restless little ass that, with a kiss, he took the top half of the other ear clean off. Then he said to the puppet, 'Get up astride your mount again; don't be afraid. That donkey must have had some bee in his bonnet; but I've whispered a couple of words in his ear, and I hope I've tamed him so that he sees reason.'*

Pinocchio remounted, and the waggon began to move off, but while the donkeys were galloping, with the waggon rolling over the cobblestones of the highway, it seemed to the puppet that he could hear a subdued voice that was barely intelligible saying to him: 'Poor simpleton! You wanted to have your way, but you'll regret it!'

Feeling a bit frightened, Pinocchio looked all around to see where the voice had come from, but he could see no one. The donkeys were galloping, the waggon was rolling along, the children inside were asleep, Candle-Wick was snoring like a top and the Little Man sitting on the box was singing through his teeth to himself:

> All the night they sleep
> And I don't sleep at all . . .

After another half-mile, Pinocchio heard the same muffled little voice which said to him: 'Remember, you silly chump! Boys who give up studying and turn their backs on books, schools and teachers to devote themselves entirely to fun and games are bound to end up in trouble! . . . I know from experience! . . . take it from me! The day will come when you weep too, as I do today . . . but then it will be too late . . .'

At these soft, whispered words the puppet, feeling more than ever scared, jumped down from his mount's back and went to lead the donkey by its bridle.

Imagine his surprise when he saw that his donkey was weeping . . . and weeping just like a boy!

'Hey, Mr Little Man,' Pinocchio called out to the waggon-driver, 'guess what's happened! This donkey is crying.'

'Let him cry; he'll laugh when he gets married.'

'And maybe you taught him how to talk, did you?'

'No, he learnt on his own how to mumble a few words, after he'd been with a team of performing dogs for three years.'

'Poor creature!'

'Come away,' said the Little Man, 'let's not waste time watching a donkey cry. Mount up again and let's go; the night is cold and the journey long.'

Pinocchio obeyed without breathing another word. The waggon hastened along again, and in the morning, at dawn, they arrived safely in the 'Land of Toys'.

This country was like no other country in the world. Its population was entirely made up of children. The oldest were 14; the youngest were just 8. In the streets there was such rejoicing, such a din, such a screaming as to numb the brain. There were troops of urchins everywhere: some were playing at five-stones, some played at quoits and others with a ball, some were on bicycles and others rode a cock-horse; some were playing blind man's buff, and others chased each other; some, dressed as clowns, played at fire-eating; some were play-acting, some were singing, some did somersaults, some amused themselves by walking on their hands with their feet in the air; some bowled hoops, some walked about dressed as generals with paper helmets and papier-mâché sabres; some of them were laughing, others shouted, others called out, others clapped their hands, others whistled, others imitated hens cackling after laying eggs. In fact there was such a pandemonium, such a chir-ruping, such a devilish uproar, that if you didn't stuff your ears with cotton-wool you'd go deaf. In all the squares you could see puppet-shows in tents which were thronged with children from morning till night, and on all the house walls there were lovely inscriptions, written in chalk, like: *Long live phun!* (instead of *fun*), *We don't want no more skools* (instead of *We don't want any more schools*), *Down with Rith Mettick* (instead of *Arithmetic*) and other prize examples.

As soon as they set foot in the town, Pinocchio, Candle-Wick and all the other children who had made the journey with the Little Man plunged into the thick of the hurly-burly, and in a few minutes, as you can easily imagine, they were friends with everybody. Who could have been happier or more content?

Amid all the perpetual pastimes and diverse amusements, the hours, days and weeks went by in a flash.

'Oh, what a wonderful life!' Pinocchio used to say whenever by chance he bumped into Candle-Wick.

'So you see I was right!' the latter would reply. 'And to think that you didn't want to come! Just fancy, you'd got it into your head that you were going back to your Fairy's house, to waste your time in your studies! . . . But now, the fact that you're free of the boredom of books and schools is all because of me and my advice and my concern, don't you agree? It's only real friends who can do these great favours.'

'That's true, Candle-Wick! The fact that I'm a thoroughly happy boy now is all your doing. But do you know what our teacher used to say to me about you? He always used to say, "Don't spend your time with that rascal, Candle-Wick, because Candle-Wick is bad company and he'll never be anything but a bad influence!" . . .'

'Poor old teacher!' answered the other boy, shaking his head. 'I'm only too well aware that he didn't like me and that he used to enjoy speaking ill of me; but I'm generous and I forgive him!'

'You're a noble soul!' said Pinocchio, hugging his friend affectionately and giving him a kiss on the forehead.

By now, they had spent five months in this lovely life of playing games and enjoying themselves the whole day long, without ever having looked a book or a school in the face. Then, one morning when he awoke, Pinocchio had, as they say, a rather nasty surprise, which put him in a very bad temper.

CHAPTER XXXII

How Pinocchio acquires donkey's ears, and then turns into a real donkey and begins to bray.

And what was this surprise?

I'll tell you, my dear little readers: the surprise was that when Pinocchio awoke, not unnaturally he happened to scratch his head, and in scratching it he noticed . . .

Can you guess what he noticed?

To his very great astonishment he noticed that his ears had grown more than six inches.

Ever since his birth, as you know, the puppet had had tiny little ears: so tiny that to the naked eye they weren't even visible! So you can imagine how he felt when his hand discovered that during the night his ears had grown so long as to seem like a couple of besoms.*

He went searching for a mirror at once to see what he looked like, but, not finding a mirror, he filled the wash-basin with water and looking into it he saw something he would never have wished to see: what he saw was his image adorned with a magnificent pair of ass's ears.

I leave you to imagine poor Pinocchio's misery, shame and anguish!

He began to weep and shriek and bang his head against the wall; but the more distracted he became, the more his ears grew and grew and grew, and now hair sprouted at the ends.

At the sound of his piercing cries, a pretty little Marmot, who lived on the floor above, came in. Seeing the puppet in such a frenzy, she asked him solicitously, 'What's the matter, my dear neighbour?'*

'I'm ill, dear little Marmot, very ill . . . and it's an illness that scares me! Do you know how to take a pulse?'

'More or less.'

'So can you tell whether I maybe have a temperature?'

The little Marmot raised her right forepaw, and having taken Pinocchio's pulse, she sighed and said, 'My friend, I'm sorry to have to give you some bad news! ...'

'Which is?'

'You have a nasty fever!'

'And what sort of fever would that be?'

'It's asinine fever.'

'I don't understand what kind of fever that is!' replied the puppet, who unfortunately *had* understood.

'Well then, I'll explain it to you,' the little Marmot went on.

'You see, in two or three hours' time you'll no longer be either a puppet or a boy ...'

'And what will I be?'

'In two or three hours' time you will become a real donkey, like the ones that pull carts and take the cabbages and lettuces to market.'

'Oh poor me! Poor me!' cried Pinocchio, taking both his ears in his hands, furiously pulling them and tearing at them, as if they belonged to someone else.

'Dear boy,' replied the Marmot to console him, 'what can you do about it? It's long been your destiny. It's long been written in the Decrees of Wisdom that all those unwilling children who take a dislike to books, schools, and teachers and spend their days in amusements, games and entertainments must sooner or later turn into so many little asses.'

'But is it really so?' asked the puppet, sobbing.

'Unfortunately it is! And now it's useless to shed tears. You should have thought about it before!'

'But it's not my fault: believe me, dear Marmot, it's all Candle-Wick's fault! ...'

'And who is this Candle-Wick? ...'

'A school-friend of mine. I wanted to go home; I wanted to be obedient; I wanted to go on studying and doing well . . . but Candle-Wick said to me: 'Why do you want to bother yourself studying? Why do you want to go to school? . . . Come with me to the Land of Toys. There we won't have to study any more; there we'll enjoy ourselves from morning till night and we'll always be happy.''

'And why did you take the advice of that false friend, that bad boy?'

'Why did I? Because, dear Marmot, I'm a puppet with no sense . . . and no heart. Oh! if only I'd had a speck of feeling, I would never have left my good Fairy who loved me like a mother and who had done so much for me! . . . By now I wouldn't be a puppet any more . . . but instead I'd be a well-behaved boy like lots of others! Oh! but woe betide if I meet Candle-Wick; I want to give him a piece of my mind! . . .'

And he made as if to go out. But at the door he remembered that he had ass's ears and as he was too ashamed to show them in public, what did he do? He took a huge cotton nightcap and, sticking it on his head, he pulled it right down over the tip of his nose.

Then he went out, and he set about looking for Candle-Wick everywhere. He searched for him in the streets, in the squares, at the puppet-shows, everywhere; but he didn't

find him. He asked everyone he met along the way, but no one had seen him.

So then he went to his house and, on reaching the door, he knocked.

'Who's there?' asked Candle-Wick from inside.

'It's me!' replied the puppet.

'Wait a minute and I'll open the door.'

After half an hour the door opened. Imagine Pinocchio's surprise when, on entering the room, he saw that his friend Candle-Wick was wearing a huge cotton nightcap on his head, which came right down over his nose.

At the sight of that cap, Pinocchio felt almost consoled and thought to himself at once, 'What if my friend is ill with the same illness as me? Maybe he too has asinine fever? . . .'

And pretending not to have noticed anything, he asked him, smiling, 'How are you, my dear Candle-Wick?'

'Fine! Like a mouse in a Cheddar cheese.'*

'Do you really mean that?'

'Why should I tell a lie?'

'Pardon me, my friend, but why then are you wearing this cotton nightcap which covers up your ears?'

'The doctor prescribed it because I've hurt my knee. And what about you, my dear Pinocchio, why are you wearing this cotton nightcap pulled down over your nose?'

'The doctor prescribed it because I've got a sore foot.'

'Oh! poor Pinocchio! . . .'

'Oh! poor Candle-Wick! . . .'

After that there followed a long silence while the two friends did nothing but eye each other mockingly.

At last the puppet said to his friend in a mellifluous, fluty voice, 'Just out of curiosity, my dear Candle-Wick: have you ever had any trouble with your ears?'

'No, never! . . . What about you?'

'No, never! And yet since this morning one of my ears has been painful.'

'I've got the same bother too.'

'You too? . . . And which is the ear that hurts?'

'Both of them. What about you?'

'Both of them. Maybe it's the same illness?'

'I'm afraid it is.'

'Would you do me a favour, Candle-Wick?'

'Gladly! With all my heart.'

'Will you show me your ears?'

'Why not? But first I want to see yours, my dear Pinocchio.'

'No, you must go first.'

'No, dear boy! First you and then me!'

'Oh well,' said the puppet then, 'let's have a friendly agreement.'

'Let's hear what it is.'

'Let's both take off our nightcaps as the same time. Do you agree?'

'I agree.'

'So, on your marks!'

And Pinocchio began to count out loud, 'One! Two! Three!'

At the word *Three!* the two boys took their nightcaps off and threw them in the air.

And then a scene unfolded which might seem incredible if it wasn't true. That's to say that when Pinocchio and Candle-Wick saw each other afflicted with the same disaster, instead of being ashamed and grieved, they began to make faces at each other's enormously overgrown ears and, after a good deal of rudeness, they broke into a hearty laugh.

They laughed and laughed and laughed so much that they had to hold their sides; until, at the height of their laughter, Candle-Wick suddenly fell silent and, staggering and changing colour, he said to his friend, 'Help, help, Pinocchio!'

'What's the matter?'

'Oh dear! I can't stand upright any more.'

'I can't any more, either,' cried out Pinocchio, weeping and swaying.

And as they said this, they both doubled up, their hands and feet on the ground and, going on all fours, they began to walk and run about the room. And while they ran their arms turned into legs with hooves, their faces lengthened and became muzzles, and their backs grew a covering of light grey fur brindled with black.

But do you know what the worst moment was for those two miscreants? The worst and most humiliating moment was when they felt a tail growing behind. Then, overcome by their shame and misery, they tried to weep and lament their fate.

If only they had not tried! Instead of moans and groans, they emitted an ass's braying and, braying resoundingly, they chorused together: '*Hee-haw, hee-haw, hee-haw*.'

Just then there came a knock at the door, and a voice outside said, 'Open up! I'm the Little Man, the driver of the waggon that brought you to this land. Open up at once, or you'll regret it!'

CHAPTER XXXIII

*How, having turned into a real donkey, he is
taken away to be sold, and the Manager of a
company of clowns buys him in order to teach
him to dance and jump through hoops; but
how one evening he goes lame and so is sold
on to someone else, for his skin to be made
into a drum.*

Observing that the door did not open, the Little Man flung
it wide with a violent kick and, coming into the room, he
said to Pinocchio and Candle-Wick with his usual little
laugh, 'Good boys! You brayed very well, and I immediately recognized your voices. So here I am.'

At these words the two donkeys were crestfallen, and
hung their heads down, with their ears bent and their tails
between their legs.

At first the Little Man stroked them, fondled them and
patted them; then taking out a currycomb he began to groom
them really well. And when, with this grooming, he had
made them shine like two mirrors, he put a halter round
their necks and took them to the market-place, in the hope
of selling them and netting a handsome profit for himself.

And in fact buyers were not long in coming forward.

Candle-Wick was bought by a peasant whose donkey had died the day before, and Pinocchio was sold to the Manager of a company of clowns and tight-rope performers, who bought him in order to train him to jump and dance* along with the other animals in the company.

Now then, my dear little readers, do you understand the nature of the Little Man's fine profession? That nasty little monster, whose appearance was all milk and honey, would travel about the countryside every so often with his waggon; as he went along, by means of promises and blandishments, he gathered up all the lazy children who disliked books and school, and loading them into his waggon he took them to the Land of Toys so that they could spend all their time playing and making a noise and having fun. When, by dint of playing all the time and never studying, those poor deluded children turned into so many little donkeys, then, thoroughly pleased and cheerful, he would take charge of them and lead them away to be sold at fairs and markets. And so in a very few years he had made a mint of money and had become a millionaire.

What happened to Candle-Wick I don't know; but I do know that right from the start Pinocchio had a very hard and cruel life.

When he was taken to his stable, his new master filled the manger with straw, but Pinocchio, having tasted a mouthful, spat it out.

So then his master, grumbling, filled the manger with hay, but he didn't like the hay either.

'Aha! So you don't like hay either?' shouted his master in a rage. 'We'll see about that, my fine donkey. I'll soon get rid of any fancy ideas you've got in your head ...'

And by way of punishment, he promptly lashed out at his legs with the whip.

In great pain Pinocchio began to cry and to bray, and his braying said, 'Hee-haw, I can't digest straw! ...'

'So eat the hay then!' replied his master, who understood the language of donkeys very well.*

'Hee-haw, the hay gives me stomach-ache! . . .'

'So you expect me to feed the likes of a donkey like you on chicken breasts and capon in aspic, do you?' his master went on, getting angrier all the time and lashing out with the whip again.

At that second whipping Pinocchio prudently fell silent and said no more.

Then the stable door was shut and Pinocchio was left on his own, and because he had not eaten for many hours he began to yawn from hunger. And in yawning he opened wide a mouth as big as an oven.

In the end, because he could find nothing else in the manger, he resigned himself to chewing a little hay, and when he had chewed it over and over again, he shut his eyes and gulped it down.

'This hay isn't too bad,' he said to himself, 'but how much better it would have been if I had gone on studying . . . Instead of eating hay, I might be having a chunk of fresh bread and a nice slice of salami! But never mind . . .'*

As soon as he woke up the next day he searched in the manger for another bit of hay, but he could not find any because he had eaten it all in the night.

So he took a mouthful of chopped straw, and while he was chewing it he had to admit that it tasted nothing like either shepherd's pie or steak and kidney pudding.*

'Never mind!' he said again, going on chewing. 'Maybe my misfortune can at least serve as a warning to all disobedient children who don't want to study. Never mind . . . Never mind!'

'Never mind, my foot!' shouted the master, who was coming into the stable at that moment. 'Well, well, my fine little donkey, don't imagine that I bought you just to feed and water you! I bought you to work and earn a lot of money for me. Come along then, be a good boy! Come into the Circus with me and there I'll teach you how to jump through hoops, how to burst through paper barrels with your head, and how to dance the waltz and the polka standing upright on your hind legs.'

Poor Pinocchio had to learn all these wonderful things whether he liked it or not; but it took three months of lessons to do so, as well as being whipped so hard that his fur came off.

At last the day came when his master could announce an amazing new show. The posters of different colours, stuck up at street corners, read like this:

GRAND GALA SHOW

This evening as usual

ACROBATIC AND OTHER AMAZING FEATS

WILL BE PERFORMED BY ALL THE ARTISTS

and all the horses of the Company, both fillies and colts,

AND IN ADDITION WE PRESENT FOR THE FIRST TIME THE FAMOUS

DONKEY PINOCCHIO

KNOWN AS

THE STAR OF THE DANCE

THE THEATRE WILL BE BRILLIANTLY LIT

As you can imagine, that evening the theatre was full to bursting an hour before the show began.

You couldn't find a seat for love or money, not in the front stalls or the back stalls or in the circle.

The tiers of seats were crammed with children, girls and boys of all ages, who were excited and longing to see the famous donkey Pinocchio dance.

After the first half of the programme, the Ringmaster, dressed in a black tail-coat, white tights and leather boots which came right up over his knees, presented himself to the crowded audience and, making a deep bow, he pronounced with utmost solemnity the following absurd address:

'Esteemed audience, Sirs and Ladies!

'Your humble servant, the undersigned, being in transit through this illustrious metropolitan, decided to procreate myself the honour, not to say the pleasure, of presenting to this intelligent and eminent auditorium a celebrated donkey, which has already had the honour of dancing before His Majesty the emperor of all the principal Courts of Europe.

'And in thanking your good selves, please support us with your enlivening presence and grant us your indulgence!'

This speech was greeted with much laughter and clapping; but the clapping redoubled and became a storm of applause when the donkey Pinocchio appeared in the middle of the ring. He was all dressed up in his Sunday best. He had a new bridle of shiny leather ornamented with horse brasses and brass buckles; he had two white camellias behind his ears; his mane was combed into lots of ringlets tied with little red silk bows; around his middle he wore a wide gold and silver sash, and his tail was all plaited with purple and sky-blue velvet ribbons. He was an altogether adorable donkey!

Presenting him to the audience, the Ringmaster went on as follows:

'Most honoured auditors! I shall not engage in laying
before you the great difficulties suppressed by me in order
to comprehend and subjugate this mammal, while he was
freely grazing from mountain to mountain in the plains of
the torrid zone. I urge you to observe how much wilder-
ness oozes from his eyes, notwithstanding the circumstance
that the vanity of all my diverse attempts to domesticate
him to the life of civilized quadrupeds obliged me several
times to have recourse to the affable parlance of the whip.
But all my kindnesses, instead of making me beloved by
him, have captivated my heart for him. Albeit adopting
the system of Gaul, I discovered on his cranium a small
bonaparte cartilage, which indeed the Medicean Faculty of
Paris recognized as the bulb which regenerates hair and
Pyrrhic dance.* For this reason I decided to school him in
dancing, as well as in the pertinent skills of jumping through
hoops and through papered barrels. Watch him! and then
judge for yourselves! Before, however, I abscess myself from
you, permit me, ladies and gentlemen, to invite you to the
diurnal performance of tomorrow evening; but in the
apotheosis that rainy weather might threaten a downpour,
then the show, instead of being tomorrow evening, will
be postponed until tomorrow morning at 11 a.m. in the
afternoon.'

And here the Ringmaster made another deep, deep bow;
then, turning to Pinocchio, he said, 'Take heart, Pinocchio!
Before the commencement of your exercises, greet this
honourable audience of knights, madames, and children!'

Obediently Pinocchio bent his two front legs at once,
and remained kneeling until the Ringmaster, cracking his
whip, called out to him, 'Now walk!'

Then the donkey got up on all four legs and began to
move around the ring at a walking pace.

After a little while the Ringmaster called, 'Now trot!'
and Pinocchio, obeying the command, changed his step to
a trot.

'Now canter!' and Pinocchio launched into a canter.

'Now gallop!' and Pinocchio flung himself into a full gallop. But while he was running like an Arab charger, the Ringmaster raised his arm in the air and let off a pistol shot.

At that shot the donkey presented to be wounded and fell down prone in the ring as if he was really dying.

Getting up from the ground amidst a burst of applause, with cheers and clapping that rose to the heavens, he naturally lifted his head and looked up . . . and as he looked, he saw a beautiful lady sitting in a box, and around her throat she was wearing a wide gold necklace from which there hung a medallion. On the medallion there was the painted portrait of a puppet.

'That portrait is mine! . . . that lady is the Fairy!' Pinocchio said to himself, recognizing her immediately, and, allowing himself to be overcome by a great feeling of happiness, he tried to call out, 'Oh my dear Fairy! oh my dear Fairy! . . .'

But instead of these words, there emerged from his throat such a resonant and prolonged braying that it made all the spectators laugh, most especially all the children in the theatre.

So the Ringmaster, to teach him a lesson and get him to understand that it is not good manners to start braying in the faces of the audience, gave him a rap on the nose with the handle of the whip.

The poor donkey, sticking the whole length of his tongue out, worked at licking his own nose for a good five minutes, probably hoping to quell the pain that he had felt.

But how great was his desperation when, looking upwards a second time, he saw that the box was empty and that the Fairy had vanished! . . .

He felt like dying; his eyes filled with tears and he began to cry copiously. Nobody noticed though, least of all the Ringmaster who, on the contrary, cracked his whip and shouted, 'Good boy, Pinocchio! Now you will show these gentlefolk the graceful way you have of jumping through the hoops.'

Pinocchio tried two or three times, but every time he reached the hoop, instead of going through, he passed more comfortably beneath it. In the end he gave a leap and went through; but by ill-fortune his back legs got caught in the hoop, which was why he fell to the ground on the other side all in a heap.

When he stood up again, he was lame and could scarcely get back to the stables.

'Bring on Pinocchio! We want the donkey! Bring on the donkey!' shouted the children in the stalls, feeling sympathetic and saddened by the unfortunate accident.

But that evening the donkey was not seen again.

The next morning the veterinary surgeon, or animals' doctor, who had examined him, announced that he would be lame for the rest of his life.

So the Ringmaster said to his stable-lad, 'What do you

expect me to do with a lame ass? He would be a scrounger of free meals. Take him back to the market-square and sell him on.'

When they got to the square, they immediately found a buyer, who asked the stable-lad, 'How much do you want for this lame donkey?'

'Twenty pounds.'

'I'll give you twenty shillings. Don't imagine I'm buying him to make him work for me; I'm buying him only for his skin. I can see he has a very thick skin, and I want to use this skin to make a drum for our town band.'

Dear children, I leave you to conjure up what a delight it was for poor Pinocchio when he heard that he was destined to become a drum!

At all events, as soon as he had paid the twenty shillings, the purchaser led the donkey away towards the seashore. Having tied a rock around his neck, and holding on to a rope attached to his leg, he gave him a shove all of a sudden so that he fell into the water.

With that block tied round his neck, Pinocchio went straight to the bottom. The purchaser, holding the rope tight in his hand, settled down on a rock to allow the donkey all the time he needed to die of drowning, so as to be able to skin him and take his hide away with him.

CHAPTER XXXIV

How Pinocchio, having been thrown into the
sea, is eaten by the fishes and becomes a
puppet once more, but how, while he is
swimming to safety, he is swallowed by the
dreaded Shark.

After the donkey had been in the water for fifty minutes, the purchaser, talking to himself, said, 'By now the poor lame donkey must be well and truly drowned. Let's pull him up again, and then we'll make a fine drum out of his skin.'

And he began to pull on the rope which he had tied to his leg. He pulled and pulled and pulled until finally he saw appearing on the surface of the water . . . can you guess what? Instead of a dead donkey, he saw appearing on the surface of the water a live puppet, which was waggling about like an eel.

Seeing that wooden puppet, the poor man thought he was dreaming and stood there stunned, with his mouth open and his eyes starting out of his head.

Recovering a little from his original astonishment, he stammered out tearfully, 'And where is the donkey that I threw into the sea? . . .'

'I am that donkey!' said Pinocchio, laughing.

'You?'

'Yes, me.'

'Aha, you swindler! So you think you can make fun of me, do you?'

'Make fun of you? Anything but, dear master; I'm perfectly serious.'

'But just now you were a donkey, so how is it that after being in the water you have become a wooden puppet? . . .'

'It must be the effect of sea-water. The sea plays tricks like that.'

'You watch out, puppet, just watch out! . . . Don't imagine you can laugh behind my back! Woe betide you if I lose my patience!'

'Well then, master, do you want to know the whole true story? If you will release my leg, I shall tell you everything.'

That silly fool who bought him, curious to know the true story, promptly undid the knot in the rope which was keeping him bound, and so Pinocchio, finding himself as free as a bird in the air, started to explain to him thus, 'You see, I was once a wooden puppet like I am now. Then it was touch and go whether I would become a boy, like all the others in this world, except that, because of my unwillingness to study and because of listening to the advice of bad company, I ran away from home . . . and one fine day when I woke up, I found that I had turned into an ass with great long ears . . . and a long tail! . . . What a disgrace that was for me! . . . A disgrace, dear master, and may the blessed St Anthony* not permit you to suffer so! I was taken to be sold in the donkey market, and was bought by the Ringmaster of an equestrian company, who took it into his head to make me into a great dancer and a great jumper through hoops. But one evening during the performance I fell badly in the ring and was left lame in both legs. So then the Ringmaster, not knowing what to do with a lame donkey, sent me off to be sold on, and you bought me . . .'

'More's the pity! And I paid twenty shillings for you. Now who's going to give me back my wretched twenty shillings?'

'And why did you buy me? You bought me to make my skin into a drum! ... a drum! ...'

'More's the pity! And now where will I find another skin? ...'

'Don't despair, master. There are plenty more asses in the world!'

'Tell me, you impertinent urchin, does your story end there?'

'No,' replied the puppet, 'there's another couple of words, then it's finished. After buying me, you brought me to this place to kill me, but then, giving way to a humane sense of compassion, you preferred to tie a rock round my neck and throw me to the bottom of the sea. This delicate sentiment of yours does you honour and I shall remember it with perpetual gratitude. However, dear master, this time you calculated without the Fairy ...'

'And who is this Fairy?'

'She is my mother, and she's just like all good mothers who love their children very much and never lose sight of them, and who lovingly help them in every misfortune, even when these children, because of their thoughtless actions and their bad behaviour, are worthy of being abandoned and left to fend for themselves. So, as I was saying, the moment she saw I was in danger of drowning, the Good Fairy immediately sent a vast shoal of fishes all round me; believing me really to be a thoroughly dead donkey, they began to eat me! And what bites they took! I would never have believed that fishes are even more greedy than children! ... Some of them ate my ears, some ate my muzzle, some ate my neck and mane, some took the skin off my legs, some the fur from my back ... and amongst them there was such a courteous little fish that it deigned even to eat my tail.'

'From now on,' said the purchaser, shuddering, 'I swear never again to taste the flesh of fish. I would not find it at all pleasant to cut open a red mullet or a fried hake and discover inside it a donkey's tail!'

'I agree with you,' said the puppet, laughing. 'Besides, you ought to know that when the fishes had finished eating all that ass's rind that covered me from top to toe, naturally they came to the bones . . . or rather, they came to the wood, because, as you see, I am made of very hard wood. But after the first few bites, those greedy fish noticed at once that wood is not fair game for their teeth, and sickened by that indigestible food they all went away, some thisaway, some thataway, without glancing back even to say thank you. So there you have the story of how it was that, when you pulled up the rope, you found a live puppet on the end instead of a dead donkey.'

'I think your story is laughable,' shouted the purchaser, turning nasty. 'I know that I spent twenty shillings to buy you, and I want my money back. Do you know what I'm going to do? I'm going to take you back to the market, and I'll sell you by weight as seasoned wood for fire-lighting.'

'You sell me on again. I'm quite happy about that,' said Pinocchio.

But saying this, he gave a great leap and landed in the middle of the water. Swimming cheerfully and getting further from the beach, he called out to the poor purchaser, 'Goodbye, master. If you ever have need of a skin to make a drum, remember me!'

And then he laughed and went on swimming, and after a bit, looking back, he shouted louder, 'Goodbye, master. If you ever have need of a bit of seasoned wood to light a fire with, remember me.'

In fact, in the twinkling of an eye he had gone so far away that he could scarcely be seen any more; or rather, all that could be seen on the surface of the sea was a little black dot, which every so often kicked its legs out of the water and capered and leapt like a good-humoured dolphin.

While Pinocchio was swimming heedlessly, he saw a rock that looked like white marble in the middle of the sea, and on top of the rock there was a dear little kid, bleating tenderly and signalling to him to come closer.

The strangest thing was this: the kid's wool, instead of being white, or black, or spotted with several colours, like the wool of other goats, on the contrary was entirely indigo, but of such a resplendent indigo that it was very reminiscent of the hair of the beautiful Little Girl.

I leave you to imagine whether poor Pinocchio's heart began to beat harder! Redoubling his efforts and his energy, he concentrated on swimming towards the white rock. He was already half-way when, lo and behold!, rising from out of the deep and coming towards him was the horrible head of a sea-monster, its mouth gaping like a chasm, with three rows of fangs that would have terrified you even in a picture.

And do you know who that sea-monster was?

That sea-monster was none other than the gigantic Shark mentioned several times in this story, which, because of his massacres and his insatiable voraciousness, had been nicknamed 'The fishes' and fishermen's Attila'.*

Just think of poor Pinocchio's terror when he saw the monster. He tried to avoid him, to change his direction; he tried to escape, but that huge, gaping mouth bore down upon him with the speed of an arrow.

'For pity's sake, Pinocchio, hurry up!' cried the dear little kid, bleating.

And Pinocchio swam desperately with his arms, his chest, his legs and feet.

'Quick, Pinocchio, the monster's coming! . . .'

And Pinocchio, gathering all his strength, redoubled his efforts to make speed.

'Watch out, Pinocchio! . . . the monster's reaching you! . . . Here he is! . . . Here he is! . . . For pity's sake, hurry or you're lost! . . .'

And Pinocchio swam faster than ever; on and on and on he went, swift as a rifle shot. And he was already getting close to the rock, and the little kid was already leaning over the sea, stretching out her little hooves to help him out of the water ... But! ...

But it was already too late! The monster had reached him. The monster, sucking in its breath, drank the poor puppet, just as it might have drunk a hen's egg, and he swallowed him with such violence and such greed, that Pinocchio, falling down into the belly of the Shark, suffered such a cruel battering that he lay dazed by it for a quarter of an hour.

When he came to himself again after that terror, not even he could make head or tail of where he was. Everywhere all around him was a dense darkness, but it was such a deep, black darkness that he thought he might have plunged head first into a pot full of ink. He sat and listened and heard not a sound; only now and then did he feel an occasional buffeting on his face of a strong wind. At first he did not understand where that wind was coming from, but then he realized that it came from the monster's lungs. Because, you see, the Shark suffered badly from asthma, and when it breathed, it felt as if the north wind was blowing.

In the beginning, Pinocchio tried to keep his courage up, but when he had the proof over and over again that he was trapped in the belly of the sea-monster, then he began to cry and shriek, and, tearfully, he said, 'Help! help! Oh poor little me! Isn't there anyone who can come and save me?'

'Who do you think can save you, you poor thing?' a cracked old voice like an out-of-tune guitar said in the darkness.

'Who's that talking?' asked Pinocchio, feeling himself freeze with fright.

'It's me! I'm a poor Tunny-fish, swallowed by the Shark along with you. And what kind of fish are you?'

'I've got nothing to do with fishes. I'm a puppet.'

'So, if you're not a fish, how did you get yourself swallowed by the monster?'

'It's not me that got myself swallowed; it's him that swallowed me! And now what are we to do here in this darkness? . . .'

'Resign ourselves and wait for the Shark to digest the pair of us! . . .'

'But I don't want to be digested!' shouted Pinocchio, starting to cry again.

'Nor do I wish to be digested,' continued the Tunny, 'but I'm enough of a philosopher and it consoles me to think that when one is born a Tunny, it's more dignified to die in sea-water than in olive-oil! . . .'*

'Nonsense!' exclaimed Pinocchio.

'It's an opinion of mine,' replied the Tunny, 'and people's opinions, as political Tunny-fish say,* are to be respected!'

'All the same . . . I want to get out of here . . . I want to escape . . .'

'Escape then, if you can . . .'

'Is it very big this Shark that has swallowed us?' asked the puppet.

'Can you imagine that his body is more than a mile long, without counting the tail?'

While they were having this conversation in the dark, it seemed to Pinocchio that he could see far, far away a kind of glimmer of light.

'Whatever can that little light be far, far away?' said Pinocchio.

'It must be some companion in this misfortune of ours, who, like us, is awaiting the moment of digestion! . . .'

'I want to go and find him. You never know, it might be some old fish who would be able to show me the way to escape.'

'I hope it is with all my heart, dear puppet.'

'Goodbye, Tunny.'

'Goodbye, puppet, and good luck!'

'Where shall we meet again? . . .'

'Who knows? . . . It's better not even to think about it!'*

CHAPTER XXXV

How in the Shark's body Pinocchio meets . . .
whom does he meet once more? Read this
chapter and you will find out.

As soon as Pinocchio had said goodbye to his good friend
Tunny, he moved off groping about in that darkness;
feeling his way through the body of the Shark, he went
forward one step at a time towards the little light that he
could see flickering far, far away.

While he walked he could feel his feet squelching in a
pool of fatty, slippery water, and that water had such an
acrid smell of fried fish that he thought it must be the
middle of Lent.*

The further he went, the clearer and brighter the light
became, until after walking and walking he at last arrived;
and when he arrived . . . what did he find? I'll give you a
thousand guesses: he found a little table all laid up, with a
lighted candle set on it in a green glass bottle, and sitting
at the table was a little old man who was completely white,
as if he were made of snow or whipped cream, and there
he was chewing over some live fish, so alive, indeed, that
sometimes while he was eating them, they even managed to
slip from his mouth.

At the sight of him, poor Pinocchio's joy was so great
and so unexpected that he all but fell into a delirium. He
wanted to laugh, he wanted to weep, he wanted to say a
heap of things; and instead he mumbled in confusion and
stammered a few unfinished and inconsequential words. At
last he succeeded in uttering a cry of delight, and flinging
his arms out wide and throwing himself at the old man's
neck, he began to yell, 'Oh my dear little Papa, at last I've
found you! Now I'll never leave you again, never ever!'

'Well then, do my eyes not deceive me?' replied the

old man, rubbing his eyes.* 'So you really are m' dear
Pinocchio?'

'Yes, yes, it's me, it's really me! And you had already
forgiven me, hadn't you? Oh, my Papa, how good you
are! ... and to think that, by contrast, I... Oh, but if you
knew how many misfortunes have rained down on me and
how many things went wrong for me! Can you believe, my
poor dear Papa, that the day you sold your cape to buy me
an alphabet book so that I could go to school, I ran away
to go and see the puppets, and the puppeteer wanted to put
me on the fire so that I would cook his roast ram for him,
and then he was the one who gave me five gold pieces that
I was to bring to you, but I came across the Fox and the
Cat who took me to the Red Lobster Inn, where they
wolfed the food, and when I left on my own at night I met
the murderers who started to run after me, and I ran off
and they were after me, and I ran faster and they were still

behind, and off I went until they hanged me from a branch of the Great Oak, where the beautiful Little Girl with indigo hair sent a carriage to fetch me, and the doctors who examined me said straight away, "If he is not dead, it's a sign that he is still alive", and then by accident I told a lie, and my nose began to grow and it wouldn't go through the bedroom door any more, which was the reason why I went with the Fox and the Cat to bury the four gold coins, for I had spent one at the Inn, and the parrot started to laugh, and instead of two thousand coins I didn't find any, which when the judge learnt I had been robbed he sent me to prison at once, so as to make reparation to the thieves, from where, when I left, I saw a nice bunch of grapes in a field, so that I was caught in the gin-trap and the peasant in his wisdom put a dog's collar on me so that I could guard his hen-house, and then he acknowledged my innocence and let me go, and the Serpent with the smoking tail began to laugh and burst a blood vessel in his chest, so I went back to the beautiful Little Girl's house, but she was dead, and the Pigeon, seeing me crying, said, "I saw your Papa and he was making himself a little boat to go in search of you", and I said to him, "Oh, if only I had wings too", and he said to me, "Do you want to go to your Papa?", and I said to him, "Rather! But who's going to take me?", and he said to me, "I'll take you", and I said to him, "How?", and he said to me, "Climb onto my back", and like that we flew all night, and in the morning all the fishermen who were looking out to sea said to me, "There's a poor man in a boat who's going down", and from a long way off I saw it was you straight away, because my heart said so, and I waved to you to come back to the shore . . .'

'I recognized you too,' said Old Joe, 'and I would have gladly come back to the shore, but how was I to do it? The sea was rough and a breaker capsized my boat. Then a horrible Shark who was nearby swam straight to me as soon as he saw me in the water and, sticking out his tongue, he caught me just like that, and sucked me down like a bit of spaghetti.'*

'And how long have you been a prisoner in here?' asked Pinocchio.

'Ever since that day. It must be two years by now, two years, dear Pinocchio, that have felt like two centuries!'

'And how did you manage to stay alive? And where did you find the candle? And the matches to light it, whoever gave you those?'

'Now I'll tell you all about it. You see, that same storm which upturned my little boat also sank a merchant ship. The sailors were all saved, but the ship went to the bottom and the same old Shark, who had an excellent appetite that day, after swallowing me, swallowed the ship as well . . .'

'What? It swallowed it all in one bite? . . .' asked Pinocchio in amazement.

'All in one bite, and it only spat out the mainmast, because it had got stuck between its teeth, like a fishbone. It was my great good luck that the ship was laden not only with preserved meat in tins, but with ship's biscuit, otherwise known as rusk, bottles of wine, raisins, cheese, coffee, sugar, tallow candles and boxes of wax matches. With all these blessings I was able to stay alive for two years, but this is the fag-end now. Today there's nothing left in the locker, and this candle that you see burning is the last candle I have . . .'

'And after that? . . .'

'After that, dear one, we shall both be in the dark.'

'In that case, dear Papa,' said Pinocchio, 'there's no time to lose. We must plan our escape at once . . .'

'Escape? . . . but how?'

'By getting out through the Shark's mouth and throwing ourselves into the sea to swim away.'

'That's easy for you to say, dear Pinocchio, but I don't know how to swim.'

'What does that matter?... You can ride on my back and, as I'm a strong swimmer, I'll carry you safe and sound to the shore.'

'That's a fantasy, my boy!' replied Old Joe, shaking his head and smiling sadly. 'Do you really think it's possible for a puppet who is barely three feet tall, like you, to have enough strength to swim with me on his back?'

'Try and see! At any rate, if heaven decrees that we are to die, we shall at least have the great consolation of dying in each other's arms.'

And without another word, Pinocchio picked up the candle and, going first to light the way, he said to his Papa, 'Follow me, and don't be afraid.'

And so they walked a long way, all through the belly and the stomach of the Shark. But when they reached the point where the spacious throat of the monster began, they thought they had better stop to look about them so as to seize the right moment for their escape.

Now, I must tell you that, as the Shark was very old and suffered from asthma and palpitations of the heart, he was obliged to sleep with his mouth open; so, Pinocchio, gazing out through the beginnings of the throat and looking upwards, could see beyond that enormous wide-open mouth a lovely expanse of starry sky and the beautiful moonlight.*

'This is just the moment to escape,' he whispered, turning towards his father. 'The Shark is sleeping like a top;* the sea is calm and it's as light as day. So come with me, dear Papa, and soon we shall be safe.'

No sooner said than done; they climbed up through the throat of the sea-monster and, arriving in his immense mouth, they began to walk on tiptoe along his tongue, a tongue so broad and so long that it seemed like a footpath in a garden. And they were standing there on the point of making the great leap and throwing themselves into the sea to swim for it, when, at that very moment, the Shark sneezed, and in sneezing he shuddered so violently that Pinocchio and Old Joe found themselves thrown backwards and hurled once more into the depths of the monster's stomach.

In the great shock of the fall the candle went out, and father and son were left in the dark.

'Well, what now?' asked Pinocchio, becoming serious.

'Now, my lad, we're well and truly sunk.'

'Why so? Give me your hand, Papa, and take care not to slip! . . .'

'Where are you taking me?'

'We have to try to escape again. Come with me and don't be afraid.'

That said, Pinocchio took his father's hand and, still walking on tiptoe, they climbed back up the throat of the monster together; then they traversed the whole of its tongue and clambered over the three rows of teeth. But before making the great leap, the puppet said to his father, 'Climb up on my shoulders piggy-back and put your arms round me very, very tight. I'll do the rest.'

As soon as Old Joe was safely astride his son's back, the good-hearted Pinocchio confidently threw himself into the water and began to swim. The sea was as smooth as oil, the moon shone down in all its brilliance, and the Shark continued to sleep such a deep sleep that even a cannon-shot would not have awoken him.

CHAPTER XXXVI

*How at last Pinocchio stops being a puppet
and becomes a boy.*

While Pinocchio was swimming fast to reach the shore,
he noticed that his father, who was riding piggy-back and
whose legs were half in the water, was trembling terribly,
as if the poor man were stricken with malaria.*

Was he trembling with cold or with fear? Who knows? . . .
Perhaps a bit of both. But Pinocchio, thinking that the
shivering was because of fear, said to comfort him, 'Take
heart, Papa! In a few minutes we'll be safe on dry land.'

'But where is this blessed shore?' asked the old man,
becoming ever more anxious and sharpening his gaze just
like a tailor threading a needle. 'Here I am looking all around
me and I can't see anything but sea and sky.'

'But I can see the shore as well,' said the puppet. 'You
know, I'm like a cat; I can see better at night than in the day.'

Poor Pinocchio was pretending to be in good heart,
but in reality . . . in reality he was beginning to feel discouraged; his strength was leaving him, he was getting
breathless and gasping . . . in fact he could go on no longer,
and the shore was still far away.

He swam as long as he had any breath; then he turned
his head towards Old Joe and said in halting phrases, 'Dear
Papa . . . save yourself . . . because I'm dying! . . .'

By now both father and son were on the point of drowning, when they heard a voice like an out-of-tune guitar,
which said, 'Who is it that's dying?'

'It's me and my poor father!'

'I recognize that voice! It's Pinocchio! . . .'

'Quite right; and who are you?'

'I'm the Tunny-fish, your cell-mate in the prison of the
Shark's belly.'

'And how did you escape?'

'I followed your example. It was you who taught me the route, and after you'd gone I escaped as well.'

'Dear Tunny, you chance this way in the nick of time! By the love you bear to your little Tunny children, I beg you: please help us, or we're lost.'

'Gladly and with all my heart. Both of you hold on to my tail and allow me to guide you. In four minutes I'll get you to the beach.'

As you can imagine, Old Joe and Pinocchio promptly accepted the invitation; but instead of holding on to his tail, they thought it best to ride astride the back of the Tunny-fish.

'Are we too heavy?' Pinocchio asked him.

'Heavy? Not in the least; it feels like having a couple of sea-shells on my back,' replied the Tunny, who was of such considerable and robust build he might have been a two-year-old calf.

When they reached the beach, Pinocchio jumped down first to help his father do the same; then he turned to the Tunny and in an emotional voice he said, 'My friend, you have saved my father! I can't thank you enough for that! Please allow me at least to give you a kiss, as a mark of my eternal gratitude! ...'

The Tunny put his nose above the water, and Pinocchio, kneeling down on the ground, kissed him most tenderly on the mouth. At this display of spontaneous and lively affection, the poor Tunny, who was not used to such things, was quite overcome and, too embarrassed to let himself be seen crying like a baby, he plunged his head beneath the waves and disappeared.

Meanwhile day had dawned.

Then, offering his arm to Old Joe, who had only just enough strength left to stand, Pinocchio said to him, 'Lean on my arm, dear Papa, so we can carry on. We'll walk ever so slowly just like ants, and when we're tired we'll rest by the wayside.'

'But where are we to go?' asked Old Joe.

'We must search for a house or a cabin, where they'll be charitable enough to give us a crust of bread and some straw to sleep on.'

Before they had gone a hundred paces, they saw sitting on the verge of the road two ugly characters who were begging for alms.

They were the Cat and the Fox; but they were unrecognizable as the same ones as before. Would you believe it, but the Cat, by dint of pretending to be blind, in the end had gone blind in reality; and the Fox, who had grown old and was moth-eaten and paralysed down one side, no longer even had a tail. That's the way of these things. Having fallen into the most abject poverty, one fine day the thieving wretch was forced to sell that most beautiful tail to a travelling pedlar who bought it to use as a fly-swatter.

'Oh Pinocchio,' called out the Fox in a whining voice, 'give a bit of charity to these two poor invalids.'

'Invalids!' repeated the Cat.

'Farewell, you masqueraders!'* replied the puppet. 'You deceived me once, but you're not going to fool me again.'

'Believe me, Pinocchio, nowadays we are poor unfortunates—truly!'

'Truly!' repeated the Cat.

'If you are poor, you deserve it. Remember the proverb that says, "Stolen money never bears fruit." Farewell, masqueraders!'

'Have pity on us...'

'On us!'

'Farewell, masqueraders! Remember the proverb that says, "Ill-gotten gains turn to ashes in the mouth."'

'Don't leave us...'

'Us!' repeated the Cat.

'Farewell, masqueraders! Remember the proverb that says, "He who steals his neighbour's cloak, likely dies without a shirt."'

So saying, Pinocchio and Old Joe calmly went on their way until, a hundred paces further on, they saw at the end of a lane, in the middle of the fields, a fine hut made of straw, with a roof over it covered in terracotta tiles.

'Someone must live in that hut,' said Pinocchio. 'Let's go and knock on the door.'

So they went and knocked on the door.

'Who is it?' said a little voice inside.

'It's a poor father and his poor son, who have no food and no roof over their heads,' answered the puppet.

'Turn the key, and the door will open,' said the same little voice.

Pinocchio turned the key, and the door opened. As soon as they went inside, they looked this way and they looked that way, but they could see no one.

'Hey, where is the owner of the hut?' said Pinocchio in amazement.

'Here I am, up here!'

Father and son immediately looked up at the ceiling, and on a beam they saw the Talking Cricket.

'Oh, my dear little Cricket,' said Pinocchio greeting him courteously.

'Now you call me "Your dear little Cricket", do you? But do you remember the time when you wanted to drive me out of your house and you threw a hammer handle at me ... ?'

'You're quite right, little Cricket! You'd better drive me away now ... and even throw a hammer handle at me; but please take pity on my poor Papa ...'

'I shall take pity on both father and son; but I wanted to remind you of your bad manners to me to teach you that, in this world, whenever possible it's necessary to show courtesy to everyone, if we want to receive equal courtesy in times of need.'

'You're quite right, little Cricket, you are righter than

right and I shall always bear in mind the lesson you have taught me. But tell me how you came to buy this fine hut?'

'I was given this hut yesterday by a charming goat, who had hair of a lovely indigo colour.'

'And where did the goat go?' asked Pinocchio with intense curiosity.

'I don't know.'

'And when will she return? . . .'

'She won't ever return. Yesterday she went away dejected and bleating, and seemed to be saying, "Poor Pinocchio . . . now I shall never see him again . . . by now the Shark must have well and truly devoured him . . .".'

'Did she really say that? . . . So it was her! . . . it was her! . . . it was my dear little Fairy! . . .' Pinocchio began to exclaim, sobbing and weeping profusely.

When he had had a good cry, he wiped his eyes and arranged a nice bed of straw, where he made Old Joe lie down. Then he asked the Talking Cricket, 'Tell me, little Cricket, where could I find a glass of milk for my poor father?'

'Three fields away from here there is Johnny, the market gardener, who keeps cows. Go and see him and you will find the milk you want.'

Pinocchio ran to the house of the market gardener, Johnny, but the market gardener said to him, 'How much milk do you want?'

'I want a full glass.'

'A glass of milk costs a penny. So first give me your penny.'

'I haven't even got a farthing,' replied Pinocchio, grieved and mortified.

'That's bad, my dear puppet,' answered the market gardener. 'If you haven't even a farthing, I haven't even a thimble of milk.'

'Never mind then!' said Pinocchio, and made as if to go.

'Wait a moment,' said Johnny. 'We can come to some arrangement, you and I. Can you learn to work the water-pump?

'What sort of water-pump?'

'It's that wooden tackle that brings water up from the cistern to water the vegetables.'

'I'll have a go . . .'

'Very well, you bring me up a hundred buckets of water, and in payment I'll give you a glass of milk.'

'All right.'

Johnny took the puppet into the market garden and taught him how to turn the pump. Pinocchio set about doing the work at once, but before he had finished drawing up the hundred buckets of water he was soaked in sweat from head to toe. He had never endured such hard work before.

'Up to now', the market gardener said, 'I have given this task of working the pump to my donkey; but now the poor animal is giving up the ghost.'

'Will you take me to see it?' said Pinocchio.

'Certainly.'

As soon as Pinocchio entered the stable he saw a hand-

some donkey lying on the straw, worn out by hunger and too much work. When he had looked very hard, he said to himself, feeling troubled, 'Don't I know this donkey? He looks familiar to me.'

And bending down towards him, he asked in donkey language, 'Who are you?'

At this question the donkey opened his dying eyes, and stammered a reply in the same language, 'I am Ca . . . ndle . . . Wi . . . ick . . .'

Then he closed his eyes again and expired.

'Oh, poor Candle-Wick!' said Pinocchio in a whisper, and taking up a handful of straw he dried a tear that was running down his face.

'Are you so upset about a donkey that's not costing you anything?' asked the market gardener. 'I paid hard cash for him, so what should I be doing?'

'I'll explain . . . he was a friend of mine . . .'

'A friend of yours?'

'One of my school-friends! . . .'

'What?!' yelled Johnny laughing loudly. 'What?! you had asses for school-friends? . . . I can just imagine the good work you put in there! . . .'

Mortified by those words, the puppet did not reply; but he took his glass of still-warm milk and returned to the hut.

From then on for five months he continued to get up before dawn every morning, in order to go and turn the pump and so earn the glass of milk which did his father's poor health so much good.* And he did not content himself with that, for as time went by he learned to make wicker baskets and rush panniers; and with the money he earned he provided—with much good sense—for all their everyday expenses. Amongst other things he built, all by himself, a stylish little wheelchair in which to take his father out for a walk on fine days, so as to give him a breath of air.

Then in the evenings he would apply himself to reading

and writing. In the nearby town he had bought for a few farthings a fat book which had lost its title-page and index, and he did his reading from that. As for writing, he used a piece of straw sharpened to make a pen; and since he had neither ink-well nor ink, he dipped it into a little bottle full of blackberry and cherry juice.

So it was that through his determination to do the best he could, to work and to support himself, not only did he manage to keep his still infirm parent in reasonable comfort, but in addition he had also been able to put forty shillings on one side to buy himself some new clothes.

One morning he said to his father, 'I'm going to the market nearby to buy myself a nice jacket, and a cap and a pair of shoes. When I get home', he added laughing, 'I shall be so well dressed that you'll mistake me for a fine gentleman.'

As he left home, he was so happy and cheerful he began to run. Then he suddenly heard his name being called out and, turning round, he saw a fine snail coming out of the hedge.

'Don't you recognize me?' said the Snail.

'I do and I don't . . .'

'Don't you remember the Snail who used to be a living-in maid for the Fairy with indigo hair? Don't you remember that time when I came downstairs to light the way for you and you got your foot stuck through the front door?'

'I remember it all,' cried Pinocchio. 'Tell me quickly, lovely little Snail, where did you last see my good Fairy? What is she doing? Has she forgiven me? Does she remember me? Is she still fond of me? Is she far away? Could I go and see her?'

The Snail replied in her usual measured way to all these questions which tumbled out one after the other, without his drawing breath, 'Dear Pinocchio, the poor Fairy has been lying for a long time in a hospital bed . . .'

'A hospital bed? . . .'

'Unfortunately, yes. Beset by so many misfortunes, she fell seriously ill and she no longer has the money to buy herself a crust of bread.'

'Truly? . . . Oh, what terrible sadness you have brought me! Oh, my poor little Fairy! poor little Fairy! poor little Fairy! . . . If I had a million pounds I would run to take it to her . . . But I only have forty shillings . . . here they are: I was just going to buy myself some new clothes. Take them, Snail, and hurry with them to my good Fairy.'

'And what about your new clothes? . . .'

'What do my new clothes matter? I would even sell these rags that I'm wearing so as to help her! Go on, Snail, and hurry up; in two days' time come back here, because I hope to be able to give you another few shillings. Up to now I have worked to keep my father; from now on I'll work an extra five hours a day so as to support my dear mother as well. Goodbye, Snail, and in two days' time I'll be waiting for you here.'

Contrary to her habit, the Snail scuttled off like a lizard in the hot dog-days of August.

When Pinocchio got home, his father asked him, 'What about the new clothes?'

'I couldn't find any that suited me. Never mind! . . . I'll buy them another time.'

That evening, instead of staying up until ten o'clock, Pinocchio was up until after midnight; and instead of making eight rush baskets, he made sixteen.

Then he went to bed and fell asleep. While he slept, he seemed to see the Fairy in a dream; she looked lovely and smiling and, after kissing him, she said these words.

'Well done, Pinocchio! On account of your kind heart, I forgive you all the pranks that you have played before now. Children who lovingly help their parents in their hardship and their infirmity always deserve great praise and great affection, even if they cannot be cited as models of obedience and good behaviour. Be sensible in future and you will be happy.'*

At this point the dream ended, and Pinocchio opened his eyes and was wide awake.

Now you must imagine for yourselves how amazed he was when, on waking, he realized that he was no longer a wooden puppet, but that instead he had become a boy like all the others. He glanced about him and instead of the old straw walls of the hut, he saw a lovely bedroom furnished and decorated with an elegant simplicity. Jumping out of bed, he found laid out ready a fine set of new clothes, a new cap and a pair of leather boots, which all looked splendid on him.

As soon as he had dressed, putting his hands in his pockets as a matter of course, he pulled out a little ivory purse, on which were inscribed these words: 'The Fairy with indigo hair herein returns the forty shillings to her dear Pinocchio and thanks him so much for his kindness.' Inside the wallet, instead of his forty shillings, there shone forty gold florins, all newly minted.

Afterwards he went to look at himself in the mirror, and he looked like someone else. He no longer saw reflected there the usual image of a wooden marionette, but he saw the handsome reflection of an intelligent and lively young boy with dark brown hair, blue eyes and a festive expression* of happiness and merriment.

Amidst all these marvels which followed one upon the other, Pinocchio himself did not know whether he was truly awake or still dreaming with his eyes open.

'And where is my Papa?' he exclaimed all of a sudden; then going into the adjoining room he found Old Joe in good health, sprightly and good-humoured, just as he once had been, and, having immediately resumed his profession as a wood-carver, he was now designing a beautiful picture-frame embellished with foliage, flowers, and the heads of various animals.

'Dear Papa, will you satisfy my curiosity: what is the explanation for all these unexpected changes?' Pinocchio asked him, throwing his arms around his neck and covering him with kisses.

'These unexpected changes in our house are all thanks to you,' said Joe.

'Why thanks to me? . . .'

'Because when naughty children become good, they have the power to bring about a happy transformation at home for all their family.'

'And where is the old wooden Pinocchio hiding?'

'There he is,' replied Joe, and pointed out a big puppet

leaning on a chair, his head turned one way, his arms dangling loose, his legs crossed over and bent in the middle,
so that it seemed a miracle that he was still standing.

Pinocchio turned to look at him; and after he had looked
for a bit, he said to himself with the greatest satisfaction,
'How funny I was when I was a puppet! And how happy
I am now to have become a proper boy! ...'*

EXPLANATORY NOTES

1 *Once upon a time... wood*: Collodi's first work for children had been his translation of Perrault's and other influential French fairy stories of the seventeenth and eighteenth centuries. Most began with the formula 'Once upon a time...' which he re-uses here, only to bring the reader abruptly and humorously back to reality from the first intimation of fantasy. This balancing trick is repeated throughout *Pinocchio*. In keeping with the many traditional—and sometimes deliberately archaic—references, the word 'How' has usually been inserted at the beginning of each chapter summary, as a means of emphasizing Collodi's stylistic sensitivity.

   Master Anthony... maestro Cherry... ripe cherry: 'mastro', deriving from 'maestro', indicated a master craftsman. The earlier form is used satirically with the nickname 'Cherry'. This character is not teased by his friend, Old Joe (Geppetto), but addressed politely as 'Master Anthony'.

2 *scratching his wig*: the wigs of *maestro* Cherry and Old Joe are anachronistic and place these figures, at least in part, within the old fairy-tale tradition.

   stone gargoyle: the original image is of a grotesque mask sculpted on a fountain, of which there must be thousands in Italy. Such masks were favoured decorative motifs in Renaissance art and derived from the comic and tragic masks of the ancient theatre in antiquity. *Pinocchio* is bespangled with theatrical allusions. The novelist Italo Calvino borrowed Collodi's exact expression to describe a character in his first novel, *Il sentiero dei nidi di ragno* ('The path to the nest of spiders') (Turin: Einaudi, 1947).

3 *Old Joe*: Old Joe's original name is 'Geppetto', an affectionate abbreviation of Giuseppe, or Joseph.

4 *semolina pudding*: Joe's original nickname is 'Polendina', from 'polenta', the cooked version of the bright yellow maize flour made in Italy. Semolina has the same texture and is well known in children's food, but is paler in colour.

   I decided to make myself... What do you think?: Master Anthony is repeatedly described as 'falegname', carpenter.

At first there is no equivalent precision as to Joe's work, but popularization has usually translated him into being a carpenter too. This is far from certain. However, at the end of the book Joe is unequivocally described as a 'wood-carver', doing skilled decorative work as distinct from ordinary carpentry. It is a skill strongly associated with Florence, but now dying out. The puppet Joe plans to make has traditional attributes; even a basic type of toy puppet, suspended between two rods, was capable of performing somersaults in children's bedrooms until quite recently, and perhaps still does. The simple, flat type is the sort of puppet depicted in the very first few illustrations, done by Ugo Fleres for the serial story in *Il Giornale per i bambini*, the children's newspaper which first published the story.

6 *basement room lit by a skylight under the front steps*: strictly speaking, Joe's room is on the ground floor under a flight of outside steps. What is important, though, is to convey the context of poverty, albeit in architectural images foreign to Italy.

7 *I'd like to call him Pinocchio... whole Pinocchio family ... The richest was a beggar*: commentaries remain remarkably silent as to why Pinocchio might have been called 'Pinocchio', or 'Pine-kernel'. It is not that he is made of relatively valuable pine wood; he is only nondescript firewood. Pine-nuts or pine-kernels were and still are a valued ingredient in Tuscan cooking. So the word, its variants used in different localities ('Pinoccolo, Pinottolo, Pinolo, Pignolo, Pinello'), and its diminutives were very familiar to all, especially as, in the country, this could be free food. Even so, there was a special term for a pine-nut vendor: Pinocchiajo. In the 1879 Tommaseo and Bellini dictionary of the Italian language, the common pine, *pinus picea*, is defined in terms of its being the source of pine-nuts ('Pinocchi'), which it calls 'frutti conosciutissimi', extremely well-known seeds. It was such a familiar object that the word had various derivatives and cropped up in popular sayings. The Tommaseo–Bellini dictionary quotes 'Pinocchina' as a substitute for 'Pollastrina', meaning a small, plump pullet—and, by extension in popular parlance, a small, plump, shapely woman; so there we have a popular connection with human beings. The diminutive form 'Pinocchino' was a term of affection when applied, say Tommaseo and Bellini, to a canary, for example.

In Florence, 'Pinocchiata' was a confection of sugar and pine-nuts. Collodi's choice of 'Pinocchio' suggests, then, a term of affection combined with overtones of both the savoury and the sweet. It may even be relevant to note that the pine-nut is inside a case which must be removed; Pinocchio is already present inside the lump of wood, which speaks and moves before the puppet has been carved out of it. This idea is poor man's Michelangelo, whose sonnet LXXXIII describes the sculptor's work as revealing what is already present within the marble.

A significant detail of Collodi's working life is that he was invited in 1868 to be a contributor to the important multi-volume dictionary, the *Novo vocabolario della lingua italiana secondo l'uso di Firenze*, edited by Giorgini and Broglio (Florence, 1877–97). His work for the dictionary will have made him even more keenly aware of 'families' of words.

Collodi had great knowledge of the theatre and it is worth noting that one of the stock characters of the Commedia dell'Arte was one Finochio.

8 *little respect for your father! That's bad, my lad, that's bad!*: Joe is the one who establishes the father–son relationship. He is evidently an ageing bachelor, like his creator.

9 *Arab stallion*: elsewhere 'Arab charger', both translations for 'barbero', a Barbary steed. The term implies a historical refer-ence to the Corsa dei Barberi, a race run by Barbary horses let loose in Rome between Piazza del Popolo and Piazza Venezia.

12 *I am the Talking Cricket* . . . : like the Fox and the Cat, the Talking Cricket has no other name (unlike the Disney ver-sion). He is often regarded by critics as the Voice of Consci-ence, but the Voice of Common Sense or Wisdom, or the Voice of one's Elders and Betters are equally viable interpretations.

great big ass . . . jokes about you?: Collodi uses three nouns in the book for the same animal. All three can be used figuratively, in criticism of people, and occur in popular phrases. This translation distinguishes between 'somaro' and 'asino' which are translated as 'ass', and 'ciuco', translated with the more everyday word, 'donkey'. This is the first reference to a theme in *Pinocchio* which will provide the climax of the puppet's misadventures. Whether that was al-ready in Collodi's mind is more doubtful, since the original version only reached Chapter XV.

13 *all finish up in the workhouse or in prison*: this has the ring of a popular saying. Collodi, as often, uses the Tuscan form 'lo spedale' for the now standard 'l'ospedale'. The word appears later meaning hospital, but here 'workhouse' is more likely.

egg to scramble . . . the scrambled egg flies away through the window: in the original, Pinocchio wants to make himself an omelette, 'una frittata', but this word, used figuratively, means 'blunder'. This is certainly an example of Collodi's wordplay. The nearest approximation to the *double entendre* is provided, not wholly satisfactorily, by scrambled egg.

14 *mouldy pasta*: originally mouldy polenta.

Oh, what a terrible disease hunger is!: the book surreptitiously provided many sidelong comments on the condition of the poor.

I'm so longing to eat it!: Collodi returns over and over again to the topic of food, a subject dear to the heart of Pinocchio. In Italian, cookery terms (like animal life and plants) are hard to pin down; this is not only the result of popular usages, but especially because language—like life—has been profoundly regional in character. The use of a preposition can alter the recipe. In this paragraph, Pinocchio is playing with and relishing food ideas, rather than considering practical cookery strategies, in which he is a beginner. He talks of frying or baking the egg, but then puts water in the pan, which will poach it. In Britain there is no native culinary concept exactly equivalent to Pinocchio's 'cuocerlo nel piatto o nel tegamino' (two methods which are sometimes identical, and are always closely related); in the USA there is, and its name is 'shirred eggs'.

15 *Oh, what a terrible disease hunger is!*: this paragraph is a good example of typical Collodian repetition.

17 *as wet as a drowned duck*: the Italian conventional expression is 'wet as a chick', which neatly reminds one of the 'dry' chick of the previous chapter.

20 *I don't know, Papa . . . Boo! . . . hoo! . . . hoo! . . . hoo!*: this is one of several long, jumbled, sometimes asyntactical recapitulations delivered by Pinocchio. They are entertaining in themselves, but also had a practical function in the original, serialized publication.

five miles away: originally five kilometres; miles have been substituted throughout.

23 *old fustian cape*: 'casacca di frustagno': 'cloak' sounds too elegant for Joe and 'cape' more appropriately workaday; the 'casacca' (derived from *kazak*/Cossack) could have sleeves, but a garment and term no longer current is indicated here. 'Frustagno' or 'fustagno' is fustian, a twilled cotton cloth, or corduroy.

26 *Harlequin and Punchinello*: in Italian they are 'Arlecchino e Pulcinella', the latter a character who degenerated into the English Punch. These are two of the leading stock characters in Commedia dell'Arte theatre; the stock situations around which the plays were improvised are implied in the words 'as usual'. The Commedia dell'Arte began in the sixteenth century as live theatre played in masks and conventional costumes; it formed an extremely important and long-lived tradition in the history of Italian dramatic art. Eventually the tradition was annexed by the puppet theatre. In this episode, Pinocchio is recognized by Harlequin and the company of marionettes as their 'brother'. This seems to go beyond the idea of one puppet simply acknowledging another puppet. Pinocchio is one of them, the troupe, and this lends weight to the theory that Collodi's theatrical expertise led to the creation of Pinocchio. The lesser character, Finochio ('Fennel' in Venetian spelling), was cunning and full of tricks, and wore a green and white costume. In a description of 1723, he was said to wear a mask like a marmot. Fernando Tempesti has suggested that Pinocchio is descended from the crafty Florentine figure of Stenterello, but Collodi's inspiration was doubtless complex and it is not appropriate to identify Pinocchio, one to one, with a single Commedia dell'Arte character. The Commedia dell'Arte itself suggests associations between fantasy and reality, between the animate and the inanimate, both of which concepts are central to *Pinocchio*.

30 *cooking that roast ram*: 'montone' is the original word, translated literally by 'ram'; 'carne di montone' is mutton, but that is not intended here where the ogre-like puppet-master is roasting a whole beast on the spit. This is fantasy (or fairy-tale) food, but in fact the word 'ram' is preserved in culinary usage in the English rural festivity (e.g. in the West Country) known as a 'ram-roast'.

30 *Hey, constables!*: Collodi uses two terms for the police, 'carabiniere' (translated as 'policeman') for realistic situations, and 'giandarmi' (from French 'gendarme') for fantasy situations; thus the two puppets are translated as 'constables' (*à la* Toy Town). The use of the French neologism 'giandarmi' derived from the political French connections of the Grand Dukes of Tuscany; so Collodi's use of the word is a sly reference to the ineffectual and ceremonial character of the old Tuscan Court and its officials.

31 *Have pity, Excellency!*: Collodi is not only satirizing the Italian penchant for titles, but indulging in a little self-referential joke. In 1878 he himself had been made a 'Sir' ('Cavaliere'), while his beloved brother, Paolo, had previously been given the title of 'Commendatore' for his work as Director-General of the Doccia porcelain factory (the title translated as 'Lord' here).

33 *the Cat who was blind was guided by the Fox*: the Fox and the Cat are two of the most distinguished—and menacing—creations in the book. While Collodi invests them with a power and certain characteristics uniquely his own, simultaneously—and paradoxically—they are derived from the tradition of fables, notably those of Aesop and La Fontaine.

34 *God willing*: a purely conventional reference to God; this is a wholly secular book.

35 *Poor Blackbird . . . feathers and all*: 'merlo' (blackbird), in popular parlance, is often used figuratively of human behaviour, meaning either a 'deceiver, cunning or sly person, rogue', or a 'fool or simpleton'. People used to exclaim 'Canta, merlo!' (Sing, blackbird!) to show that someone's lying or deceiving conversation had been understood ('Pull the other one!'). Here, it is the 'merlo' doing the warning and Pinocchio is the gullible simpleton.

36 *five florins*: the gold pieces are called alternatively 'monete' (coins) or 'zecchini', as here. This word indicates the Venetian coin, the sequin, and is used in expressions concerning true gold or the glittering of gold. Secondly, the 'zecchino gigliato' (the sequin with the lily) was the Florentine florin (or 'fiorino', the gold coin with the flower, 'fiore', on one face), which was first minted in 1252. The flower or lily is, in fact, the heraldic fleur-de-lys which was one of Florence's symbols; the emblem was based not strictly on a lily, but on the Florentine iris, still native to the city.

land of Boobies: the 'land of Boobies' is an approximation to the original 'paese dei Barbagianni', meaning barn owls. These beautiful birds have quite a different cultural significance in Italy from any English connotation. Figuratively, the word means 'stupid individual, dolt or blockhead', and that kind of dual interpretation is essential here.

sacred ground, which everyone calls the Field of Miracles: this sentence is probably a reference not only to people's gullibility generally, but also specifically in the religious context. The place in the original Italian is the 'Campo dei miracoli'. This exists in reality as part of the topography of Venice, where the word 'Campo' is widely used instead of 'Piazza' or Square. In standard Italian 'campo' means 'field'. The renowned tiny church of Santa Maria dei Miracoli is in this Venetian 'campo'.

37 *That's a very easy sum . . . gold shiners in your pocket*: this is a lesson both on the notion that statistics and damned lies can go hand in hand and, at the same time, on the importance of education.

38 *tripe and onions . . . grated cheese!*: tripe ('trippa') is a traditional Florentine food, but the half-hidden resonance here is provoked by the cognate word 'trippaio', meaning either a tripe-seller or a cat's meat man.

jugged hare: the almost literal translation—'hare in sweet and sour sauce'—sounds too Chinese; 'jugged hare' is preferable, being richly flavoured country food.

hotchpotch of game-birds, partridge, . . . green grapes: the word 'cibreo' means a fricassee or hotchpotch or hotpot, normally made with chicken giblets and eggs. Collodi gives it a diminutive ending and plays tricks with the ingredients, the first two being 'pernici' and 'starne', both of which mean partridge. *Cibreo* is the name of a well-known restaurant in Florence.

40 *blundering nocturnal birds . . . 'Who goes there?'*: owls have rather a bad press in *Pinocchio*. The word Collodi uses here for 'nocturnal birds' is 'uccellacci', a now obsolete meaning of which is 'simpletons'.

'Who are you?' Pinocchio asked him: Pinocchio never recognizes the Talking Cricket (or voice of conscience?), but always asks him who he is.

41 *'Listen to my advice and go back.'*... *'I want to go on.'*: an antiphonal conversation utterly characteristic of Collodi's writing.

42 *'Really,' the puppet said to himself*... *'that would be the end of it*...*'*: Pinocchio often talks to himself. This long paragraph shows Collodi's acute observation of children and how they chat to themselves to explain things to their satisfaction and, as here, to reassure themselves. This could also be seen as a kind of stream-of-consciousness passage, *avant la lettre*.

46 *Then there appeared*... *from the other world*: the beautiful Little Girl has 'a face as white as wax'; Collodi uses the same description of a young woman's looks in his novel for adults, *I misteri di Firenze*. It appears simply to be a definition of beauty rather than a quasi-religious or occult allusion. She is like a doll who does not open her eyes. Her most famous attribute is her blue hair, and 'blue' is the term generally used by translators. One argument in favour of 'blue' is that in his *I racconti delle fate* (Fairy Tales) of 1875, Collodi had translated Madame d'Aulnoy's 'L'oiseau bleu' as 'L'uccello turchino'. This was partly to avoid a French-sounding neologism in Italian, and partly no doubt for euphony: 'blu' is very abrupt. The other Italian words for different shades of blue ('azzurro', 'celeste') sound awkward with the word 'uccello' (too many initial vowels, or too many letters c). In *Pinocchio*, Collodi's use of 'turchino' is unforced, and requires special treatment. It does *not* mean 'turquoise' (for which the noun is 'turchese'), and indeed it is not a light blue. 'Turchino' is an unusual word (unlike 'blue'), meaning a deep or dark shade, while 'turchinetto' is the noun for indigo or laundress's blue. (There is also 'indaco'.) These words are related to 'Turchia' (Turkey), just as indigo is related to India. Thus, 'indigo' both describes the colour and captures the special mood accurately. Needless to say, 'turchino' has a cognate expression 'farne delle turchine' which means 'to be up to all sorts of tricks'.

Rumour has it that, in his youth, Collodi had fathered a girl-child whom he was never able to acknowledge and who died young. This may, perhaps, shed a different light on the Little Girl from the rather sickly sweet, rather mawkish first impression in the story. She seems, at first, to strike the only false, sentimental, note.

48 *hung there as if frozen stiff*: Pinocchio seems to be dead and the Little Girl has said that she is dead. This is the tragic point in the story where, horrifyingly, the serial in *Il Giornale per i bambini* originally came to an end, on 27 October 1881. The eight parts had appeared intermittently since 7 July of that year (some of the parts containing two or even three chapters). In November a new serial was announced but the story did not resume until 16 February 1882. The original newspaper serial, ending with the hanging of Pinocchio, had appeared under the title *La storia di un burattino* ('The story of a puppet'). The paper was besieged by children writing to ask for the story to be continued. When the second part was launched, it appeared under the definitive title of *Le avventure di Pinocchio* ('The adventures of Pinocchio').

49 *Girl with indigo hair . . . very good fairy*: the dead doll is transformed into a Good Fairy with magic powers. The first section of the serial had talking animals, but no magic, properly speaking. The advent of magic and of an all-good, re-deeming, protecting female figure signals a change of tone in the writing. There is less realism and more fantasy; the first section is altogether more acerbic, tougher, more pessimistic, more original. For the time being, Collodi has reverted to the traditional fairy-tale mode. Shortly this is to be overlaid by overt didacticism. The distinctive appearance and nature of Collodi's fairy is undermined by the many English transla-tions which term her the 'Blue Fairy' (and even illustrate her in a blue dress), thus reducing her to the bland and the banal.

50 *The Poodle-dog . . . if the weather turned to rain*: the Poodle (a French poodle, no doubt) has stepped straight from the pages of the French fairy tales previously translated by Collodi. He even wears the fancy court costume and wig of the period of Le Roi Soleil or one of the other Louis, and is rescued from triteness only by the umbrella-cover for his tail, in the Fairy's indigo livery, of course.

good boy Medoro: the Poodle's name, Medoro, is taken from the Renaissance poet Ariosto, in whose great chivalric poem, *Orlando furioso* (1515–33), Medoro is a young Moor of humble birth; Angelica falls in love with him, causing Orlando's madness.

51 *sky-blue carriage . . . lined inside with whipped cream . . . drawn by a hundred pairs of white mice*: this is a traditional

fairy-tale image, or rather two: a combination of Cinderella's carriage and the witch's house in 'Hansel and Gretel', made of foodstuffs and sweets.

51 *The doctors . . . a Crow, a Little Owl, and a Talking Cricket*: the first two are seen as portentous creatures, suitable for a mordant lampooning of the medical profession.

55 *Oh my dear Fairy . . . Quick, hand me the glass . . . Hurry up, for mercy's sake*: the changed relationship between the Fairy and Pinocchio is evident in the Italian at this point. When he speaks to the 'Bambina'/Doll in Chapter XV, he uses the informal 'tu' form of address. Now that the Fairy is his 'sister', and has already adopted a quasi-maternal role, she seems still to be young, but not little, and from now on Pinocchio addresses her with the more respectful 'voi' (which Collodi used to his own mother throughout her life).

58 *Lies are quickly recognized . . . yours is the long-nosed sort*: the Fairy is referring to well-known sayings. Italian has the proverb, 'Le bugie hanno le gambe corte' (Lies have short legs), meaning 'Truth will out'. There is also the saying 'La bugia ti corre su per il naso' (Your lie is running all up your nose), meaning that it is 'written all over your face' or 'it sticks out a mile'. The two parentheses are added to the translation to clarify what would be self-evident to the Italian reader. In the second expression lies the origin of Pinocchio's tell-tale nose, though it will be remembered that in Chapter III, while carving the puppet, Joe was unable to control the size of the nose, which grew long of its own accord, one of many signs of rebelliousness in the lump of wood. In Italian there is a huge array of popular sayings concerning noses, several of them to do with deceit. Collodi was fond of noses: in 1881, the same year as the publication of the first section of the serial, he published a volume of short pieces under the title *Occhi e nasi* ('Eyes and noses'), in which he focused on single features in human psychology and behaviour, as well as appearance. Pinocchio's long nose is reincarnated in Salman Rushdie's *Midnight's Children*.

62 *bald dogs . . . fleeced lambs . . . gone for ever*: all these creatures have allowed themselves to be 'fleeced' in the figurative as well as the literal sense. Several of the verbs used in the Italian are *double entendres* of this kind.

some Fox, or Thieving Magpie, or bird of prey: Collodi chose these creatures for their popular reputations and symbolic value, and doubtless also had Rossini's *La Gazza ladra* ('The Thieving Magpie') (1817) in mind, being a devotee of opera in general and Rossini in particular.

65 *The judge was a great ape... for many years*: the medical profession has already been lampooned; now it is the turn of the legal profession and the police. The face of the gorilla was evidently not familiar at this time, as Mazzanti's illustration of the judge shows not a gorilla but a baboon (with similar satirical effect).

71 *pain from the gin-trap... nearly fainting*: the gin-trap in Italian is 'tagliuola', from 'tagliare', to cut. Literally it 'saws' ('segare') into his shins with its sharp edges. The language is apt, for Pinocchio's wooden legs are in as great danger as those of flesh and blood would be.

74 *beech martens, little carnivorous animals*: 'faina' is beech marten (*Mustela faina*), a relative of the pine marten which exists, though rare, in some wild parts of Britain (in mountainous Scotland, for example). It would have been possible to translate this as a more familiar animal, a stoat perhaps, but as usual there is a double meaning. 'Faina' is used figuratively of people to indicate an ugly person (or an old fogey, indeed). The nearest approximation might have been 'weasel' but its symbolic value would not have been obvious, so literal accuracy was preferred.

Good evening, Impala: the dead dog's name was 'Melampo', meaning (incongruously) the Impala antelope. Hardly a gazelle, this dog was rather sluggish.

76 *Your chastisement is my due, but I'll not stoop so low!*: this improbable remark from the peasant is a parody of operatic style (yet another allusion to the theatre). In particular it bears a close resemblance to an aria in Act I of Bellini's opera *Norma* (1831). In Felice Romani's libretto, Norma's words, referring to her errant lover Pollione, are:

'... Punirlo io posso,
Ma punirlo il cor non sa.'
(... Punish him I can,
But punish him my heart cannot.)

The peasant's words are:

'Potrei punirvi, ma sì vil non sono'
(I could punish you, but so vile I am not).

Nicolas Perella in his 1986 edition of *Pinocchio* is mistaken: it is the first part of the sentence, not the second, which most closely resembles *Norma* in its wording. However, the inversion of the second half is the essential indication of operatic, rather than rustic, diction.

81 *I would never have believed that tares could be so good!*: the original word for 'tares' is 'vecce', plural of 'veccia', vetch (*Vicia sativa* or *Vicia hirsuta*). The old English word 'tare' means any of the small vetches, or any other weeds of wheatfields, or their seeds. The basket in the dovecote contains the seeds. This is both a reference to practical country lore and a symbolic and moral tale to teach that one should eat bad bread as well as good, and be thankful. As so often, there is an Italian proverb to clinch the meaning: 'In times of famine, even bread made of tares is wholesome.'

Pinocchio's ride on the pigeon's back is not unique. Young boys ride astride flying birds in several works of Swedish children's literature of the same period. Nils had such an experience thanks to a goose in Selma Lagerlöf's *The Wonderful Adventures of Nils* (1906–7), an episode derived, it is thought, from an illustration to Madame de Ségur, while the steed is a pigeon in Gotthold Kurz's *Jakob Fingerlång* (1878). For this John Beer's illustration was rather similar to Mazzanti's later drawings for *Pinocchio*.

83 *'Poor lad!'... they went off to their houses*: the repetition of this paragraph with almost identical words has something of the operatic about it: a chorus this time, rather than a solo aria. It is also reminiscent of Giovanni Verga's writing about Sicilian fishing villages; his novel *I Malavoglia* had been published in 1881, and demonstrated the harsh reality of fisherfolk's lives, but also used a theatrical, choral technique to convey the life and talk of the community.

85 *a Dolphin*: like Collodi's gargoyle in Chapter I, Mazzanti's illustration of the Dolphin was clearly inspired by the magnificent fountains of Florence, often adorned prominently with conventional, decorative dolphins, whose heads are quite unlike the reality.

90 *knee-high to a cricket*: the Italian popular saying is 'tall as a piece of cheese'.

93 *Old Nick*: the original is 'berlicche', a joking reference to the devil.

98 *the volumes... all fell into the sea*: Collodi includes a joke at his own expense here: two of the books thrown in the

water are his own hugely successful *Giannettino* (1877) and *Minuzzolo* (1878). Easily recognizable late nineteenth-century schoolbooks and children's stories in English have been substituted for the Italian titles. Collodi's original collection includes 'Sillabari' (easy reading- or spelling-books), 'Grammatiche' (grammar books), copies of *Giannettino* and *Minuzzolo*, Pietro Thouar's *I Racconti per i fanciulli* ('Stories for children'), which had begun to appear in penny numbers in 1836, and Ida Baccini's *Le memorie di un pulcino* (1875) ('Memoirs of a chick').

103 *set a big mastiff on him*: in the courtroom in Sillybillytrap (Chapter XIX), the police constables were themselves mastiffs. ('Mastino' in Italian can be used figuratively to indicate roughness, crudeness.)

Mercury (for this was the mastiff's name): the dog's grandiose Italian name is Alidoro; 'ali d'oro' means wings of gold, so 'Mercury', the name of the winged messenger of the gods of Ancient Rome, has been substituted.

105 *baker's peel*: long 'paddle' or shovel used by bakers to place bread in the oven.

112 *'little sack where I keep lupin seeds.'... lupin sack, which was empty*: the lupin seeds may be a reference to Verga's novel *I Malavoglia* (1881), written according to his precepts of Verismo, or strict adherence to reality. The disasters that befall the Malavoglia family begin with the sinking of their fishing-boat with a cargo of lupin seeds. Thus, lack of lupin seeds equals destitution.

113 *large snail... with a glowing night-light on her head*: there is a play on words in the original: the snail ('lumaca') carries a light ('lume') in the form of a night-light ('lumicino').

115 *counting all the ants*: in Chapter II, Joe found Master Anthony on the floor 'teaching the ants their numbers'.

117 *That day promised... there are always buts, which spoil everything*: just as Pinocchio is promised his longed-for rite of passage to real boyhood, the serial publication stopped again. The previous cessation happened when Pinocchio had apparently died. Chapter XXIX was published in *Il Giornale per i bambini* on 1 June 1882. Since 16 February, the serial had appeared weekly with regularity, with the exception of April during which month no parts appeared. The new break in publication was long, nearly 6 months in fact, so eclipsing

the 3½ months of delay after the hanging, published in late October 1881. The new interruption covered the whole summer holiday period. Indeed, the third section did not begin to appear until 23 November 1882, when Chapter XXX was published.

118 Candle-Wick ... *wick of a night-light*: 'Candle-Wick' (i.e. the wick of a candle) is a literal translation of 'Lucignolo'. It is notable how many of Collodi's characters, human and animal, have an association with light.

119 *a land of pleasure and plenty!*: in the original, the land of pleasure and plenty is 'una vera cuccagna', a real land of Cockayne (or Cockaigne). This old myth is no longer sufficiently familiar in English for a literal translation.

every week is composed of six Thursdays and one Sunday: in the 1880s there was no school on Thursdays, and indeed Thursday remained a half-day until relatively recently. Collodi used the same notion, jokingly, in several other writings, including *Giannettino*.

121 *What a nice place!*: 'What a nice place!' translates 'Che bel paese!' This may be an allusion to the book *Il bel paese* ('The lovely land') (1875) by the priest and scientist Antonio Stoppani. It was written to instruct children about the new nation of Italy and to cultivate a sense of one-ness. It was the first such work responding to the needs of the post-Unification period. In his didactic mode, Collodi addressed the same educational need in the three volumes of *Il viaggio per l'Italia di Giannettino* (1880–6), the first volume of which had been published before *Pinocchio*. If the echoing of Stoppani was intentional, it is possible that the reference encompasses Collodi's political scepticism.

123 *Try to conjure up ... winning over the tender-hearted mistress of the house*: the Little Man (significantly with no other name), one of Collodi's great creations, is insinuatingly sinister, an incarnation of the devil himself.

126 *bee in his bonnet ... sees reason*: the original for 'bee in his bonnet' is 'grillo per il capo' (a cricket in the head), meaning a whim. This popular phrase is particularly pointed here, of course, since the Grillo/Cricket is the voice of conscience or common sense.

130 *couple of besoms*: brooms the shape of witches' broomsticks made of a bunch of twigs or heather.

pretty little Marmot . . . dear neighbour: the marmot is a mountain creature found in Italy, amongst other regions of Europe (though not Britain). This character is clearly not simply female, but feminine; Collodi clearly chose her for her metaphorical allusiveness. 'Una marmotta' is a sleepy individual or lazy-bones, and the dictionary translates 'dormire come una marmotta' as 'to sleep like a dormouse'. Both animals hibernate in nature. An Italian folk tale, 'Queen Marmot', is analogous to the story of Sleeping Beauty.

133 *Like a mouse in a Cheddar cheese*: in the original the mouse is in a whole Parmesan cheese.

137 *to train him to jump and dance*: the irony here is that when Joe first fashioned his puppet, his object was to make one that would 'dance, fence and do somersaults', so as to travel about presenting it as a side-show. In addition to exploiting the symbolic value deriving from the popular sense of 'ass' or 'donkey', Collodi may have been prompted by Apuleius' *The Golden Ass*, in which the transformed man learns about the vices of humankind by being owned by a series of different masters. Collodi's translation of the French fairy tale *Peau d'Asne* ('Donkey-Skin') may also have a bearing on the humiliation of Pinocchio in the guise of a donkey.

138 *understood the language of donkeys very well*: the 'language of donkeys' translates 'dialetto asinino'. Until recently the first language of most Italians was their local dialect, Italian being learned at school. In Collodi's day (the early years of unified Italy), the 'Question of the Language' was still a burning issue, especially as to the nature of the standard Italian language of culture. In Collodi's lifetime the Florentine and Tuscan forms of literary Italian became pre-eminent. Mutually incomprehensible dialects, used for everyday conversation, still abounded. Hence Collodi's use of the word 'dialetto' in a formulation similar to, for example, 'il dialetto aretino' (the dialect of Arezzo). 'Asinino' is meant to be understood also as 'asinine'.

This hay isn't too bad . . . But never mind: for the umpteenth time Pinocchio has to learn to eat something he does not like.

shepherd's pie or steak and kidney pudding: the original delectable dishes were 'risotto alla milanese' (risotto with saffron), and 'maccheroni alla napoletana' (pasta with a tomato sauce), in other words two basic, traditional recipes.

141 *Most honoured auditors! ... Pyrrhic dance*: this passage is a
farrago of confusions. The 'system of Gaul' is, in the Italian,
that of 'Galles' (Wales), and this mixes up a place-name with
Franz Josef Gall (1758–1828), who developed phrenology. A
'bonaparte cartilage' was 'cartagine ossea' (bony Carthage),
and 'Facoltà medicea' muddles the Medici family with Medical Faculty. The Pyrrhic dance was a war-dance.

146 *the blessed St Anthony*: St Anthony: the patron saint of swine-
herds, or St Anthony of Padua, a follower of St Francis.

150 *fishermen's Attila*: Attila the Hun (d. 453), barbarian invader
of the Roman Empire, notorious for his brutality.

152 *... more dignified to die in sea-water than in olive-oil*: tunny
(or tuna) preserved in olive-oil is nothing new.

... people's opinions, as political Tunny-fish say: another
Collodian side-swipe at the hypocrisy (a favourite theme)
of politicians.

... better not even to think about it!: this chapter appeared
on 28 December 1882 in the original serialization. Two issues
of *Il Giornale per i bambini* then came out without further
chapters of the story. The penultimate part (definitive Chapter XXXV) was printed on 18 January 1883.

153 *the middle of Lent*: traditionally in Lent, the period of mourning before the commemoration of Christ's death on Good
Friday and Resurrection on Easter Sunday, good Catholics
fasted; whereas the eating of meat and rich foods was re-
nounced, fish was permitted.

154 *the old man, rubbing his eyes*: there is a long and varied
cultural tradition of men being swallowed by sea-monsters
and living safely inside their vast bodies. The biblical example is the story of Jonah and the Whale, and in ancient times
Lucian provided another, but Collodi may have had Ariosto
uppermost in his mind, whose narrative poem *Orlando furioso*
(1515–33) had already supplied the name of Medoro (see note
to p. 50). A section, the *Cinque Canti*, eventually omitted from
the definitive *Orlando*, described just such an episode. He
was not necessarily as familiar with Bible stories as northern
Protestants used to be, and, besides, the cultural frame of
reference of *Pinocchio* is literary rather than religious. Pinocchio's quest, like Orlando's, put him through a long series (or
comic Odyssey) of bizarre challenges and adventures.

156 ... *a bit of spaghetti*: one 'tortellino di Bologna', to be precise, i.e. a mini-raviolo.

157 *gazing out... could see beyond that enormous wide-open mouth a lovely expanse of starry sky and the beautiful moonlight*: there is something Dantesque about this image; at the end of Dante's *Inferno*, the first canticle of the *Divine Comedy*, Dante (the character in the poem) and Virgil, his companion (with whom he has developed a son–father relationship), look out from the tunnel as they emerge from Hell and gaze up at the stars in the night sky.

The Shark is sleeping like a top: in the original, this is 'Dorme come un ghiro' (is sleeping like a dormouse).

159 *malaria*: Collodi's expression here is 'tertian fever', a form of malaria. This disease was common in Italy at Collodi's time, including in Tuscany, especially the low-lying coastal areas such as the marshy Maremma.

161 *Farewell, you masqueraders!*: masqueraders ('mascherine') are deceivers, but they also provide yet another link with the cultural traditions so closely woven into the fabric of *Pinocchio*. They wear masks and costumes like the characters of the Commedia dell'Arte; they dance the night away at Carnival balls (in the period of festivity between Christmas and Lent). In the issue of *Il Giornale per i bambini* of 16 February 1882 (when the second section of *Pinocchio* began), there was a front-page article by Ugo Fleres, entitled 'Mascherine'. Let's have a masquerade, the writer says, and proceeds to describe a number of typical costumes in which children (and adults) might dress up, starting with Pulcinella, and including the Count, Countess, Spaniard, Flower-girl, and Devil.

165 *for five months he continued... did his father's poor health so much good*: Pinocchio redeems himself for five months, having played the fool in the Land of Toys for five months.

168 *Be sensible in future and you will be happy*: although the final chapter reintroduces the reader to many characters from earlier passages, the one whom Pinocchio most wants to see again (as does the reader) does not reappear *in propria persona*. The only glimpse we now get of the Fairy is through Pinocchio's dream. It is both psychologically and structurally satisfying that throughout the story the Fairy and Joe never coexist within a single scene. Besides, the Fairy does

not need to return here: her work is done. Like Virgil with Dante in the Earthly Paradise, she vanishes when no longer useful.

168 *festive expression*: 'Pasqua' (Easter) has previously been used to indicate happy festivity. Here Pinocchio is as festive as Whitsun ('una pasqua di rose').

170 *a proper boy!*: the Italian for the final phrase (which has been used many times) is 'un ragazzino per bene'. The translation chosen ('a proper boy') is intended to convey something of the double meaning of the original. Pinocchio means that he is glad to be both a *real* boy and a *good* boy.

The last chapter, which was printed in the original, serialized version on 25 January 1883 (eighteen months on from the beginning), is by far the longest chapter. The very short chapters of the first section double in length in the second, making a kind of progression in terms of substance (literally *and* metaphorically, of course).

American Literature

British and Irish Literature

Children's Literature

Classics and Ancient Literature

Colonial Literature

Eastern Literature

European Literature

Gothic Literature

History

Medieval Literature

Oxford English Drama

Poetry

Philosophy

Politics

Religion

The Oxford Shakespeare

A complete list of Oxford World's Classics, including Authors in Context, Oxford English Drama, and the Oxford Shakespeare, is available in the UK from the Marketing Services Department, Oxford University Press, Great Clarendon Street, Oxford OX2 6DP, or visit the website at www.oup.com/uk/worldsclassics.

In the USA, visit www.oup.com/us/owc for a complete title list.

Oxford World's Classics are available from all good bookshops. In case of difficulty, customers in the UK should contact Oxford University Press Bookshop, 116 High Street, Oxford OX1 4BR.

JANE AUSTEN	Emma
	Mansfield Park
	Persuasion
	Pride and Prejudice
	Sense and Sensibility
MRS BEETON	Book of Household Management
LADY ELIZABETH BRADDON	Lady Audley's Secret
ANNE BRONTË	The Tenant of Wildfell Hall
CHARLOTTE BRONTË	Jane Eyre
	Shirley
	Villette
EMILY BRONTË	Wuthering Heights
SAMUEL TAYLOR COLERIDGE	The Major Works
WILKIE COLLINS	The Moonstone
	No Name
	The Woman in White
CHARLES DARWIN	The Origin of Species
CHARLES DICKENS	The Adventures of Oliver Twist
	Bleak House
	David Copperfield
	Great Expectations
	Nicholas Nickleby
	The Old Curiosity Shop
	Our Mutual Friend
	The Pickwick Papers
	A Tale of Two Cities
GEORGE DU MAURIER	Trilby
MARIA EDGEWORTH	Castle Rackrent

ANTHONY TROLLOPE

An Autobiography
The American Senator
Barchester Towers
Can You Forgive Her?
The Claverings
Cousin Henry
Doctor Thorne
The Duke's Children
The Eustace Diamonds
Framley Parsonage
He Knew He Was Right
Lady Anna
The Last Chronicle of Barset
Orley Farm
Phineas Finn
Phineas Redux
The Prime Minister
Rachel Ray
The Small House at Allington
The Warden
The Way We Live Now